The Midnight Book Club

By
E.W. Andersen

For my family, who taught me to love books
And for book lovers everywhere

1

It had been a difficult day at the end of a difficult year.

Maybe that was why Aurelia's nerves were on edge that night when, awakened once again by noise from the flat next door, she threw back her covers and clambered out of bed.

"That's *it*," she muttered to herself as she fumbled around the room, trying to find something to wear for her march over there. "If they think they can party all night and keep the rest of the neighborhood awake, they can just..." Aurelia struggled to come up with what, exactly, they could do before finishing lamely, "Think again!"

Voices from next door echoed through the room in a steady drone, clearly oblivious to her half-hearted threats. The noise had woken her every night since she'd moved in a few days ago, and the lack of sleep had worn her usually cheerful demeanor to the breaking point. She'd never had the courage—or the need—to yell at a disrespectful neighbor before, but her mind was made up and she was determined to put an end to it.

If only she could find something to wear besides her pajamas, which Aurelia was fairly certain would undermine the authoritative look she was aiming for. With a final peek under one of her moving boxes, she sighed and gave up the search. The flat was her aunt's old place and was in total disarray now that she'd moved in. She kept meaning to unpack, but she'd been busy running the bookshop downstairs, which, like the flat, had been her aunt's and was now hers.

Aurelia stomped out of the bedroom, earning a scowl from Fezz, the tuxedo cat she'd also inherited.

"Sorry," she whispered as she watched him stalk past her.

She moved more quietly as she followed him through the open kitchen and living area. He was headed for the sofa, while she went down the stairs to the door that led into the shop. She pulled a jacket off one of the pegs on the wall and then froze, one arm halfway through a sleeve. From where she was standing, she could now hear that the voices were coming from *inside* the shop, not the neighboring flat.

Aurelia's anger drained out of her in an instant and her eyes widened. Could it be burglars? There wasn't much to steal in the shop, apart from old books. But maybe they knew there was a flat upstairs? She put her ear to the door, though she could barely make out what the voices were saying over the sound of her heart slamming against her chest. Then it suddenly occurred to her—there were voices, plural, meaning more than one burglar was downstairs.

Time to call the police, she told herself. *Just as soon as I can move my legs again.*

Struggling to find her courage from moments ago, Aurelia stepped away from the door, ready to head back upstairs for her phone. That was when she spotted a strip of light coming through the gap at the threshold. Had she forgotten to turn out the lights when she'd closed up? Or were these people bold enough to turn on the lights while doing their burgling? Only... their voices didn't seem all that rowdy or threatening. Aurelia hesitated, then leaned toward the door again. There was a woman's voice mixed in with the deeper male voices—two or three, in fact. No one was whispering; it seemed like they were all just having a chat. Her eyebrows drew together, and she pushed her ear full against the door to listen.

"Oh, yes, I am sure you would find much to recommend Pemberley. What a pity we cannot find a way to bring you there."

Aurelia jerked back. *Pemberley?*

Deciding she must have misheard, she felt her body relax for a moment before she stiffened again. Whoever these people were, the door was the only thing separating her from them. They might be harmlessly chatting now, but there was no telling how long it would be before they wondered what—or who—was on the other side of the door.

She pulled her other arm through the sleeve of her jacket as she climbed the stairs to the flat, then found her phone and quietly padded back down again. But as her fingers hovered over the buttons, ready to dial the police, she heard a chorus of 'goodbyes' and 'farewells.' Were they leaving, then? She leaned against the door and registered a sudden hush just as the light at the threshold faded away.

Aurelia dialed the police and then unlocked the door and slowly pushed it open. She stepped onto the shop's mezzanine and swept her eyes past its bookshelves and down to the ground floor. For a split second, she thought she saw a small puff of smoke hovering above the round table near the front of the shop. Her breath caught in her throat at the possibility of a fire, but when she stepped forward and looked again, there wasn't any smoke at all.

Though it was dark inside, the first light of dawn was just visible through the large window at the other end of the mezzanine, and she could see the shop was empty. Hearing a noise, it took Aurelia a moment to register that someone was speaking to her through the phone.

"Hello?" she asked, bringing it to her ear.

"Yes, what's your emergency?"

"I'm sorry," Aurelia said, shaking her head. In her confusion over walking in to find the shop deserted, she'd forgotten she'd dialed the police. "No—I... There's no emergency, actually. Everything is fine."

Then, remembering those voices, she wondered, *But is it, really?*

2

Despite her exhaustion, Aurelia couldn't fall asleep after going back up to the flat. Those voices had seemed incredibly real. And yet, the way they'd disappeared almost instantly... She would have heard the bell over the shop door if people had filed outside. But instead, they'd vanished within seconds.

All evidence suggested that it was a very vivid dream. Or, Aurelia acknowledged, perhaps it was the emotional by-product of a tragic and terrible year.

She made herself a cup of tea and sat in one of her aunt's cozy armchairs. Fezz the cat, having apparently forgiven her for waking him up in the middle of the night, hopped up and created room for himself at her side. Aurelia petted him absentmindedly as she looked out over the square that bordered the front of the building. She'd grown up loving her visits to the bookshop and had worked there on and off over the years. True, she'd always imagined she would take over the shop one day, but it was all too soon. Her aunt was supposed to retire in a dozen or so years, giving Aurelia time to write a few novels of her own before she started selling other people's books. The shop, once as beloved as one of her favorite novels, had become an anchor weighing her down, tying her to a future she wasn't yet ready to face.

All the same, Aurelia hadn't written so much as a haiku recently. Her aunt had died three months ago, and her mother nine months before that. One year ago, yesterday, in fact. It had been an unbearable year; each week brought a new high or low as first her mother and then her aunt worked their way through various treatments that seemed promising before, each time, they failed and cancer took its hold.

Grief seemed to ooze out of her every pore these days, and she was afraid of the very real possibility that it might spill onto the page. She was sad enough living through it all without subjecting an audience to her misery. Part of her longed to write again, but another, stronger part of her felt almost repelled by the thought of opening her emotional floodgates any further.

A year's worth of grief—maybe that's what had brought on last night's hallucination. She'd spent the day walking around the city and visiting her mum's favorite spots: Chelsea Physic Garden and tea in the café; a walk down the hidden lanes tucked off ancient Fleet Street; then sitting alongside the Thames at dusk. Aurelia and her sister, Antonia, had debated whether to travel to Yorkshire to spend the day with their father or meet in Paris, where Antonia lived with her husband and three children. In the end, they'd decided to wait to see each other at Christmas as it was just over a month away.

Trudging home yesterday in the chill air of late autumn, Aurelia thought maybe she should have spent the day with her father and sister after all. Now, after last night's misadventure, she felt certain of it. Those voices, that light under the door—her mind returned to it all again and again. Could it have been real, as it had seemed to her then? But she'd heard them talking about Pemberley, which wasn't a real place at all.

Aurelia frowned and drew her knees up to her chin, chiding herself for thinking that last night could be anything other than the result of being overtired and overly sad. She felt a sudden need to talk to her sister and, almost as soon as she had the thought, her phone rang.

"It really is amazing," Aurelia said as she answered. She smiled and nestled deeper into her chair.

Antonia gave the slightest pause as she processed this. "Did we do it again?"

"We did. I was *just* about to call you."

"I know you think it makes us special—"

"And I know you think it makes us freaks," Aurelia laughed.

She could hear the faint sound of children's voices raised in either a game or an argument; she couldn't tell which. Her heart ached to hear how distant their voices sounded.

"How are my darling niece and nephews?"

"Well, Julia's been reading *Little Women* and is now making up her own plays."

A shriek made Aurelia pull the phone from her ear.

"As you can no doubt hear, she and the boys are in the other room practicing one right now," Antonia added.

"Aw, Mum's favorite book. I'm glad Julia likes it."

"Yeah, it felt like the right time to share it with her." Antonia paused, her signal for a shift to serious talk. "How are you doing?"

"Fine? Fine, I suppose," Aurelia said before adding the obvious. "Sad."

"Me too."

"It's not like I haven't missed her all year, it's just hard having it be the end of the first year. 'The first anniversary.'" Aurelia swallowed down a few threatening tears.

"I know," Antonia said softly just as the children's voices reared up through the phone again, punctuated by a high-pitched scream. "It helped having the kids to distract me. I talked to Dad—did you?"

"I did. He sounded okay, didn't he?"

"I might have rung up a few of his friends to remind them to check in on him," Antonia said without a hint of guilt. "What did you get up to after we talked yesterday?"

"Oh... I went on a sort of pilgrimage and walked around some of Mum's favorite places."

"Did it help?"

"I don't know." Remembering last night's events, Aurelia amended that, saying, "I don't think so."

"Are you alright?"

"Yeah, it's just... The strangest thing happened. I woke up convinced people had broken into the shop. But I checked and no one was there."

"You *checked*?"

"I called the police," Aurelia reassured her. "But the shop was empty—there was no sign of anyone breaking in." She gave a mirthless laugh and added, "I thought I heard them talking about Pemberley."

"What's that?"

"You remember—Darcy's place! From *Pride and Prejudice*."

"Oh, right. Well, leave it to you to have literate burglars."

"I know," Aurelia said, rolling her eyes at herself. "Still, it did spook me a bit. I'm just getting used to Aunt Marigold's flat, the different noises."

She thought again of those voices. They weren't exactly the hum and creak of an old building, but she was determined to move past it.

"I'll bet after another week or two I won't even notice."

"How are you managing? I mean, it's a great flat and all, but everything in there must remind you of her."

"It does," Aurelia admitted, looking around at the mess of her moving boxes mixed in with her aunt's things. "But it's free. My old lease was up anyway, and it doesn't make sense to pay rent somewhere else when I'm here running the shop every day."

There was an awkward silence. The shop had been in their family for generations, passed down from aunt to niece since the early 1900s. With Antonia's life firmly rooted in Paris, Marigold had left the shop to Aurelia—giving her no choice but to keep the family business going.

"I know I've said it before," Antonia said sincerely, "but I wouldn't blame you if you wanted to sell the place."

"I can't let it go. And what if Julia wants to run it one day? I'll make it work." Aurelia tried her best to sound convincing.

"Are you at least keeping up with your writing?"

"No." Quickly cutting her sister off, she added, "Not right now anyway. I'm not in a good place these days."

"Exactly. You're tucked away with all of Aunt Marigold's old things."

The children's voices reached fever pitch; Antonia's teasing tone was gone when she spoke again.

"I'd better go. Try to think happy thoughts, Relia. Know I love you."

Aurelia held her breath, trying not to let loose her tears.

"I do. You too."

She hung up and rested her head on the back of the chair as she closed her eyes. She and her sister had started saying 'know I love you' whenever they spoke. It had been their mother's way of saying goodbye ever since they were little, her way of sending them off into the world safe in the knowledge that they were loved. A tear slid down her cheek and Aurelia swept it away before opening her eyes and sitting up in her chair.

"Right, then."

Nodding decisively, she stood and walked toward the kitchen. As she passed a box filled with her old notebooks and journals, she paused, brushing a hand across their spines. Would she ever again feel that need to hold a pen in her hand and scribble down her ideas? Pursing her lips in frustration, she turned from the notebooks and resolved to start her day in earnest.

3

An hour later and Aurelia was standing in the stairwell at the door to the shop, willing herself to walk through it and go about the business of opening for the day. She felt a chill run up her spine at the thought of stepping into the shop again, but it was broad daylight and there were no voices coming from the other side of the door. Last night had to have been a dream, no matter how very real it might have seemed. Inhaling deeply as though the air could supply her with courage, Aurelia opened the door and walked onto the mezzanine.

It was empty, just as it should be.

She exhaled and looked around. Whenever she walked into the shop, she was always conscious of the hush that came from the dense books; the worn, sky-blue carpet underfoot; and the yellow curtains with their blue tasseled tiebacks. On her visits to the shop as a child, she'd been dazzled by its blue and yellow décor, so evocative of moonlit skies and magicians' capes. She was less dazzled once she was old enough to vacuum and dust what to her had felt like miles of blue carpet and rows and rows of books.

There was a wrought iron railing overlooking the floor below, and Aurelia stepped over to it. Like the ground floor, bookshelves ran along the mezzanine, though there were gaps for artwork and built-in benches where customers could sit and read. Opposite the door to the flat stretched a wide cushioned window seat set below the oversized window at the front of the building, facing the street. The only sounds were her own breathing, the soft ticking of the clock downstairs, and the distant noises from the street outside. She reminded herself that a quiet shop was a good sign; it was further proof that what she'd experienced last night was all in her imagination.

Satisfied that everything was as it should be, Aurelia walked down the spiral staircase that led from the mezzanine to the back of the shop, where she passed a large semicircular desk with a high ledge running across the top. The desk was home to a register and a small typewriter that had sat there for so long that it was practically a fixture. Heading toward the front of the shop, she surveyed the overstuffed yellow velvet armchair and the round table with its rotating stock of books marked as 'Recommended Reads.' She was nearly past the table when one of the books on display, *Pride and Prejudice*, caught her attention.

Ah, she told herself, *I must have spotted it yesterday and had it in the back of my mind.* Relief washed over her until she realized that might explain why she thought she'd heard a reference to Darcy's home, but not why she'd heard voices in the first place.

Her anxious thoughts were displaced by the sound of the old mantel clock at the back of the shop chiming to let her know that it was ten o'clock and time to open for the day.

Moving to the front windows, she raised the blinds and looked out across the street, which formed one side of a small and leafy square that had inspired the shop's name—On the Square Books. The shop's building was tucked in amongst others on the street like a slim book between heavier volumes on a bookshelf. Though it was in central London, somehow the square was an oasis from the general hubbub of city life, and this morning was no exception.

Usually Aurelia appreciated the stillness, but now she wished for a bit more noise and activity to distract her from the thoughts that kept surfacing—strange noises in the shop, the odd light under the door. At least it was a Saturday, she told herself, which was sure to bring customers and, with them, something different to occupy her mind.

In spite of Aurelia's hopes, not a single customer crossed the threshold until just before noon, when one of Aunt Marigold's old regulars arrived.

Just as she did now, Mrs. Smith always seemed to arrive and depart in a rush with her corgi, Alfie, trotting behind her as fast as his short little legs could carry him. Whenever Fezz saw Alfie, he slunk to the spiral staircase and let out a few non-threatening hisses as he affected to nonchalantly climb the stairs. Alfie would stand below, whimpering his desperation to follow Fezz, but too afraid to venture far from Mrs. Smith—likely afraid she'd race out of the shop without him.

The two animals began their standoff as soon as Mrs. Smith breezed inside. Mrs. Smith—she was always 'Mrs. Smith' since she'd never invited Aurelia to call her by her first name—didn't so much as look at Aurelia but headed straight for the shelves stocked with Agatha Christie's works.

"Good morning, Mrs. Smith," Aurelia said somewhat feebly. "Can I help you find something?"

"Oh, it's you."

It had been three months, but she still seemed surprised every time she found Aurelia in the shop instead of Marigold.

"Where's *The Unexpected Guest*?" Waving her hand at the shelves, Mrs. Smith continued, "Do you have it in stock?"

"Um, yes. *The Unexpected Guest*... I know we have the novelization."

Mrs. Smith grunted her disapproval.

"Let me just see—we also have the script if that's what you're after?"

"It is," Mrs. Smith said, taking the book from Aurelia and giving it a glance before striding toward the register.

"You know, we have some excellent mysteries by other authors. *The Moonstone* is just there, on the table, if you'd like to have a look."

Mrs. Smith had her handbag open and was digging inside, which Aurelia took as her version of 'No, thank you.'

"*The Unexpected Guest* it is, then."

Once Mrs. Smith had paid for the book, she smiled as she looked down at its cover.

"I've never seen it performed, but since I've read all her other books at least once, I thought I might as well read the script."

Mrs. Smith looked up and startled when she saw Aurelia standing in front of her. Aurelia was certain that, for a moment, she had thought Marigold would be there in her place.

"Well, thank you."

"You're very welcome."

Aurelia felt she ought to say something more—comfort her in some way—but Mrs. Smith had already turned and walked to the door. Aurelia watched as Alfie ran to her side, barely managing to pass through the door alongside her.

"Come again," Aurelia called out, just as the door closed behind them.

It wasn't exactly the distraction she'd been hoping for, but at least instead of worrying about hearing voices, she was now back to wondering whether the shop would ever feel like her own.

4

It was four o'clock in the morning and Aurelia was standing in her pajamas at the door that led from the flat to the shop. She'd woken to the sound of voices again and had gotten to the bottom of the stairs only to hear them more distinctly and to see that same light coming from under the door. Once again, the voices didn't seem angry or aggressive. It was all playing out just like last night, making it harder to believe she might be dreaming.

This time, she'd brought her phone with her straight away and she clutched it in her hand, debating what to do. She was scared but also... curious. Were people actually in the shop, or was she just hearing things? Last night she'd seen for herself that no one was there; perhaps they would go away again if she opened the door? It was mad, but she made the snap decision to do it—to open the door and check. She had her phone, she reassured herself, so she could quickly call the police if she discovered that the voices were attached to bodies.

Aurelia's hand was shaking, but she managed to turn the door handle. Peeking through the smallest possible gap, she ran her eyes over the mezzanine but saw no sign of anyone. It seemed as though the voices were coming from the first floor of the shop; she'd have to get closer to be sure. She stepped through the door and took a few steps toward the mezzanine railing. Blinking in the soft light emanating all around her, she stood still as her eyes adjusted after the darkness of the stairwell.

Within the same instant, she registered two things: the voices had gone quiet, and people were standing downstairs looking up at her.

Feeling as though she'd opened the wrong door into the wrong room, Aurelia quickly stepped back into the stairwell and closed the door. For a moment she was embarrassed by her mistake before remembering it wasn't a mistake at all—she'd definitely walked into the shop, and she'd certainly seen a group of people there. With that reality confirmed, she fumbled for the lock, then closed her eyes and tried to steady her erratic heartbeat.

Well, she thought, *not only did the voices not disappear, but they are now officially connected to bodies.* She couldn't decide whether that made her feel better, or worse.

It took her several tries to dial the police, thanks to her shaking hands. Once they promised they were on their way, her tension eased, but only just.

As she waited, she replayed her brief encounter with the people. They were all wearing suits and dresses that looked like costumes from a period drama, not exactly the sort of outfits you'd expect to see on a group of burglars. Was it some sort of fancy-dress party? The thought shifted her feelings from fear to anger—just who did these people think they were, making themselves at home in the wee hours?

Curiosity and annoyance did battle with her fear. Maybe she ought to go back out and shout at them to leave? The police were already on their way, and the people she'd seen were all downstairs. If she went in again, she was certain she could get back to safety quickly if anyone made a move toward her. She was still trembling slightly, in spite of her resolve, but managed to open the door again.

Taking a step toward the mezzanine railing, she leaned forward. There they were! A whole gathering of people looking up at her. She let out a mangled scream as she stumbled backward, falling to the ground as she tripped over Fezz, who had appeared underfoot.

She heard gasps from below and someone saying, quite calmly: "Oh, dear. She is not taking it well at all, is she?"

All thoughts of shouting at the people and telling them to leave were gone—Aurelia's only instinct now was to escape. She scooped up the cat and got herself back into the flat's stairwell, slamming the door behind her. After locking it, she held Fezz tight against her chest, breathing hard. She had the urge to scream again but couldn't seem to find her voice through her shock—it seemed she'd used up her minute of pluck.

Aurelia's knees practically gave way beneath her as she sat on a stair and counted the seconds until she heard a police siren signaling their arrival to rescue her.

———— ☾ ————

The shop was a scene of chaos. Police were milling about, their badges catching the lights and their shoes crunching broken glass into the carpet. When they had arrived at the shop, they told her, there was no sign of forced entry. Having been informed that she was barricaded upstairs, they broke the glass door themselves in order to get in and look for intruders. They reported seeing what looked like smoke near the table at the front of the shop, but after they'd turned on the lights, it was gone and there was no sign of a fire or smell of smoke on the air. Nothing had been disturbed—the books were in order and the register hadn't been tampered with.

The police were kind, but it was clear they'd written it all off as a false alarm. One of them gave her the number for a twenty-four-hour glazier who could fix the glass panel on the door, and they left once the glazier had arrived and started his work.

When Aurelia was by herself in the building again, dawn light was coming in through the blinds of the shop windows, reflecting off the glass shards on the floor. Another sleepless night, another baffling encounter, and now add to that—a mess to clean.

5

It was Sunday, the shop was closed, and the day seemed to stretch out before Aurelia in an unpleasant way. Even after vacuuming up broken glass and downing several bracingly strong cups of tea, she still had hours to fill. But she knew her mind would be stuck on repeat, playing over what had happened.

She considered the evidence: she could see and hear people in the shop in the middle of the night, and they seemed to disappear quite suddenly. There was also that strange light that came and went along with them. Narrowing the possibilities, she thought she was either dealing with ghosts or hallucinations. While neither was particularly appealing, she was leaning toward ghosts since that option was preferable to losing the power of rational thinking.

Aurelia thought of her sister and father, who'd known Aunt Marigold almost as well as she had. Maybe Marigold had mentioned something to them about the shop being haunted? If so, it would go a long way toward easing her mind.

She decided to try calling her father first. He must have heard the tension in her voice because he soon asked if everything was alright.

"Yes, everything's fine."

She was determined not to tell him or Antonia about the police since they'd be guaranteed to worry about her.

"It's silly, really, but I was wondering... Do you remember if Aunt Marigold believed in things... like, supernatural things?"

"What, like ghosts and spirits?"

"Right, that sort of thing. Did she ever mention anything like that?"

"I'd have to think."

He paused, giving Aurelia time to appreciate that, as a retired philosophy professor, he was game to indulge her by carefully considering an entirely random question.

"I suppose I'd say Marigold was a very practical person," he reasoned. "She loved her books, same as you, but I think she left fiction to her novels."

Aurelia sank back into her chair. She had to agree with him; Aunt Marigold *had* been a very practical, rational person. If she'd ever encountered something out of the ordinary in the shop, she likely felt as Aurelia did now—unsure if it were actually happening and unwilling to tell anyone and risk them thinking she was unstable.

"Do *you* believe in those sorts of things, Dad?"

"Do I?" After another thoughtful pause, he replied, "I suppose I believe there are still a few unanswerable mysteries in the world—things that can't be explained by modern theories. Don't you?"

Aurelia had to admit that she did. Not only because of recent experience, but other incidents that, so far in her life, she couldn't explain away with rational explanations. Like the calls to and from Antonia that one or the other usually anticipated before the phone rang. Since they never set a date for their calls, it seemed as if one sister could simply sense when the other was about to call. And how many times had Aurelia seen Marigold hand a customer a book right before they'd asked for it?

"I do, yeah. I like answers, though."

Her father laughed and said, "Well, mysteries make life a little more enjoyable and unexpected. Just think if your novels answered every question. It wouldn't leave much room for the imagination, would it?"

"Hmm." Aurelia smiled. "I see your point, but I still don't like it."

"We rarely like what's good for us."

"Like Brussels sprouts."

"Or flossing," her father added.

Aurelia's smile widened at the smile she could hear in his voice. He reminded her that he'd be coming down to London later in the week and they made plans to meet for dinner. They soon rang off, leaving Aurelia to think about whether what she'd seen in the shop was one of those unanswerable mysteries he'd mentioned.

When she still couldn't come up with a good answer, she decided to sound out Antonia. She dialed her number and Antonia picked up after the first ring.

"I was just about to call. How're you doing?" Antonia asked, unfazed by the apparent coincidence.

"Oh, good." Aurelia tried for a casual tone but failed.

"What's wrong?"

"Nothing's wrong," Aurelia fibbed. "I was just thinking about Aunt Marigold this morning."

Antonia made a vague noise that suggested she was growing distracted, so Aurelia forged ahead.

"Do you remember... Did she ever... I mean—"

Aurelia couldn't make up her mind how to casually ask her sister about ghosts. It had been easier with her father, somehow.

"Spit it out, Relia."

Aurelia closed her eyes—nothing for it now.

"Did Aunt Marigold ever mention seeing or hearing anything strange in the shop?"

That had got Antonia's attention; Aurelia could hear her growing still.

"Strange like what?"

"Just... strange. Unusual."

"Like noises? Did you hear something again last night?"

Antonia was a bloodhound for intrigue and seemed to sense there was more to Aurelia's question. Of course, Aurelia *had* heard something again last night, but it was what she had *seen* that concerned her.

"I did, but it wasn't like someone had broken in. It was more like there was... a presence."

"What, like ghosts?"

"Something like that."

"Um… I remember her saying she thought there were mice in the walls."

"I can confirm—there are," Aurelia groaned.

"Other than that, no. I don't think she ever talked about feeling a 'presence' or seeing a ghost." Antonia grew serious. "Is it too much, Aurelia? Living there and running the shop? You were out of sorts yesterday, and now—"

"No, I'm fine. Really. I was just curious, that's all."

"You're sure?"

"The shop, the flat—everything's fine." Aurelia hoped she sounded convincing.

"The shop's closed today, right? Can you get out for a bit? You said you went for a walk the other day—are you doing your 'idea walks' again?"

"No," Aurelia said with a sigh. She hadn't been writing, so she hadn't needed to go out wandering the city in search of ideas and inspiration like she used to do. After her mum died, Aunt Marigold had joined her for a while, insisting that she keep up with her walks—and her writing. Now, with Marigold gone too, Aurelia had lost the habit of it. "But I could probably do with some fresh air."

"Go. Maybe you'll see something out in the world that'll inspire you to start writing again. Or *someone*."

Trust Antonia to seamlessly shift from concern over Aurelia's well-being to concern over her stagnant love life.

Like her writing, Aurelia's romantic prospects had tapered off in the wake of her mother's death. She'd been dating a nice-enough guy named Brendan for a few months when her mother had gotten sick, and he'd stuck by her through the difficult months that followed. Aurelia had liked him well enough but knew he wasn't 'the one.' Still, she'd hung onto him—perhaps selfishly, she could admit now—as she'd needed to lean on someone who wasn't torn up by grief the way her father, sister, and aunt had been.

But when Marigold became sick soon after her mother died, Brendan had broken things off with Aurelia, declaring it all 'too much.' She'd been hurt by it, but another, deeper, part of her understood. She'd wanted to say, 'Right there with you,' and walk out on herself. It had all *felt* too much—she couldn't blame him for wanting a relationship with someone who wasn't wrung out from crying on a daily basis. Now, months after Aunt Marigold's death, Aurelia was certain she was still too much for someone new to want to take her on.

"I'm not looking for anyone inspiring just yet, Tonia."

"Well, keep your eyes open while you're out, anyway."

Aurelia returned from a walk, clutching a nearly empty coffee cup as if it might still warm her hands. Standing in front of the shop door, she peered through the new glass panel, trying to decide whether it was safe to go in. She'd done the same thing on her way out of the flat as she left for her walk—opened the door a crack and peeked through to confirm the shop was deserted, as it always was on Sundays. Now, putting up a brave front, Aurelia opened the door and walked inside. A light gust of wind blew in behind her, sweeping her hair around her face. She closed the door and turned the lock, then looked around. There was no one there but her.

Hearing a thump above her, she flinched in surprise only to realize it was Fezz hopping down from the window seat. Not a ghost, then. She sighed at her jumpiness, then climbed the spiral staircase to the mezzanine and waited as Fezz made his way toward her. Aurelia smiled and shook her head at his glacial, nonchalant pace, then bent down and rubbed his cheek.

"Desperately missed me as usual, hmm?"

She stood and opened the door to the flat, then watched Fezz scramble up the stairs. Turning back, she looked across the shop, through the mezzanine window, and out to the trees in the small square. She used to love this view, but now—between taking over the shop and losing sleep over her mysterious nightly visitors—she felt trapped, as though she were looking through the bars of a well-appointed cage.

6

Lying in bed with a pillow over her head, Aurelia knew the voices were still coming from downstairs, even if she temporarily couldn't hear them. She'd woken just after two in the morning to their steady prattling. At first, she tried to convince herself that they were simply a group of social ghosts meeting for a chat. Eventually, though, the voices became more distinct, making it harder to tune them out. Whether the product of her own delusions or the paranormal, she decided to get up rather than pretend she could possibly ignore them. She tossed the pillow back onto the bed and stood, pulling on the clothes she'd left on the floor a few hours earlier when she'd changed for bed.

From the top of the stairs, she could hear the voices more clearly. She carried her phone down to the doorway, though she doubted the police would appreciate another call from her. She felt vexed and anxious to be standing here once again, but those feelings were tempered by her memory of the night before. Whoever they were, they hadn't exactly seemed like the criminal element in their fancy dress. And, despite seeing her on the mezzanine, no one had come toward her or threatened her.

Determined to investigate, she crouched to the ground and slowly opened the door into the shop. She couldn't see anyone, which meant they must be downstairs again. The lights were on—but were they? Looking up, she could see the bulbs were dark, but there was light coming from somewhere. She couldn't get a good view of the shop floor from the doorway, so she crawled forward with her phone clutched in her hand.

As she peered through the mezzanine railing, Aurelia could see people standing about and talking to one another. No one noticed her, giving her a chance to take it all in. There were about ten people there, men and women. Once again, they were wearing old-fashioned clothes, complete with cravats, full skirts, and long hemlines. Standing together, they looked like the cast of an Austen or Dickens adaptation and didn't seem at all concerned about the fact that they were trespassing. Instead, they appeared to feel right at home, just as a group of ghosts might.

Her focus was drawn to a woman in a silk dress with a feather sticking out of her carefully coiffed hair. She was speaking with a man in a black suit who had large mutton-chop whiskers. He was pointing to a book on the Recommended Reads table and then moved his hand as if to pick it up. Only—his hand went right through it, turning into a white mist with what looked like black dots running across it... or were they letters? He pulled his arm back, shaking his head and chuckling as the mist reformed into his hand once again.

Aurelia couldn't contain her gasp of surprise, which was loud enough to turn several heads in her direction. The woman in silk gave her an inquisitive smile and Aurelia, panic-stricken at being spotted, crawled backward, bumped into the doorframe, then got behind the door and quickly locked it.

Ghosts, she told herself, remembering the misty hand as though it were being projected right in front of her. *Definitely ghosts.*

She leaned against the door with her head thrown back and legs splayed out. It was then that she realized she'd left her phone on the floor of the shop, near the railing. She covered her face with her hands and then slowly lowered them. Even if she'd had it with her, what on earth would she say to the police this time? 'I'm calling to report a haunting'?

7

When Aurelia woke the next morning, it was because of pain instead of her alarm. She was curled into a ball at the bottom of the stairwell and had to slowly unwind her limbs and stretch them out before she could stand up.

She'd fallen asleep listening to the voices coming through from the other side of the door, fascinated by the bits of conversation she could make out as their volume rose and fell. There was a heated discussion about whether the Royal Navy could continue to outmaneuver Napoleon and excited theorizing about what type of sleeves would be popular in the coming season. It wasn't exactly the stuff of current affairs. Still, once Aurelia had gotten over her initial panic, she'd almost enjoyed hearing the voices transition from the annoying noise that had kept her awake at night, to conversations between people with unique personalities and points of view.

The vaporizing hand had dispelled Aurelia's fear of intruders once and for all. She was now almost certain they were ghosts, but so many? In one shop? She'd heard of one ghost haunting a place before, but a whole crowd? She tried to think if there was anyone she could confide in but felt certain that everyone she knew would likely say the same thing—her imagination was running wild because of too much time spent alone, too much time reading books, too little time spent processing her recent losses... And maybe they'd be right.

Aurelia focused on the routine of her morning to distract herself from thoughts of ghosts and hauntings. Moderately alert after breakfast and a shower, she headed down the stairs that led to the shop and stopped at the bottom to pull an oversized cardigan from a peg on the wall. Slipping her arms into the sleeves, she hesitated for a moment and then pushed open the door. All was quiet below.

She picked up her phone from where she'd left it on the floor, then headed downstairs and went into the back room to make tea. Pulling a box from a shelf, she found a single teabag left inside, but she'd need two this morning since she was expecting a visitor. She poked around the shelf and countertop, then bent down to rummage through the cabinets. At last, she wrapped her hand around a likely box at the back of a cabinet and pulled it out. It was tea, but there was a small note attached to it, scrawled out in her aunt's handwriting: *Marigold's tea! Consume at your own peril.*

Aurelia laughed, remembering their battles over whose turn it was to buy tea. She'd been convinced that Marigold had a secret stash somewhere, and she'd finally found it. But then her smile wavered, giving way to tears, and she was lost in missing her aunt.

When she heard the click of the electric kettle switching off, the water now ready, Aurelia knew she had to pull herself together. She'd need to open the shop soon and couldn't greet customers with tears streaming down her face, so she ran up to the flat to sort herself out. Once she was mostly back to normal, she grabbed a half-empty box of tea—one that wouldn't make her cry—and slumped back down the stairs, willing herself to put on a brave face.

Tea made, she left one mug at the desk and carried the other with her as she moved to the front of the shop. Pausing at the Recommended Reads table, she placed her hand on each stack of books, almost believing a mist might appear. But no—she was as solid as ever, as were the books.

Sighing, she moved to the front windows and raised the blinds, then unlocked the door and opened it, taking in the morning. It was cool enough to see a few wisps of her breath as she exhaled. Aurelia felt her sadness ebb as the chilly air brushed her skin and she watched the square come to life. She waved to a neighbor passing on the other side of the street, then retreated inside with her shoulders hunched and her hands wrapped around her mug for warmth.

Her phone rang from where she'd tucked it in her pocket and she jumped, nearly spilling her tea. As she walked to the desk, Aurelia pulled her phone out and saw it was David, one of her oldest friends. She answered as she leaned against the desk to watch for customers.

"Why aren't you at school?" she asked, knowing his days usually started early since he taught history at a local secondary school.

"Good morning to you too," he said, his voice muffled. "And I *am* at school—I'm in between classes, so I can't talk long, but I wanted to check on you."

"Me? I'm fine."

"That's not what Antonia says."

"What did she say?" Aurelia felt defensive even though she knew Antonia had plenty to report about her—like questions about ghosts and worries over burglars.

"She said you've been weird and need to get out of the shop. So, you're going on a date tonight."

"No, I'm not," Aurelia insisted before her curiosity took over and she added, "With who?"

"With Oliver. He works with James at his publishing house."

Aurelia bit back a smile; David loved calling the publisher where his boyfriend worked a 'publishing house,' even though James insisted it was a tiny company that was more like a publishing closet than a house.

"I've never heard James mention someone named Oliver—and I'm not going."

"That's because Oliver just started working there a few weeks ago. Listen, I can't raise my voice right now because my students are filing in, but you're going," David informed her.

"Have you even met this man?"

"Of course I have."

"How old is he?" Aurelia challenged.

"Mid-thirties?" David guessed. "He's our age," he added defensively.

"What's his surname?"

"Just call him Oliver."

"You don't know it, do you?"

"Look, I've got to go," he whispered urgently. "I'll text you the details later."

David hung up before she could keep arguing, leaving her to shake her head indignantly.

"I'm not going," she muttered to herself as she sipped her tea.

A date was the last thing she needed after sleepless nights and strange happenings in the shop. Antonia was just meddling and, as one of Aurelia's closest friends, David was only too happy to join in. His parents had moved to the outskirts of London from Kenya when he was in primary school and the two of them had bonded after an eventful school outing when they discovered that they both became carsick on buses. Their long friendship meant he knew her sister well since Antonia was only two years older than them, and they'd spent plenty of time together over the years. It was fun when they were all plotting something in tandem but far less fun when Aurelia was the one being plotted about. She would just have to ring him back during his afternoon break and tell him to call the date off.

Aurelia was still grumbling to herself when she spotted an older man walking past the square and heading for the shop. The sight of him instantly lifted her mood and she smiled as he opened the door and set its bell ringing.

"Good morning, Mark!"

"Morning, Aurelia."

He walked slowly toward her, favoring an old injury in his right knee, and greeted her with a wistful smile. Mark was in his late sixties and had rumpled salt-and-pepper hair and stubble that was less an aesthetic choice than a sign that he wasn't taking particularly good care of himself. He wore an old tweed coat and a maroon scarf that had seen better days, but Aurelia knew he wouldn't part with it for the world. Marigold had knitted it for him many years ago after tutting to see him underdressed for midwinter. Mark quickly became a regular visitor to the shop, but it had taken him years to confess his feelings for Marigold. She had let him down gently, but they remained friends, with Mark ever pining for her.

"How've you been?" Aurelia asked, sliding the extra mug of tea across the counter.

"Oh, doing alright," Mark said, pausing to take a sip. "I was wondering how you were doing, since... Well, it was a year ago this week, wasn't it?"

Aurelia blinked hard and only just managed to keep from crying again. She hadn't expected Mark to remember, though he'd witnessed Aurelia and Marigold struggling through the difficult days and weeks after her mother's death.

"It was, yeah. Thanks, Mark."

He reached out a tentative hand and patted her arm.

"It's been a hard year, but you've come through just fine," he said encouragingly.

"I don't know about that," Aurelia said, rubbing at a muscle in her neck that was still sore from last night's cramped sleeping position.

"No, you've got to give yourself credit," Mark scolded, though not unkindly. "Taking on the shop all on your own... I know Marigold would have been so impressed. She was lucky—she had her aunt to lean on for help when she first started."

"Mmm... I'm trying, anyway," she said with a half-hearted laugh.

"This place is very special to me—to a lot of people." Mark stooped to catch her eye and then nodded. "It means a great deal to us, knowing it'll always be here."

After Marigold's death, Mark had stopped visiting the shop, leaving Aurelia to worry over him. A few weeks after the funeral, however, he appeared on a Monday morning, just after Aurelia had opened for the day. They didn't exchange a word; she just walked over and threw her arms around him. They'd shared a long hug that both of them needed, then she made him tea and let him wander. After that, he'd made it a habit to stop by on Monday mornings and Aurelia always looked forward to seeing him.

"I've spent so many happy hours here," he continued.

"Lately it feels a bit... like a place to clock in each day," Aurelia said quietly.

"I'd hate to think that were true."

Aurelia saw the concern in Mark's face and felt guilty for not sharing his enthusiasm.

"I think I'm still just settling in, getting used to running it myself," she said, repeating what had become her now-constant refrain.

"You've got to find a way to put your own stamp on the place," Mark said knowingly. "This carpet, those curtains—that was all Marigold. And she was very particular about the books she set out on the table," he added, nodding to the Recommended Reads table.

"I keep meaning to rearrange those," Aurelia admitted with a frown.

"Well, I'm going to need a new recommendation one of these days," Mark said kindly. "When you're ready."

8

During a lull that afternoon, Aurelia stood in front of the Recommended Reads table. Marigold used to swap out the table's display of books once a month, but Aurelia hadn't changed them since her aunt died. It had been three months of keeping the status quo for Aurelia's own sake, but maybe Mark was right and it was time to think about the shop's customers instead of herself.

Marigold had a 'system' for picking books for the table. She'd told Aurelia that she chose the books based on whether she thought the characters would get along. Keeping in mind that system, Aurelia wandered the shelves to make her selections. Family lore was unclear on exactly when or why it had happened, but the shop only carried novels written by authors born before 1900 and books about those novels and authors. Her aunt had sometimes dabbled in rare books and first editions, but even those were by the authors she carried in stock. Aurelia had come to love the shop's limited inventory and had lots of favorites, but the table's small size meant she would have to be choosy.

Anna Karenina was an obvious choice as it was Aurelia's favorite book. The first time she'd read it was the summer after her first year at university. Reading that book, she could almost feel the flakes of snow against her cheek as Anna said goodnight to Count Vronsky in St. Petersburg; she could feel the sun beating down as Levin sowed clover at his country estate; and, most of all, she remembered feeling the heartbreak of Anna's doomed romance with Vronsky.

Her mother had seen Aurelia reading the novel that summer and admitted that she'd never read it herself. She then bought her own copy from Marigold so they could read it together. Each week, one of them would read ahead before the other eventually caught up, but they both finished the book on the same day in August. They were forlorn that day, sitting outside in the shade in an unsuccessful attempt to escape the stifling heat, their hearts still in Russia with Vronsky as he mourned Anna's death. Aurelia remembered her mother had shivered as though there were a chill in the air as she said, 'You never get over a love like that. A love that powerful is written across the heart in indelible ink.' Looking at the book now, Aurelia put her hand to her own heart and tried to ignore the prickle of tears in her eyes. The truth in her mother's words seemed just as applicable to the pain Aurelia had experienced over the past year.

She gathered a few copies and put them on the table.

Antonia had just reminded her of their mother's favorite book, *Little Women*, and that was Aurelia's next pick. Their mother had read it to them when they were in primary school; each night they had burrowed onto the sofa together, ready for a new chapter in the adventures of the March sisters. With her natural bent toward writing, Aurelia felt her heart swell with pride when her mother said that she reminded her of the second-oldest sister, Jo. Aurelia had started calling Antonia 'Meg,' her mother 'Marmee,' and her father 'Papa,' driving the family to finally ban the book for a solid year. It was only with Aurelia's solemn promise not to try to live out the story that her mother agreed to read it to them again.

An armful of copies went on the table.

Sense and Sensibility was a must. Aurelia had been in secondary school when she first read it. She'd been assigned *Emma* in her English class and her mother, seeing the book amongst Aurelia's school things, had complained that her favorite Austen novel, *Sense and Sensibility*, was often overlooked. Aurelia had fished out her mother's copy from the family bookshelves and read it over a bank holiday weekend, succumbing to the lure of Elinor and Marianne Dashwood and the sisters' triumphs and woes.

On the table it went.

There was room for one more title. Aurelia looked at the spot where her next selection would go, which was now occupied by two copies of one of her aunt's last selections: *The Moonstone*. It had been her aunt's favorite book, and it had frequently made an appearance on the Recommended Reads table. Aurelia hadn't read it until Marigold, shocked to learn this, sent her home with a copy and refused to let her return to work until she'd finished it. Aurelia liked it, though she had to admit it wasn't a favorite, even with its quirky old detective, Sergeant Cuff. She didn't know what the allure was for her aunt and, much to her regret, she'd never asked what her aunt liked most about it. Aurelia hesitated before deciding that maybe she'd made enough changes for one day, and she left *The Moonstone* on the table.

After arranging the books just so, she stepped back and surveyed her work. She smiled, knowing Mark would be happy to see she'd taken his advice. Glancing up at the mantel clock, she saw it was a quarter to five. It occurred to her that she might go upstairs to make her mark on the flat too, and she started toward the shop door to close a few minutes early. But as she turned the lock, she remembered standing in that same spot hours earlier when she'd gotten the call from David.

"Oh no!"

She'd forgotten about his call, the random date he'd planned for her, and her own plan to call him back and refuse to go. She barely had her head on straight these days—how was she supposed to pretend to be normal on a date? She'd probably break down in tears, driving another man away with her 'too much'-ness.

Phone in hand, she paced in front of the shop windows as she waited for David to answer.

"Need help picking an outfit?" was his greeting.

"No—no, I don't because I'm not going. You've got to cancel."

"I'm not canceling. It's too late now."

"It's only just five! Your text said to meet him at eight."

"Exactly. Much too late to cancel. I'm sure he's looking forward to it and you don't want to disappoint him."

"Seriously, David—I'm not ready to meet anyone right now."

"As your oldest friend, I'm insisting that you go. One date."

Aurelia pulled a face, trying to think of a way to get out of it.

"Look, it's been a wild week—truly. The idea of going on a date right now—"

"It's not just an idea, Aurelia. It's happening."

"How about next week instead?"

David said nothing, prompting her to add quietly, "Or never?"

"I heard that, and no. You're going."

"I'm sure he's lovely, but—"

"He is. You're going to like him, but even if you don't, it'll be good for you to get out again. Have some fun. Drink some wine. Snog a boy."

"Oh, now we're snogging?"

"Don't scoff—he's cute. You'll want to snog him," David said with what she just knew was a wicked smile, even if she couldn't see it. "Meet the man for a drink and see where the night takes you."

She looked around the shop, at the Recommended Reads table where she was sure she'd seen a man's hand vaporize and reappear in the wee hours; at the mezzanine, where she'd peered down and been certain she'd seen people gathered in the shop late at night. Maybe getting out for a bit wasn't such a bad idea after all.

"You're really going to make me do this?" she asked, her resistance fading.

"I am. And you can thank me later," David said, clearly pleased with himself.

"Fine," she said on a dramatic sigh.

"And put in some effort," he said bossily. "I've talked you up, so don't go meeting him in a frumpy old jumper." He paused, then added a little more gently, "It's just a date, Aurelia. You'll be fine."

9

While Aurelia didn't want to doom the evening with low expectations, her expectations still weren't particularly high. After changing out of an oversized jumper (David *did* know her all too well), she tried to strike a balance between looking like she'd tried to smarten up without going overboard, though she wasn't sure she'd actually succeeded. It didn't help that she looked drawn and tired after so many sleepless nights.

Aurelia walked to the hotel bar in South Kensington where David had told her to meet Oliver for drinks. Once she was in the lobby, she spotted the bar, which was very posh and not at all the kind of place she usually liked. Standing in the doorway, she glanced around, trying to identify a lonely-looking man who might be waiting for her. No one seemed a likely candidate and she was just about to wander around the lobby to wait for him when she sensed someone standing behind her.

She turned and found herself uncomfortably close to a man who was a few inches taller than her. He had dark brown hair that was creeping backward, and brown eyes to match, though they were a lighter shade of brown than his hair. He was wearing a black jacket over an ice-blue oxford shirt, open at the neckline by only one button.

They both took a step back, which gave them more room to assess each other.

"Are you Oliver?"

"Yes. Oliver Pearce."

She had to admit he was attractive—David hadn't misled her there. But he had the slightly haughty, bored look of someone who was fulfilling an obligation, which instantly annoyed her. She was fulfilling the same obligation, after all.

"I'm Aurelia Lyndham. Hi," she said, leaning in for a friendly kiss on the cheek in greeting. Her movement was halted by Oliver's hand, however, which shot out to shake hers.

"Oh, right," she said, reaching out and shaking his hand.

"I should give you my card," he said, pulling a business card from his inside breast pocket.

"Your card?" she asked, staring down at the small rectangle in his hand.

"It has my contact info," he said offhandedly.

"Ah, okay. I don't exactly have a business card..."

Aurelia fumbled in her bag and found a bookmark from the shop, then handed it to him.

Oliver looked as confused by her bookmark as she'd been by his business card, but he eventually took it and tucked it into his pocket. He looked away from her and into the bar, saying "Shall we go in?"

She followed him and inwardly groaned when he chose a high-top table with tall barstools. She hated those types of tables as she always felt awkward sitting with her feet dangling.

As soon as they were seated, Oliver took hold of the cocktail menu and stared down at it. Watching him, Aurelia wondered whether he was just nervous or entirely disinterested. She looked around the bar, which was sparsely populated, probably because it was a Monday night and most people—lucky people—were tucked up at home.

"I'm not sure why David picked this spot," she observed, feeling like she ought to make an effort at conversation.

Oliver looked up as she wrinkled her nose.

"It's not really my kind of place. Too sterile," she added conspiratorially.

"David didn't pick it. I did," Oliver said, returning his attention to the cocktail menu.

Crap.

"Ah! Put my foot right in it, didn't I?" she acknowledged with a laugh.

"That you did," Oliver said, sliding the menu across to her.

His lip had quirked and Aurelia thought she caught a momentary sparkle in his eye. He had a sense of humor buried in there somewhere.

"What's your kind of place, then?" he asked.

"I like a bar that's a little more lived-in. Somewhere that has furniture that's been knocked about a bit, maybe a fireplace."

"More like a pub, then?"

"Sure, beer-stained tables and all," she said with a warm smile.

"Mmm," Oliver intoned, still not giving a smile of his own. He seemed to hold himself back with a reserve that gave Aurelia a quick shiver.

A server came to the table and asked for their drinks order.

"She hasn't had a chance to look at the menu," Oliver said, preparing to dismiss him.

"She doesn't need to," Aurelia cut in, sitting up taller to remind them that she was sitting right there. The server gave a chuckle, but Oliver still wouldn't crack. "I'll have a glass of cabernet."

"They do a good cocktail here," Oliver said, frowning.

"That's alright—I'm happy with a glass of wine," she said, smiling first at him, then at the server.

Once they'd ordered, it felt like an eternity until the drinks finally arrived. Aurelia tried not to take an obvious gulp when their server set her glass down on the table.

They talked about Oliver's work, which led to a discussion of how she knew James, which led to a discussion about where they'd gone to university. It was all very polite and surface-level, like they were guests at a party where they only knew the host.

During the first awkward pause, Aurelia tried and failed to hide a yawn.

"What do you do for work? James didn't say."

"I..." *I'm a writer who can't write anymore* was the first answer that came to her, but she bit her lip to keep it in. Instead, she said, "I run a bookshop. Thus the bookmark," she added, nodding to his jacket pocket.

"Oh, right," Oliver said, taking the bookmark out of his pocket to inspect it. "I wondered about that."

"You thought I just hand out random bookmarks?" she teased.

"It seemed a bit odd," he said with a laugh.

His smile spread over his features, momentarily melting his reserve. Aurelia smiled back, taken in by it. She told herself it was just because that smile had been so hard-earned, but maybe it was also because his smile made his eyes squint in a way that was almost endearing.

Looking back down at the bookmark, he read, "'On the Square Books.'"

"The shop's on a small square with a park in the middle," Aurelia explained, feeling a little silly when he'd probably guessed as much.

"Well, it's brave of you to open a bookshop with everything going digital," he declared, tucking the bookmark back into his pocket.

"Well, I didn't open it. My great-great aunt did in the early 1900s. We do alright, actually. There are lots of people still devoted to hard copy."

"Are there?" he asked, quirking an eyebrow.

"You should know—being a publishing man, and all."

"Yes, but it's going to get more and more difficult to sell hard copies. I think exclusive digital sales are in the future."

"Not mine," she retorted with a bite in her voice. She took back the idea that anything about him might be endearing.

Despite her insistence, Oliver started detailing sales forecasts and predictions for publishing's future and Aurelia tried to stifle yet another yawn. He spouted one last statistic, then they were both silent again. She started wondering what time it was and longed to get back to the flat so she could try to catch up on sleep—if the ghosts in the shop would keep it down for once. Or maybe she should try to stretch the date out, after all, since the alternative was dealing with a haunting at home. But it was hard to show an interest in Oliver when she was so preoccupied—and tired. Besides, he didn't have much to say aside from rambling on about publishing.

"Are you alright?" he asked.

"Yes, I'm sorry. I was in my own world for a second."

He began talking about what he liked and didn't like about the publishing company where he and James worked. She hadn't asked, but he dove right in—though, in fairness, she wasn't exactly winning points for offering up any sparkling conversational topics of her own.

"It's a small boutique-type place," Oliver explained. "We put out a few books a year and only do a limited distribution. My goal is to work there for a year or two before going somewhere larger. I want access to more authors and bigger budgets."

Aurelia frowned. She didn't like to think Oliver was just using the publishing closet—*house*, she corrected herself—as a launchpad to something bigger. He sounded aggressively ambitious, a five-year-plan man who would stop at nothing to get ahead. She took in his jacket, his buttoned-up shirt, and started recasting him as a *Mad Men*-type.

There was a sudden silence and she snapped-to as she realized she must have missed her cue to respond to something he'd said. She reached for her glass of wine, hoping to give herself another few seconds to try and figure out what to say. Yet, somehow, she managed to knock the glass with her hand, sending red wine sloshing over the lip as she fumbled to keep it upright.

"Oh! Damn," she spluttered as she mopped up the spill with her tiny cocktail napkin before leaping up to grab extras from an empty table. "Did I get you?"

"No, I think you just missed," he said, patting at his jacket.

"What a mess—I'm so sorry."

She made a pile of wet napkins between them, and even though the table was clean now, she kept uselessly swiping one last napkin over its surface. Oliver reached out and put his hand on hers, stopping her.

"It's fine—no harm done. I'm sure it's not the first time the table has seen some red wine. Or my jacket, for that matter."

Aurelia stilled, taken in by the gentleness of his touch and tone. There was a warmth there that he'd kept locked away before, and it was disorienting to suddenly see another side of him. She sat back down, her hand slipping from beneath his as she added the napkin she'd been holding onto the pile.

"Let's try that again," she said lightly.

She reached slowly for the glass, carefully lifted it to her mouth, took the daintiest of sips, and then used both hands to put it back on the table. His face bloomed into a smile as he laughed with her, and she was distracted by how it lit up his features. Her eyes lingered a bit too long, their silence stretching from a shared moment into something more awkward and unsure.

She dragged her eyes away and looked around the nearly empty bar again, desperately searching for something to say as she stifled yet another yawn.

"We can call it a night," Oliver said abruptly.

"Sorry?"

"You're tired—or bored. We can say goodnight." He began reaching into his pocket for his wallet as Aurelia scrambled to catch up with what was happening.

"No—I'm sorry—it's just been a bit of a mad week." She almost laughed to think of everything that had happened. "I mean, that is truly an understatement."

"It's fine," he said as he waved over their server.

"I really am sorry."

Aurelia reached for her bag, but Oliver shook his head to signal he'd pay.

"I... Look," she began, flustered that she'd come across as rude with her yawning and distraction. "I tried explaining it to David, but he insisted we meet each other. I'm... I'm not really ready for this just now."

"This?"

"This. Dating," Aurelia said, waving her hands to sweep in Oliver, their table, the bar.

"Bad breakup?" he asked, sitting back in his chair, his tone almost amused.

Aurelia only just managed to hold back her first response—*No, dead mother*—and her second—*No, I just seem to have inherited a haunted bookshop*. One was unfair, the other wasn't likely to improve his first impressions of her.

Instead she simply said, "Something like that."

He nodded and said, "Me too."

As he said it, his stiff shoulders relaxed for the first time that evening, giving Aurelia another glimpse of what seemed like the 'real' Oliver.

"To be honest," he continued, "I didn't really want to meet tonight either, but James was fairly adamant."

"I'm going to guess it was David's plan, and James went along since he knew David wouldn't take 'no' for an answer."

"That does seem to be how they work," Oliver said with a laugh.

"It's how he and I work too, apparently," Aurelia said, laughing back and feeling relieved to be on even footing with him.

He paid for their drinks and they walked out of the hotel together, then stood on the pavement to pull on scarves and button up coats.

"Thank you for the drink," she said. "I'm sorry again. And I hope you get over your breakup soon."

"Thanks for that," Oliver said with a smile.

Aurelia was momentarily caught off guard by a fluttering in her stomach—he really was handsome when he smiled.

"You as well," he added. "So, what should we tell David and James?"

"We can tell them... It was nice meeting each other, but we just weren't a match," Aurelia offered, shrugging her shoulders.

"Alright. Well, it *was* nice meeting you, Aurelia." He stuck out his hand once again and she shook it.

She started to pull her hand away but he held it in his. She stared down at their joined hands, then looked up to see a question playing on his face.

"Would you mind—since... Well... Could I try something?" he asked.

"Try something..."

Aurelia had meant it to be a question, but Oliver seemed to take it as a request or a command. He quickly leaned forward and kissed her. It happened so quickly, in fact, that her eyes shut reflexively before popping open again in surprise. She saw his hand rise to touch her cheek and she closed her eyes again, willing to lose herself in the moment as he was, against all odds, doing an excellent job of kissing her.

When he pulled away, he had a bemused look on his face and seemed shocked at his own daring.

"I was just... curious," he said, flashing a shy smile before wrinkling his brow, looking for a moment as confused as she felt. "Take care, Aurelia."

He walked away and she stared after him, eventually managing to say "Take care," to his back.

He turned and gave a small wave, then continued on his way.

"What on earth was that?" Aurelia wondered under her breath.

Though she had to admit, she hadn't minded it all that much. It'd been too long since she had kissed someone, and what was the harm when they would never see each other again? Besides, it was an awfully good kiss.

10

Aurelia had practically fallen asleep at the bar, but she felt more alert as she walked home and thought about her very odd first date—*only* date—with Oliver. David and Antonia had been pushing her to get out, to leave the shop and spend time in the world again after holing herself up over the past year. It felt like everyone was pushing and prodding her—running the shop before she was ready, going out on dates when she didn't want to, and getting haunted as an unwelcome housewarming present.

As she got closer to the shop, her thoughts started turning over the last few nights and what she might find—or wake up to—later. She felt anxious to go back inside, but also irritated to think that whatever she'd been experiencing was keeping her from sleep and from feeling safe in what was now her home.

Standing outside, she peered through the windows and confirmed there was nothing, ghost or human, lurking around. She unlocked the door and stepped inside, then shrugged off her coat as she headed toward the spiral staircase. But when she passed the Recommended Reads table, she paused. Looking at the books she'd set out earlier in the day, she thought again of the man's hand passing through one on that very table just last night. She'd watched those people, or ghosts, from between the bars of the mezzanine railing, then listened from behind the door to the flat—too scared and bewildered to face them. But perhaps it was time for her to take a stand when everything and everyone seemed to be conspiring to move her along like something caught up in the tide. She wanted to plant her feet and refuse to budge for once.

Confronting these late-night visitors rather than hiding from them seemed like a good place to start. And wasn't that what films and books insisted you were supposed to do when you were being haunted by ghosts? You had to ask them why they were there and then help them to 'move on.' She'd been in the shop with them twice now, and no one had tried to harm her. Surely she'd be safe in the same room with them if they weren't solid enough to touch a book, she reasoned.

Resolved to face whatever it was she'd been experiencing, she went to the back room, made a strong cup of coffee, and stationed herself at the desk, ready for the arrival of the crowd of people she'd seen the night before. But minutes passed, then an hour, then two, and still she was the only person in the shop. After so many nights with so little sleep, Aurelia struggled to stay awake, and her eyelids grew heavier and heavier with each blink.

Aurelia couldn't have said how long she'd slept, but at some point, she began to regain consciousness. She heard voices all around her; some were quietly intense, some were boisterous and loud, some were nearby, and some seemed to be coming down to her from the mezzanine.

She opened one eye. Her head was resting against a book she'd opened just before falling asleep, her cheek pressed to its pages. With both eyes open now, she tried to take in her surroundings but she couldn't see above the ledge that ran the length of the desk. She knew, at least, that she was in the shop, but there was something different—some element that was unlike its familiar setting.

The voices seemed to solidify so that she could now make out specific conversations. The ghosts or hallucinations—whatever she'd been seeing in the shop—must be here, all around her! The realization gripped her in a panic that stopped her heart for a beat before it began pounding in her chest.

Sliding off her chair, she crouched under the desk. Her bravery and insistence that these people weren't real had vanished now; she was terrified to find herself in their midst. She carefully peered out and grabbed the nearest item that could serve as a weapon—a stapler that had never seemed dainty until now—and pulled it back under the desk with her. As she strained her ears again, she realized that the voices weren't hushed or rushed. Just like the other nights, whoever was there didn't seem in a hurry to leave. The conversations seemed to be light and excitable, as though they were all gathered for a polite round of drinks. So what was she afraid of?

Collecting her wits, Aurelia tried to convince herself that, as the shop owner, she ought to take control and assess the situation. She slowly rose up so that she could just see above the raised ledge of the desk, the stapler gripped in one hand. There were women in fine gowns and one in a more humble, homespun dress. There was a man in a frock coat and another in a slightly worn suit. As she took in the scene, she realized that she didn't seem to recognize anyone. Gone were the feathered woman and the mutton-chopped man. How had this new group managed to take their place? And why?

The man in the frock coat caught Aurelia's eye and started to smile in acknowledgment. Her eyes widened and she dove under the desk, not yet ready to face them after all.

She thought through what she had just seen. The people looked very real and solid—no misty hands tonight. Had they, in fact, broken into the shop? But she'd checked that the door was locked as she had waited for them to appear, so where had they come from? Were they the ghosts of departed customers who had come back to haunt the shop?

She slowly raised her head above the desk again. Two people were talking about someone named Joe. An elderly man was speaking with a young woman about a rose garden. These two looked a little familiar, but Aurelia couldn't say for certain whether she'd seen them last night. And on the mezzanine, two women were talking about plans to have their mother and younger sister join them for Christmas at a place called Barton Park.

She was still trying to make sense of these snippets of conversation when an accented male voice sounded immediately to her right and made her scramble to her feet.

"Good evening, madame."

Aurelia spun around, one hand clutching the stapler and the other holding onto the edge of the desk for support. The voice belonged to a man of medium height and build, with dark hair that was receding at his forehead. He was dressed in a navy-blue military uniform with gold epaulettes on his shoulders that caught the light, but despite the formality of his uniform, he carried himself with a relaxed air—as though he were wearing a tracksuit.

"Madame, you must forgive me, I have frightened you," the man said, his face full of concern.

Aurelia took a moment to catch her breath. *One of them was talking to her.*

"You did frighten me," she managed to say at last. "More to the point, all of this—all of you—frightened me." She looked around briefly before settling her eyes back on the man in front of her.

"Were you not expecting us?" His lip twitched to one side, as if amused by her surprise.

"Definitely not." Aurelia looked again at the people who were still talking to one another, unaware of, or unconcerned by, her presence. No one moved toward her, making her feel reasonably safe, all things considered.

"Where are the other people? The woman with the feather? The man with the... the hand?" Aurelia asked, pointing at her hair and then waggling her hand in the air.

The uniformed man looked around the room.

"I have not seen a woman with a feather," he said slowly, as though Aurelia might be slightly mad. "But there are several men here. Is there a particular gentleman with whom you wish to speak?"

His accent was difficult to place—perhaps French or Scandinavian? And there was something about him that seemed almost as though he was from a different time—or century—than this one. It wasn't just the way he was dressed, but also his bearing, the way he inclined his head to her, and the formal way he spoke. It all seemed too genuine to be an act.

"Do you... Does this..." She paused, before demanding, "What's going on here?"

At that moment, the elderly man she'd seen earlier stepped forward to stand beside the man in uniform. He looked seemingly ancient, with his lean figure dressed somberly in a simple black suit with a white cravat.

"Sergeant Cuff, at your service, miss," he announced, nodding toward her in greeting.

Aurelia nodded back, not fully processing his words. Within seconds, though, her brain began to work and she understood he'd given his name. A name she knew. A name she'd read in a book. A name that couldn't possibly belong to what looked like the very real man standing in front of her.

Aurelia's hand reached for the edge of the desk, and she managed to drop into the chair rather than fall to the ground.

11

B oth men stood over Aurelia, their faces mirroring each other's worry.

"Are you unwell, madame?" the man in uniform asked.

"I... You..." Aurelia stared at the elderly man, her breath coming rapidly as she tried to keep from passing out. "You're... *Sergeant Cuff*?"

"I am, miss."

"But... Sergeant Cuff? From *The Moonstone*?" The words were ridiculous, but she didn't know what else to say.

"Yes, I am depicted in that novel."

"You're—you're *from* the novel?"

"I am."

Aurelia wanted to stare at them, run from the shop, hide under the desk—she just couldn't decide which should take priority.

"But you just... You rented a costume and this is some kind of party?" she asked hopefully. "Or are you ghosts?"

"Not ghosts, miss, certainly not!" He laughed. "As for a costume, this is merely what I was wearing when I left my story this evening."

"When you left your story," Aurelia repeated, as though hearing it again might make it sound in any way rational. She blinked a few times, trying to sort her rushing thoughts. Characters from books, come to life... *Sanity very much at risk*, she told herself.

"You must be Miss Aurelia. Marigold told me to expect you."

"Aunt Marigold? *You know who I am?*" In her shock, Aurelia managed to get to her feet.

"If your aunt is Marigold Clarke, then yes," Cuff said, barely managing to suppress a teasing smile.

"Marigold... Marigold *was* my aunt..."

This is bizarre, Aurelia thought, shaking her head. She couldn't believe she had to break the news of her aunt's death to a character from a novel who apparently knew her.

"Well, she passed away recently."

"Oh, that is sad indeed. May I express my heartfelt condolences." He bowed his head, looking truly sad. "She did warn me that she was ill. Then, after so many nights without her company, I began to suspect the worst."

"It happened very quickly—at the end. None of us were ready for it."

Aurelia hated to think of Sergeant Cuff sitting in the shop wondering where Marigold had gone, and the strangeness of the situation hit her once again. If her aunt had talked to him and told him she was sick, was it possible this was all really happening?

The man in uniform stepped forward, elegantly maneuvering past Cuff to stand before Aurelia.

"My deepest sympathies for your loss." He gave a slight bow. "I did not have the honor of making your aunt's acquaintance, but I am honored to make yours." He inclined his head toward her.

"Thank you," Aurelia said, trying to keep the quaver from her voice as she stared at the two men in front of her. "Are all of you from *The Moonstone*, then? But no, that can't be right."

She once again took in the varying costumes—clothes, she corrected herself—of the people gathered in the shop. Some of them were clearly from a different period than *The Moonstone*'s mid-nineteenth-century setting.

"No, miss. As you guessed, that is not the case. I am from that novel, along with Rachel. Others are from their own novels."

Aurelia looked around the shop, trying to place each individual in their literary home. Those two women chatting together on the mezzanine: they looked like they were from a Jane Austen novel, but which one? That man with the tumble of curly brown hair wearing the stylish frock coat: he kept mentioning someone named Joe and seemed to have a different accent—American?—but Aurelia couldn't place him. And the man in uniform—he was still a mystery. If she really was surrounded by characters, which book was his?

Catching her eye, the uniformed man quirked an eyebrow at her.

"It is a unique circumstance, is it not?" he asked. "I myself was amazed to learn of it."

Recognition was beginning to dawn on her—his manners, his demeanor—yet still she couldn't put her finger on who he was. He had a stiff way of standing that suggested military service but also had the casual, confident air of someone who felt at home wherever he went. Aurelia's curiosity got the better of her.

"I'm Aurelia Lyndham. And you are?"

He reached out his hand in greeting. Remembering the stapler still clutched in her grip, Aurelia quickly deposited it on the desk, then lifted her hand to his. But rather than shake her hand, he bowed and made as if to pull it to his lips. To their mutual surprise, however, his hand moved through hers, momentarily dissolving into a misty cloud of white studded with a swirl of what looked like printed black words before seeming to become solid once again.

A gasp caught in Aurelia's throat as she looked from the man's hand to his face. Another disappearing hand! Although, unlike last night, the uniformed man appeared just as astonished as Aurelia to have seen his hand disappear. Again, he tried grasping her hand, but again his hand passed through hers, dissolving and reforming as if he were made of vapor and air. They stared at each other; despite what she had just seen, he looked as solid as she was.

"Have you never been in the shop before, sir?" Cuff asked.

"No, this is my first visit to this establishment."

"Then I shall explain one of its unique features," said Cuff. "We are never able to touch or manipulate persons or things which do not come forth from books, as we ourselves do."

The man in uniform cast a glance at Sergeant Cuff, looking like he preferred to be the person delivering information rather than the one receiving it.

Aurelia's hand flew to her mouth—she knew exactly who he was.

"Vronsky? Count Vronsky?" Aurelia's voice came out in a whisper. "From *Anna Karenina*?"

"How intriguing that you seem to know me, madame, when I am only just making your acquaintance." He again quirked one of his dark eyebrows at Aurelia as she looked him up and down. Her face drained of color and she lost her balance.

"Please, Miss Lyndham, let me help you to your chair. You look as though you have taken ill."

He tried to guide her to the desk chair, only to recall—as his arm passed through her—that he couldn't. Instead, he pointed at her chair, which was a few steps away. Aurelia backed slowly toward it and plopped down. She hadn't stopped staring at him and he was starting to look uncomfortable.

"I'm sorry. I think I'm alright now, thank you." Aurelia took a few deep breaths before adding, "That was very... Victorian of me."

"Victorian?"

"Fainting couches, the vapors, and all that." She waved her hand vaguely. "Are you... Are you *really* Count Alexei Vronsky?"

"I am indeed. It is a pleasure to make your acquaintance." He straightened to his full height and inclined his head to her again. "I take it my reputation precedes me, as usual?"

"In a manner of speaking," Aurelia mumbled.

"I hope you have only heard of my best attributes and qualities. Any ill ones I deny wholeheartedly," he said, his face lighting up with a smile.

"I... It's just that—"

Aurelia shook her head, muddled at how to put into words everything she felt about him and his novel. How could she explain that she felt like she knew him, like they were friends? She knew more about his thoughts and feelings than David's, and they'd been friends for ages. But she was saved from having to explain herself when the man with abundant curly hair and an older woman in a brown muslin dress approached the desk.

"Pardon our interruption, miss, but we hoped to introduce ourselves as well." The man made a short bow, and the woman dipped into a brief curtsy.

Aurelia stood to greet them.

"Hello, I'm Aurelia Lyndham."

She reached out to shake their hands, then—remembering that it hadn't worked with Count Vronsky—she turned it into a wave instead.

"Miss Lyndham, I am Theodore Laurence, and this is my mother-in-law. You can call her Marmee—we all do. And you can call me anything you like, but I'm quite partial to the nickname Laurie."

Aurelia's eyes widened. She felt for the arm of the chair and dropped into it again.

"Laurie... and Marmee?"

The two characters exchanged amused glances, then smiled at her. The warmth of Marmee's smile almost undid Aurelia—it was the smile of an indulgent mother, of hugs when you're sad or even when you're happy—and she had to keep holding onto the chair to stop from flinging herself into Marmee's arms as if she were her own mother.

Aurelia closed her eyes and took a deep breath. She had just met Count Vronsky from *Anna Karenina*, and now Laurie and Marmee from *Little Women*. This was the stuff of dreams and fantasies! Any booklover would jump at the chance to sit and talk to their favorite characters, and here Aurelia was trying not to pass out. She took another deep breath and opened her eyes. Laurie, Marmee, Vronsky, and Cuff were watching her with a mixture of curiosity and concern. Maybe it was a dream, or maybe she was hallucinating; either way, they were standing in front of her, waiting for her to talk to them.

"I'm sorry, I think I've recovered now." Aurelia stood again. "I don't quite understand what's happening here—or how it's happening—or if it really is happening... But, anyway," she continued with a shake of her head, "I feel like I know all of you, like I've known you for years. I'm sure that sounds very strange."

"Not strange at all, dear. Though I am glad to see you standing and the color returning to your cheeks," Marmee said, smiling.

"I've read your books—you're in novels that I've read and loved. Is that... Do you know about your novels?" Aurelia still couldn't quite grasp whether these people knew that they were, in fact, fictional.

"Oh, yes. We know all about them." Laurie nodded enthusiastically.

"Laurie and Marmee, I've read your book so many times and know, or feel like I know, you and your family." She was struggling to keep her tone polite, not to fawn over people who, just a few hours before, had existed only in her imagination.

"Thank you, Miss Lyndham. What very nice things to say. I have no doubt my girls would be pleased to hear you speak so fondly of them." Marmee gave Aurelia another warm smile. "I visited the shop several times before with my daughter, Jo, who enjoyed talking with Marigold—your aunt?—about all things literary."

"Of course! Jo, not Joe," Aurelia said, remembering the conversation she'd overheard earlier. "Is she here?" Aurelia looked around, hoping to catch a glimpse of Marmee's bookish daughter.

"Not tonight." Marmee looked thoughtful. "Just Laurie and me."

Sergeant Cuff stepped forward, inserting himself into the conversation by announcing, "I believe you will find, miss, that no more than two people from each book may appear at any given time. I first discovered this with Cristobel."

"You knew my great-great aunt Cristobel?" Aurelia asked, incredulous. "And you said Aunt Marigold also knew about you?"

"Yes, as did Lucy, your great aunt."

Everyone in her family who had run the shop had met a collection of characters from books, then. *And now me*, Aurelia thought.

"I have visited the shop on countless occasions. I seem to be quite popular with the ladies of this establishment." Cuff straightened himself and puffed out his chest.

"But Aunt Marigold never said—she never told me anything about this." Aurelia wasn't fully convinced of the reality of this new discovery but still felt hurt at the idea that Marigold might have kept it all a secret.

"No, indeed. She and I discussed how to tell you and determined it best if *I* explained things," Cuff said importantly. "She thought you might not believe her if she told you herself, before you'd met us. But then, you said her time came sooner than expected. She must not have had the chance to make our introductions."

"No, but... She didn't even give me a hint."

"I cannot speak for Marigold, but I can understand why she might not have shared such an incredible tale," Marmee said gently.

"Would you have believed her if she had told you?" Laurie asked. "I don't think I would have believed even Jo if she had told me that her favorite characters from Charles Dickens or Sir Walter Scott had appeared before her."

Aurelia nodded, conceding the point.

"You were here, when I came in last night, and the night before?" she asked Cuff, though she was certain she knew the answer.

"I was. As was Rachel."

"Why didn't you call out to me or say something?"

"You didn't give me a chance, miss!" Cuff said, laughing. "You scampered away each time, scared of your own shadow."

"Well," Aurelia said defensively, "in fairness, it was pretty shocking to walk into what should have been an empty shop only to see it full of people."

Cuff inclined his head, though his mischievous smile suggested he still found her reaction amusing.

Other characters began to venture closer to the circle around Aurelia, including the two women from the mezzanine who had come down the spiral staircase to join them.

"Were my aunts the only people you've met in the shop? The only people other than characters from other books?"

Many around her nodded.

"I have only ever met Marigold and Lucy," Marmee said.

"And I have only ever met Cristobel," said Laurie. "This is my first time back in the shop since then."

"Do you have any choice over whether you come here?"

"Apparently not. It was a surprising turn of events to find myself here tonight, but not unpleasantly so," Vronsky said with a smile.

"Indeed, we have no foreknowledge as to whether we shall appear or not. We simply arrive here and return home as though no time had passed." Cuff seemed unable to resist adding his account of things.

"That must be a bit alarming?"

"Oh, no. It's rather an adventure," Laurie insisted.

The others chimed in to agree.

"Do you know when it's about to happen, or is it very sudden?"

"When it's time for a visit, it feels as though a child is pulling at me, wanting my attention," said Marmee. "Once I feel that, I know that within a few moments I'll find myself here in the shop. The same happens in reverse—I feel a gentle pull when it's time for us to return."

Aurelia nodded, taking it all in and trying to order the dozens of questions that kept multiplying in her head. But she began to realize that no matter how well explained, she might never fully understand it. She looked around at the characters and decided she might as well enjoy the experience while it lasted.

"Could someone introduce me to the others?" she asked.

Laurie stepped closer and swept his hand forward, indicating that she should lead the way.

"Miss Lyndham, this is Elinor and her sister, Marianne."

I must have slept for a good while if they're already on a first name basis with one another, Aurelia thought as Laurie gestured to the two women who had been discussing Barton Park on the mezzanine.

Nodding a greeting to each woman, she recognized them now as the Dashwood sisters from *Sense and Sensibility*.

"Good to meet you—and please, you should all feel free to call me Aurelia."

"Well then, Aurelia," Laurie said with a smile, "this is Rachel."

He was gesturing to the other young woman Aurelia hadn't been able to place. She had to think for a moment before remembering that Rachel was the strong female character at the center of *The Moonstone*.

A dawning realization spread over her and she swung her head around to look at the Recommended Reads table. Her eyes ran over the books, one by one. She looked up, taking in the roomful of characters around her. The only characters in the shop tonight were from the books on the table: Laurie and Marmee from *Little Women*; Rachel and Sergeant Cuff from *The Moonstone*; Elinor and Marianne from *Sense and Sensibility*; and Count Vronsky from *Anna Karenina*.

Putting the pieces together at last, Aurelia remembered Aunt Marigold's insistence that the Recommended Reads table and its display of books remain a fixture in the shop. Marigold must have wanted to ensure that Aurelia would discover the shop's secret in time. She watched the characters as they began circulating around the room, talking and laughing with one another. A jumble of emotions ran through her—elation at this night and its discovery, frustration that it had taken her this long to find out about it, and, overriding everything, a lingering fear that she would wake up to find that it was, in the end, all a figment of her imagination.

Deciding to focus on her excitement, Aurelia walked back into the crowd of characters, resolved to enjoy this remarkable magic.

12

Aurelia woke to the sounds of birds calling through the square and a loud lorry passing the shop. In her half-asleep state, her eyebrows drew together as she pondered this—lorries passed the front of the building, never her bedroom at the back. She opened one eye, then the second quickly followed as she sat bolt upright. She'd been asleep in the shop, tucked up on the window seat on the mezzanine. Checking her watch, she saw that it was nearly ten o'clock. She continued to stare at her watch, trying to process this information—nearly ten, nearly ten...

"Oh, damn!"

It was almost time to open the shop and Aurelia was still dressed in yesterday's clothes, her hair matted from sleep. She jumped up from the window seat and started heading toward the flat before memories of the night before came rushing back. Walking to the railing of the mezzanine, she looked down to where she'd talked with Marmee and the others. Had it really happened? Could it happen again?

A loud meow from the flat brought her back to the present. She opened the door and Fezz burst through, sounding another meow of annoyance.

"Yes, I realize breakfast is late. Up you get." She started up the stairs and Fezz dashed past her.

Driven by habit, Aurelia fed the cat and took a quick shower. It wasn't until she was running her fingers through her wet hair as she stood before the bathroom mirror that she finally took a moment to think back on all that had happened. She paused, staring at her reflection. Something strange and wonderful was happening to her. If it was a dream, it wasn't a bad one—in fact, it was one she'd often wished she could experience. If it was a hallucination, what could she do about it? See a psychiatrist and hope the characters would disappear?

But she didn't want them to disappear, not anymore. Not now that she knew they were characters from books and not restless spirits or random strangers coming into the shop uninvited. Maybe her mind had instructed the characters to tell her about Aunt Marigold and her ancestors to reassure her, but somehow, the pieces fit together to suggest there was something real there. The table, Marigold's system for setting out books with characters that would get along—wasn't it just possible that it was all true?

Aurelia wanted to call her sister to tell her what she'd discovered, but even with her growing certainty that it was real, she couldn't imagine how to share the news with Antonia—or anyone, for that matter. Who would believe her without experiencing it for themselves? She'd have to get Antonia to come for a visit to show her—but would her sister be able to see the characters too? Sergeant Cuff had mentioned meeting Aurelia's aunts, but they'd all owned the shop at various times—maybe shop owners were the only ones who could talk to characters? She was sure he'd know the answer and the idea of talking to him, to all of them, again brought a smile to her face even as she rushed to finish getting ready for the day.

Soon, Aurelia was hurrying downstairs with two slices of toast. She made a cup of coffee in the back room—tea wasn't going to cut it after the night she'd had—then unlocked the shop door and raised the wooden blinds on the front windows. Sitting at her desk with her coffee and breakfast, Aurelia's mind once again worked through the previous night's events.

She had spent the night talking with characters that had only ever lived in her head.

She had stood just there when she met Marmee, Laurie, and the rest.

She had met Count Vronsky!

Each time Aurelia came up with a new question about the characters she'd met, the same persistent one ran through her mind: had any of it really happened? Every time she convinced herself that she hadn't been dreaming—that Marigold had experienced it too—she convinced herself right back to believing that it couldn't have been real.

A series of customers shifted her focus and kept her busy through lunchtime, but as she spoke with each of them she tested herself, wanting to be sure she seemed as rational as she felt. Their conversations seemed perfectly normal, though. She decided to test herself outside the shop too, so she closed up to walk a few streets over to her favorite café for a late lunch. Everything was just the same—no one gave her funny looks and the world seemed no different than yesterday.

Once she was back, she pulled out a stack of paper from a desk drawer and began writing out her questions so she could organize her thoughts. Aside from the obvious relating to dream versus reality, there was the question of why she'd met those particular characters. Marmee said she'd been to the shop with Jo, but why was Laurie in the shop this time? Aurelia also remembered that only two characters from each book on the table had appeared in the shop, with the exception of Vronsky. Why hadn't he appeared with another character from his novel?

With each new question, Aurelia grew more excited for the night ahead, but also worried that the characters might not appear again. What if last night had been her first and only opportunity to meet characters from her favorite books? All those nights of hearing voices and being scared—had she wasted the few chances she would get to be with them?

Between her racing thoughts about last night and customers coming in and out of the shop that afternoon, Aurelia was caught off guard when the phone rang and it was David. She had no doubt he was calling to check on how her date with Oliver had gone, but in all the excitement of last night she'd nearly forgotten him. Well, not entirely—the mysterious kiss was memorable, but not quite enough to displace her thoughts about what she'd come home to discover.

Aurelia tried letting David down gently, but he didn't believe her when she said it hadn't gone well; he kept asking her to try again and to let him and James arrange another meeting.

"No and no," Aurelia insisted. "The only thing we connected over was what a schemer you are. We barely learned anything about each other."

"What's there to know? You're both good people and I think you'd like each other."

"He doesn't even know I'm a writer—he only knows about the shop."

But maybe that's all there is to know about me, she thought, tuning David out for a moment as she considered that new truth. She hadn't written anything in ages—maybe she never would. Maybe running the shop was all she'd do now, and maybe that was alright. After what she'd learned about the shop's after-hours happenings, that ought to be enough. But even the excitement over her discovery didn't seem like it could replace what she felt when she was working on a new story. What she used to feel. What she hoped she might feel again.

Aurelia tuned back into David as he said, "That's why you need to go on at least one more date with him."

She wanted to ask him to repeat himself and tell her why, but now more than ever—when she'd gone from thinking the shop was haunted to discovering it hosted fictional characters—seemed like the wrong time to give in to David's plotting.

"No, David, I'm sorry," she said, putting on her best attempt at a firm tone. "It's just not meant to be."

13

Aurelia decided to stay awake that night to see whether the characters would reappear. Though calling it a 'decision' wasn't quite right when she wouldn't have missed the chance to see them again for anything—not even another forced date.

As her dinner simmered on the stove and one of her aunt's old rock albums spun on the record player, Aurelia went to the bookshelves where she'd only recently unpacked her many boxes of books and pulled out her own copies of each of the novels that were on the Recommended Reads table. Carrying them into the living room, she dropped them onto the coffee table, then brought in her dinner and a glass of wine. Sitting cross-legged on the floor, she began paging through each of the books in turn.

After re-reading her favorite passages, she decided she wanted to ask Elinor and Marianne about their lives in Barton Park. Were they happy? Was Elinor's sister-in-law still mean and snobby? Aurelia also began to wonder about what the characters knew and understood about their novels and how she could and should interact with them. Did Marmee and Laurie know what happened in their sequels, *Little Men* and *Jo's Boys*? Should Aurelia offer her condolences to Marmee over Beth's passing a few years ago, or would it be too insensitive to bring up such a painful subject?

Similarly, paging through *Anna Karenina* raised questions that had less to do with Aurelia's curiosity about Vronsky and the other characters in the novel, and more to do with how to actually talk to him. She was sure it would be rude to ask him about Anna directly, but what else was there to talk about when the book revolved around their relationship? At the end of the novel, Vronsky was on his way to fight a war. Would it be any less intrusive to ask him about that experience?

Aurelia slid her knees to her chest as she closed her well-worn copy of *Anna Karenina*, holding it between her hands. Her eyes lost focus as she remembered meeting Vronsky the night before. In the novel he was a bright, energetic man who had suffered a great deal to be with the woman he loved. Would they be able to find common ground without her alienating the one character that had appeared from her favorite novel?

A bump across her shin signaled Fezz's arrival, and she reached out to pet him.

"Did Aunt Marigold ever tell you about what happens in the shop at night?"

Fezz was impassive, his steady purr and continued interest in being petted giving nothing away.

"Did *you* ever see anything strange?"

He turned around to signal a need to have his other side scratched, leaving Aurelia none the wiser about what he might have seen in the shop after hours. She obliged him, then stood and gathered her dishes. It was just past nine o'clock, and she was eager to get downstairs.

A few minutes later, Aurelia caught sight of herself in her bedroom's full-length mirror. She was dressed in jeans and a fuzzy jumper. Would it be silly of her to change into something more formal? All the characters last night had been in dresses and suits, so maybe she ought to smarten up for the occasion? She opened the doors to the closet, eyes wandering over her options. A simple black dress with white spots might work—it had an empire waist, similar to Elinor's and Marianne's Regency dresses, and wasn't too low-cut or short for a gathering of nineteenth-century characters. Aurelia changed into the dress, then realized she'd also need a pair of tights. She sighed; if she was going to do the thing, she might as well do it properly.

Once she was at the top of the stairs that led down to the shop, she called Fezz, but he remained curled up in the warm spot she'd left on the living room floor.

"Suit yourself."

Aurelia made her way down the stairs, suddenly nervous for what may or may not be on the other side of the door. She closed her eyes for a long beat. What a difference a day made—tonight she was no longer hoping to see an empty shop.

Exhaling, she opened the door to find it quiet and dark, and her heart sank. The shop looked just as it had when she'd gone upstairs for dinner—the blinds were closed; the lights were off; and there wasn't a living soul, or embodied fictional character, to be found.

Although disappointed, Aurelia quickly reminded herself that last night the characters hadn't appeared right away, but instead she had woken up to find herself surrounded by them. Heartened somewhat, she walked down the spiral staircase. Strong coffee was in order if she was going to stay awake to meet them, so she set about making it and then sat at her desk, mug in hand, waiting. It was nine forty-five.

Two hours later, and Aurelia was struggling to keep her eyes open. The novelty and excitement had worn off, multiple cups of coffee were no longer working to keep her awake, and she was now tired and finding it more and more difficult not to assume the worst—that the characters wouldn't reappear and that the past few nights had been unique, one-off events borne out of her own exhaustion and grief. How much longer should she wait for something that might never happen again? Something that might never have happened in the first place...

Slowly, she began to tidy up the desk, taking her coffee mug and a box of biscuits to the back room. As she stood at the bottom of the spiral staircase, she could hear Fezz rattling the door handle upstairs. Picturing him on the other side of the door, standing on his hind legs to bat at the handle, Aurelia sighed. She knew if she went upstairs now, she likely wouldn't return to the shop that night. What was the point, really? Clearly she'd gotten herself worked up over a dream, or a delusion brought on by the heightened emotions of the past few days. It had been interesting to consider that the shop might hold some secrets left undiscovered, but it was all too unlikely.

She pulled herself up the spiral staircase, turned off the lights, and opened the door to let Fezz out. He wound around her legs, then walked directly to the window seat, ignoring her now that he'd gotten what he wanted.

"You're here for the night, Fezz. Keep an eye on things, eh?"

The mantel clock below began tolling midnight. Aurelia looked back across the shop and was about to pull the door closed behind her when something glimmering and white caught her eye. No, not white exactly, more like the color of parchment or the pages of a book. She stepped toward the railing of the mezzanine and looked down into the shop.

From the stacks of books on the Recommended Reads table rose a collection of off-white mists, each bearing printed words that moved and shifted as the mists swirled above the table. They were just like the mist that had appeared when Vronsky tried to touch her hand the night before, or when that other man had put his hand through a book. Each grew and expanded above the books, then spilled over the table and onto the floor. Aurelia felt goosebumps spread over her skin as she gripped the handrail.

What was happening?

When each mist touched the floor, it rose into a column, forming a human shape. Soon the parchment and ink swirls resolved into skin, clothes, and hair, so that once again she saw the characters she'd met the night before. As each one materialized from their respective cloud of printed words, they looked around the shop but didn't seem at all surprised to find themselves outside of their own stories. Some patted down their clothes or hair, while others seemed to hardly consider their surroundings as they continued conversations or found places to sit with needlework or books they'd brought with them.

As the characters took shape, the shop's dark interior brightened. It was as if the shop were illuminated by the soft glow of a dozen chandeliers with wax candles reflecting across the wrought iron of the mezzanine's railing and the rows of books. Though the mysterious light wasn't coming from the shop's fixtures, but some hidden source.

A smile spread across her face as each character appeared and made themselves at home in the shop. Tears filled her eyes but, unlike her tears of the past few months, these were tears of joy and absolute wonder at what she was seeing. *It was happening again—they were here again!*

Aurelia surveyed the crowd below and saw Laurie standing near the table, looking up at her. She smiled and nodded to him, and he made a modest bow.

"Won't you join us, Aurelia? We require a hostess."

Although she would have been happy just to observe the characters from afar, Aurelia quickly walked to the spiral staircase and did her best not to trip down it in her excitement. Sergeant Cuff was waiting for her at the bottom.

"I am gratified to see you again, miss. Thank you for your hospitality."

"I'm happy to see you again, Sergeant Cuff. I wasn't sure whether I would—or could."

"You doubted, even though many here indicated they had met your aunt and ancestors?" he teased.

"I'm ashamed to say that I did," Aurelia admitted. "It seemed too wonderful to be true, but I'm glad I was wrong."

She caught herself beaming, happiness radiating out of her like the mysterious light that filled the shop.

One by one, the other characters approached her to say hello. As she greeted them she spotted Fezz, who'd come down from the mezzanine behind her, winding through the characters to claim a spot on the armchair. He seemed to see or at least be aware of them, though he clearly wasn't any more troubled by the characters as he was by the customers that came in and out of the shop each day. As he passed Marianne, his tail twitched and caught at the edge of her dress, momentarily releasing a cloud of words. Neither Fezz nor Marianne seemed to notice. He simply leapt onto the chair and promptly began a bath.

Soon, Aurelia started talking with Rachel from *The Moonstone*, who was interested in learning more about how she ran the bookshop all on her own. But Aurelia had a hard time focusing because she was constantly thinking of new questions for Rachel and the other characters. Time felt precious when she was unsure whether she would get another night with them. Just as she had the night before, though, she tried to relax into the experience and—as Antonia would often tease her—'live in the now.' The 'now,' at this moment, was a miraculous adventure and she was content to sink into it.

14

E ven after a few hours of chatting with the characters, Aurelia's questions about what she was experiencing kept multiplying. Determined to find answers, she found Sergeant Cuff, who seemed to know the most about the magic of the shop, and asked if they could sit and talk. He agreed, and they made their way to the window seat upstairs.

Cuff waited for Aurelia to sit, then lowered himself onto the window seat. She had to stifle a laugh as a few puffs of mist and words rose from where he'd sat down, like dust rising from an old cushion. But just like Marianne with Fezz's tail, Cuff seemed unbothered by it.

"I was hoping to ask you a bit about the shop," Aurelia began.

"Certainly, miss. In fact, Marigold had hoped we would have the opportunity to speak so that I could help explain things to you. I believe that is why she left my book on the table for you, at the end."

"Really?"

Aurelia thought of how close she'd come to putting something new on the table and was grateful for her last-minute change of heart.

"Well, actually, I'm not all that surprised. She must have known I'd have a million questions. I mean, all of this is very unusual," she said, sweeping her hand toward the other characters.

"It is unusual, miss. I certainly never had encountered such a thing before my first evening here. I cannot say I was a frequent customer of bookshops when I lived in London, but on the few occasions when I did visit one, I never came across characters from the very books on the shelves."

"I still can't believe this has been happening for years without me knowing anything about it. You mentioned that you visited the shop when Cristobel, Lucy, and then my aunt—Marigold—owned it?"

"Yes, I visited with each of them on several occasions."

"Did they seem surprised when you appeared?"

Sergeant Cuff thought for a moment before responding.

"It is my recollection that they were not surprised to see characters in the shop, though they were surprised, at times, by which characters appeared."

"What do you mean?"

"It seems that each time a book is placed on the table below, different characters appear to the owner of the shop. As you know, Rachel and I have appeared to you from our novel. Were you to place our book on the table again several months from now, it is my understanding that two different characters might appear. Or perhaps I might appear again with someone other than Rachel, or she might appear with someone other than me."

"Interesting... And do you know why a major character like Anna Karenina hasn't appeared from her own novel?"

Sergeant Cuff looked around the room, his lips pulled tight as though he were trying to keep from speaking.

"I don't suppose you have a theory about that?" Aurelia asked.

"As it happens, I do. It is my supposition—mind, simply a supposition—that only characters who survive their novel may appear in the shop. Count Vronsky has indicated that Mrs. Karenina, his novel's namesake, was not so fortunate as to have survived hers."

Aurelia considered this. If it were true, she would never meet Anna, or Marmee's Beth. The shop's magic apparently reflected reality—those who were lost could never return.

"Why do you think that is?" she asked Cuff. "It seems very unfair."

"Some things are too mysterious for even me to understand, despite my best efforts," Cuff said philosophically. "Do you know, there is a rose variety at my cottage that will not bloom when planted on the left side of my fence post, but which grows quite abundantly when planted on the right side. The light, air, and water are the same, thus I cannot account for it using rational processes of deduction. Yet I know by observing with my own eyes that the rose prefers one side to the other. Regardless of the reason, the fact remains. Some aspects of this phenomenon"—Cuff raised his hand to signal the shop and its population of characters—"elude me, but they are no less evident, even if I am unable to define or categorize them."

"Unanswerable mysteries," Aurelia said quietly, recalling her recent conversation with her father.

"Indeed," Cuff agreed.

They sat in silence for a few moments, reflecting on the mysterious.

"There is one question I felt convinced you would ask me."

"I hate to disappoint you, Sergeant," she said with a wry smile. "Okay, let me think."

Aurelia's mind ran back over the list of questions she'd written out earlier in the day.

"Well, I waited a few hours for you tonight, but you didn't arrive until midnight. Is that when you always appear?"

"Yes. We arrive at midnight and depart at first light."

"Oh." Aurelia drew out the word, remembering the sudden disappearance of the people—other characters—she had spotted on that early morning just days ago. "What about your novel: do you know everything that's been written in it—what happens to other characters, their thoughts and feelings?"

"Not at all! I know what I observed and what was told to me in the course of my story, but nothing else. It would be very intrusive if I did, would it not?"

"Right, yes." Aurelia felt foolish before reminding herself that she couldn't possibly know, let alone guess, the 'rules' of the shop and its characters after only a few nights with them. So she asked another question.

"And your ending—I remember you went back into retirement, but what happened after that?"

"I am still living the ending. I returned to my cottage and assume that I will continue to enjoy the life I lead there—cultivating my roses and infuriating my housekeeper."

"You don't know what happens after your book ends?"

"I do not, no more than you or I know what will happen tomorrow, or the day after."

She thought for a moment, then asked, "Were any of those the question you had in mind?"

"No, none was the question I referred to earlier."

"Are you willing to tell me without my guessing?"

"I think the question will occur to you when the time is ripe for an answer. Therefore, I will keep my counsel until then."

Trying hard to keep from huffing in disappointment like a nineteenth-century heroine, Aurelia nodded.

"I am happy to discuss any other topics that may interest you. Might I suggest rose propagation? It is one of my favorite topics, and I have much occasion to reflect upon it in my retirement."

Opening her mouth to come up with an excuse—in his novel, Cuff was like a dog with a bone when it came to roses—Aurelia was saved by the arrival of Elinor and Marianne at the top of the stairs.

"May we join you?" Elinor asked.

Cuff stood, bowing to them.

"Please, ladies, you are very welcome. Were you, perchance, seeking to discuss the propagation of rose varieties?"

Marianne pulled a face, while Elinor said smoothly, "We were not, Sergeant Cuff. We had hoped to discuss literature with Aurelia."

"Then I shall leave you and allow you to pursue that topic to your contentment."

Sergeant Cuff made another slight bow to the women, then walked to the spiral staircase and descended to the floor below. Marianne and Elinor joined Aurelia on the window seat, setting off their own small, momentary wisps of words before Marianne leaned toward Aurelia, her entire body tense with excitement.

"Rachel was telling us about the modern literature of her time! She mentioned an author called Dickens and another called Trollope. Have you read their works? I wish I could—they sound delightful."

Marianne paused for a breath and Aurelia realized it was her turn to speak.

"Dickens and Trollope, modern?" She thought for a moment and then remembered that *Sense and Sensibility* was set in the 1790s, decades before Dickens began publishing his work. "Well, I guess you could say that."

"I once met David Copperfield in the shop. He is one of Mr. Dickens' characters," Elinor explained to Marianne. "I found him very amiable and well-mannered."

"Who were you with on that occasion?" Marianne seemed to struggle to keep the envy from her voice.

"Margaret and I were together. She liked Mr. Copperfield very much and said she wished she could return to his book instead of ours."

"As do I," sighed Marianne.

"Dickens was a fantastic writer. His stories are full of vivid characters, and twists and turns."

From Marianne's dismayed look, Aurelia realized she might have overdone her enthusiasm.

"But your author, Jane Austen, is also known for writing really engaging characters. Have you met her other characters when you were visiting the shop?"

"I once met a woman named Elizabeth Darcy and her father, Mr. Bennet," Marianne offered. "I understand they also came from Miss Austen's pen."

"Yes, they're in *Pride and Prejudice*, her best-known novel."

Once again, Aurelia noticed Marianne's look of disappointment.

"I, uh... I'm overstating that, really," Aurelia stammered. "I'd say both *Pride and Prejudice* and your novel are her most popular books."

Elinor and Marianne exchanged pleased glances and Aurelia let out a quick breath of relief to have saved the moment. She started thinking of questions she'd like to ask about Lizzy, but was distracted when she spotted Count Vronsky looking at a bookshelf filled with literary criticism along the back wall of the mezzanine.

Glancing toward him, Elinor observed, "Count Vronsky appears to be widely read on a great deal of subjects."

"Does he? I met him last night but haven't spoken to him much since then."

"He was very complimentary of your shop. He said it had some fine examples of the fiction of his day. In fact, he was with us when we were discussing the merits of Dickens and Trollope."

"Really? I don't remember a scene in his novel where he read their books." Aurelia turned to Marianne. "I know some of the poets you like because Austen wrote that you liked them, but are there other poets you've read, like... William Wordsworth? I don't remember her mentioning him in your book."

"Oh yes, Wordsworth's poems are a dear favorite," Marianne said in what Aurelia recognized as her typically passionate manner. "I often feel as though his poems travel straight into my soul and roost there. His work has been a source of comfort in difficult times and a source of joy in happier ones."

"So, you have experiences and memories that aren't on the pages of your book?"

Aurelia looked up as she asked her question. Out of the corner of her eye, she'd noticed Vronsky slowly making his way toward the window seat. He now stood in front of them and bowed deeply.

"Forgive my unaccountable rudeness, ladies, but I could not help overhearing a portion of your conversation. I myself was a great admirer of Dickens. My life's vagaries may not have been captured on the page, but thus far I have lived a full life, though it has not come without its sorrows."

At these last words, Vronsky's charming smile faded.

"I, too, have lived a full life beyond the page, Count Vronsky," Marianne agreed. "Not every pastime, happiness, or hurt was described in my novel, but by no means has that limited the scope of my pursuits." She seemed to understand he'd been alluding to romantic difficulties and perhaps sensed a kindred spirit.

"Do you disagree with anything your authors wrote about you? Are there things you believe didn't happen the way they described them, or feelings your authors didn't capture?"

"I do not dispute Miss Austen's description of events. It may be difficult at times to reflect back on painful moments, but they are true to my experience of them," reported Elinor.

"I concur completely, Elinor," Count Vronsky joined in. "At times knowing the patterns of your life have been depicted in stark black ink can be bruising, but on reflection I have not found cause to dispute an occurrence in which I was involved."

"Sergeant Cuff mentioned that he only knows about things he saw or experienced, or things other people told him about events that he didn't see for himself."

"That is true. We cannot know what takes place when we are not present," said Marianne.

"We know what we think, see, and are told by others, just as you do," Elinor added.

"I own I do envy readers who know and see all," said Marianne.

"Yes, but even so, readers only know and see what an author reveals," countered Aurelia, warming up to their debate. "Writers leave lots of questions unanswered for us."

"Quite so, Miss Lyndham," Vronsky said enthusiastically. "Though I am undecided as to whether I like an author who leaves much to the imagination, or one who explicates every moment in such detail that the reader is in no doubt as to what is occurring."

From just below them, Rachel called up to Elinor and Marianne, asking them to come down and tell Marmee 'that amusing story' about their younger sister. Marianne smiled and said they'd be happy to, and she and Elinor stood and curtsied their goodbyes to Aurelia and Count Vronsky.

They looked on as Marianne and Elinor made their way down the spiral staircase, and Aurelia suddenly felt self-conscious. She was finally alone with Vronsky, able to ask him anything, and yet she was tongue-tied and couldn't think of a single thing to say.

15

V ronsky sat next to Aurelia on the window seat and was first to
break the silence.

"It might be easiest, Miss Lyndham, to comprehend us to
be as real as you are: capable of thought, emotion, and action. I
understand that a man named Count Lev Nikolayevich Tolstoy
wrote a novel in which he described aspects of my life, but I view him
as one might view a parent. He created me, but I live a life distinct
from him and from the confines of my book."

Vronsky paused, his lip quirking into a smile.

"Do I bore you with my philosophizing? I am amenable to any
subject of interest to you, apart from banalities about the weather."

"No, please! I'm enjoying it. I was thinking that it reminded me
of discussions I had at university in my literary theory courses."

"You have taken courses at a university?"

"Yes, I graduated from UCL with a degree in English literature."

"U-C-L?"

"Oh, sorry—that's short for University College London."

"And you obtained a degree! How very fascinating. I believe we had one university in Russia that admitted women, but it closed not long after it opened. You say this university with women is in London?"

"It is. In my time, most universities admit men and women."

"*Your time*, you say—when exactly are we? I presumed from what I have observed of the shop and its wares that we are not in my own time, but I am undecided as to how many years beyond it you and your shop exist."

"I think your novel started in the early 1870s?"

"Yes, I believe that is when Count Tolstoy chose to begin his account of my life."

"Then I live over one hundred years later—we're a little way into the twenty-first century here."

"The twenty-first..." Vronsky trailed off as his eyes widened in surprise. "Can it be? I guessed a few dozen years, but... well over a century?"

"I imagine it's a lot to take in, but some things are just the same as they were in your own time. Like... Well, people still read books. Some people still ride horses, though I never learned. We still like wine, and parties, and the theatre."

"That is a comfort. It would be difficult to believe that such pastimes could fall out of fashion entirely."

Aurelia decided not to mention that some people rode in cars instead of carriages, or read books on screens instead of on paper.

Vronsky shifted gears, then, saying softly, "I have observed you asking others in the shop about their lives and stories. You must feel free, Miss Lyndham, to ask questions of me."

Her heart went out to him at his offer. Knowing everything he'd gone through in his novel, his willingness to be an open book was extremely generous.

"Thank you. First, though, please call me Aurelia. I've been asking the others to do the same."

He seemed taken aback, then recovered himself.

"I must remind myself that we are in modern times in this shop. If I am to call you Aurelia, then you must call me Alexei."

Aurelia held out her hand, as though to shake his. He quirked an eyebrow at her.

"If we're being thoroughly modern, Alexei, we should shake hands—or at least pretend to," she said, laughing. "In modern times, men and women shake hands when they introduce themselves."

A wide smile broke across his face as he said, "Then I should hate to be left behind."

He reached his hand toward Aurelia's and, as close as he could get without passing through her, they both motioned a single shake, up once and down once.

With that settled, Aurelia's brow creased as she started debating where to begin with her questions.

"Well, Alexei, I do have questions for you. I've read your novel many, many times—probably more than any other."

His eyebrows rose in surprise.

"It's very odd to be sitting next to a—"

Aurelia stopped herself from saying 'character,' feeling it wasn't quite right to use the word to refer to someone who seemed as real as herself.

"Next to a *person* who feels like a friend even though we've only just met."

Vronsky looked down at his hands before responding.

"I struggle to place myself in your position. If I were to wake tomorrow, confronted with characters from the novels on my shelf, I would presume I had gone mad."

"I did think I might have lost my grip on reality. I also wondered whether I was dreaming all of you. Honestly, I wonder that still."

She gave a smile, which Vronsky returned.

"But here you are, sitting next to me and seeming as real as the customers who came in and out of my shop earlier today. Or yesterday, rather," Aurelia added as she noticed the sky outside the window slowly morphing from deep cobalt to a soft violet-blue as dawn approached.

Vronsky also made note of the changing light and his eyes took on a worried cast.

"Are you alright, Alexei? Is something wrong?"

"The night is ending," he said with a regretful smile. "It has been a pleasure."

He stood and made a slight bow.

"I don't understand—are you leaving?"

Aurelia stood too, confused by his change in tone. A moment ago, they were going to talk about his novel and he'd invited her to ask him about his life. Had she said or done something wrong?

Vronsky smiled reassuringly and took a step backward, toward the spiral staircase. As her eyes followed him, his body began to shift and change, melting back into a parchment-colored mist littered with words. Startled, Aurelia jumped back and fell neatly onto the edge of the window seat. She saw mists appear all around the shop as the figures that had been solid a moment before were changed back into their literary forms.

Dropping to her knees, she crawled to the mezzanine railing to watch Vronsky's mist join the others that were making their way back to the Recommended Reads table, back into their books, and back to their own lives and stories. She stayed at the railing long after they'd vanished, watching the table and its copies of their books.

Was it really that simple, that easy for them to disappear? Just like that, swept up in a breath of air, they were gone and she had stood by, unable to stop them. She was sure that Vronsky, at least, had been disappointed to leave. Eventually, Aurelia sat back, stretching her aching legs before sitting cross-legged on the floor.

They'd come to the shop two nights in a row now. Was it unreasonable to hope they'd come for a third night? A fourth? She smiled, remembering Cuff's teasing words: '*You doubted?*'

Maybe hope wasn't such an unreasonable thing after all.

16

B y her third cup of coffee, sipped at her desk soon after opening the shop the following morning, Aurelia felt her cognition slowly reignite. She wasn't used to these late nights in the shop, and her internal clock was revolting.

It was during that third cup that she realized she hadn't heard from David again. She was surprised but also relieved not to have to discuss the date any more than they already had. She hadn't told David about that kiss and she wasn't sure she had the fortitude to keep it to herself if he really pushed her. He would almost certainly see it as a sign that his matchmaking was successful rather than, as she did, just an odd ending to an awkward first date.

Aurelia soon had to shift her focus back to the shop, as customers kept her busy through the early afternoon. They included Sophie, a UCL undergraduate who was fast becoming one of the shop's regulars. She'd found Aurelia and the shop through one of Aurelia's old literature professors and was one of the first customers who felt like hers rather than Marigold's.

They were standing near the armchair as Sophie was explaining why she preferred George Eliot to the Brontës. That was when Aurelia's eyes drifted to the window for a moment, only to spot Oliver walking past, holding something in his hand as he looked up at the shop. Aurelia frowned as she watched him looking up and down, from the windows to whatever it was he held in his hand, until she realized he was holding the bookmark she'd given him.

"Aurelia? Is everything alright?" Sophie asked.

Aurelia pulled her attention back to Sophie just in time to realize that her frown had turned into a smile.

"I'm sorry," she said as she watched Oliver approach the door. "I just... There's just someone—"

Sophie's eyes followed Aurelia's.

"Ah, I see," Sophie said with a knowing smile.

The bell above the door rang as Oliver came into the shop.

"No, it's not... It's nothing like that," Aurelia began explaining in an undertone.

"That's alright," Sophie said, grinning now. "I'll leave you to it," she added in a whisper as she headed toward the door.

Aurelia felt the color rise in her cheeks as she watched Sophie pass Oliver.

"It's a brilliant shop," Sophie said to him as she swept out the door. "I'm sure you'll find something here to pique your interest."

Oh, honestly, Aurelia thought as she struggled not to roll her eyes. *First David and James, now Sophie.*

Once they were alone, Oliver and Aurelia stared at each other.

"Hi," she said at last. "Uh... welcome."

"Thanks."

They stood in silence for another moment until she blurted out, "How's your jacket?"

"Sorry?"

For some reason it had been the first thing she could think to say, but of course he'd be confused by it.

"The other night—my wine, your jacket," she clarified. "No permanent damage, I hope?"

"Right. No, not at all."

They both nodded uselessly in the ensuing silence, and then Oliver took his first proper look around the shop. She watched as he gazed at the shelves with their books, the mezzanine, and Fezz—who was asleep in the armchair—and saw a smile creep across his face.

"I get it now," he said at last.

Aurelia knew without asking what he meant. After all his talk during their date about digital being the future, he now understood why she would run a bookshop. She smiled, looking around for herself. It wasn't often that she had a chance to share the shop with someone new, and she liked seeing it through the eyes of a person who seemed to feel in his bones what made it so special.

He walked over to a bookshelf and ran his eyes over the spines.

"A healthy collection of the classics," he said, moving to another bookshelf. "More classics." He looked around the shop again, then up at the mezzanine. "Are all your modern books upstairs?"

"I don't have any 'modern' books. The shop only stocks novels written by authors born before 1900."

He let out a laugh and then his face fell.

"You're serious?"

"I am."

"That's... oddly specific."

"I know," she said with a shrug of her shoulders. "One of my aunts—I can't remember if it was my great-great aunt or my great aunt—had this thing about hating modern literature, how the writing was stilted or the stories were dark and twisted... I can't remember exactly, but it sort of became a shop thing—not to sell anything after a certain period."

Oliver grimaced and Aurelia cocked her head at him.

"What?" she asked.

"I'm just not a fan of the old stuff."

"*The old stuff*? Well, that's oddly non-specific," she teased. "You know, some people consider authors like Dickens or Trollope modern," she added, thinking of Elinor and Marianne.

Oliver laughed. "I'd like to know who."

Aurelia avoided answering that, saying instead, "There are countless 'old' authors here—I'm sure there's someone you like."

"Not really," he said, wrinkling his nose. "Give me dark and twisted Vonnegut over, what..." he said, looking around and spotting the Recommended Reads table, "Collins or Austen."

Aurelia's mouth was open but she couldn't find her words. Oliver's face broke into a broad grin and she couldn't help but smile back. Had he been baiting her, or did he really not like Austen and Collins? She was mentally planning a reading list for him, but he spoke up again before she could start reciting the books he needed to read.

"Believe it or not, I didn't come to argue about books," he said, his smile fading. "I came to apologize."

"Apologize?" she asked before realizing she knew exactly what he meant.

"The other night—the way I... Well, the way I ended our date. I should have explained myself."

She was about to insist that it wasn't necessary then thought better of it. She was curious to hear what he had to say.

"I dated someone, for a long time. We broke up a few months ago—I think I mentioned it?"

Aurelia nodded and he paused. It looked as though he were struggling to let down his usual wall of reserve, and she had the good sense to let him speak in his own time.

"I hadn't kissed anyone else in years," he continued. "That night, I just had this sudden impulse to see what it might be like. Maybe in part because... Partly because I thought we'd never see each other again. Of course, later I realized we might very well do, since we both know David and James. Afterwards, I felt bad. I didn't want... I mean..."

As he spoke, Aurelia's face fell and she quickly tried to rearrange it into something neutral. Had he come all this way just to make sure she understood he didn't like her? The fact that he'd seemed to think it was necessary—as if she'd been crossing fingers, hoping he'd ask her out again—made her face flame with embarrassment.

"No, of course not," she cut in before he could stumble on. "We both said the other night that neither one of us is looking to date anyone, least of all each other. Right?"

"Right," he echoed, though his face wasn't registering the relief she'd expected.

She gave a curt nod, as though that settled things.

"Okay, then. Well. I'd best get going," he said, his words sounding clipped. "Take care, Aurelia."

"You too."

She walked him to the door, and he leaned in to kiss her cheek. Aurelia felt that fluttering in her belly again, like she had during their date, as he lingered a moment too long. She'd enjoyed that kiss the other night, but he'd come to the shop with the sole purpose of telling her that it—and she—didn't mean a thing to him. And so even though the moment felt full of something, she'd take him at his word that it wasn't.

Oliver's brow crumpled in confusion, just as it had after he'd kissed her days ago. It shadowed his smile as he pulled open the door and left the shop. Aurelia watched him through the window, feeling just as confused as he looked.

He turned back to the shop as he walked through the square and, spotting her, gave a small wave. She waved back until he turned and continued on his way.

"Seriously, what on earth was that?" she muttered as she watched him disappear on the other side of the square. The inscrutable Oliver had struck again, but no—he wasn't all that inscrutable; he'd made his intentions clear regardless of that final moment at the door.

Best to take him at his word, she reminded herself before turning back into the shop with a sigh. Dusting the bookshelves wasn't an ideal task to take her mind off Oliver, but it would have to do until midnight, when she'd have a much more exciting distraction.

17

I n a state of half-consciousness, Aurelia felt a tickling sensation on her cheek. There was something touching her face and there was... music? As she shook off the fog of sleep, she realized that Fezz was nudging her with his wet nose, and the music was coming from her alarm clock.

"Fezz!" She rolled onto her back and he climbed on her chest, his nose and whiskers now taking turns on her face. She turned her head from side to side, finally covering it with her arm.

"What time is it?"

Looking at her alarm clock, arm still blocking the cat's attentions, she saw that it was just past seven thirty.

"Seven—what?"

Aurelia was suddenly wide awake. She shifted Fezz off her as she sat up and grabbed the clock to check the display—it was indeed seven thirty-four in the morning. She turned off the radio; it must have been playing for hours, set off when the alarm kicked in at eleven thirty last night to wake her from what she'd intended to be a short nap before meeting the characters at midnight.

Racing to the top of the stairs, she took the steps as fast as she could without tumbling down them. She wrenched open the door to the shop and saw sunlight streaming in the mezzanine window through the filter of the branches in the square outside.

"No! No, no, no!"

She dropped down to sit on a stair, staring out at the shop and the early morning light that was growing brighter as it stretched across the floor toward her feet. She felt awful for having missed the characters. Would they wonder what had happened to her, like Cuff had worried over Marigold?

Fezz gave an annoyed meow from the top of the stairs, reminding Aurelia that he had worked very hard to wake her for his breakfast. Heaving a deep sigh, she looked across the shop and down to the Recommended Reads table. *There's always tonight*, she reminded herself, and tried to believe it.

Her missed night with the characters, combined with several days of getting less sleep than she needed, put Aurelia in a strop for the rest of the morning. She scolded Fezz when he attacked the sheets as she was making the bed and nearly came to tears when she broke one of her aunt's old mugs after dropping it in the sink. And memories of Oliver's visit to the shop yesterday—just to confirm he didn't like her—weren't helping her mood either. She'd even cried in the shower when she'd had the thought that her mother would never meet the man she'd end up with one day, whoever he might be.

If only she'd had more time to sleep before midnight had arrived, she wouldn't have slept through her alarm. She'd need to catch up on sleep since she'd be spending late nights in the shop, so she decided to commit to napping after closing up in the evenings.

After yawning in between helping customers for most of the day, she perked up when an old friend from her university days, Kali, appeared at the shop door later that afternoon.

Kali was a small woman who usually wore her dark hair parted in the middle and pulled back into a low bun, not unlike a beloved ballet teacher from Aurelia's childhood. That afternoon, she was dressed in a stylish coat and was pushing a pram that seemed twice her size. Inside was a toddler, her son Ben, who was wrapped up in blankets and a large coat.

"Good afternoon, love!" Kali's gravelly voice carried across the shop to where Aurelia was sitting.

"Hello, you!" Aurelia made her way over and gave Kali a hug before dropping down to greet Ben.

"How are you? Are you keeping Mummy busy?"

He stared back at Aurelia, his sleepy, half-lidded brown eyes suggesting that he had just woken up or was about to fall asleep—perhaps both.

"I'm trying to tire him out. Tom and I are off to dinner tonight and I don't want Tom's parents to have a struggle over bedtime."

"I think you've succeeded. Though it looks like he might fall asleep any moment."

"Oh no." Kali dropped to a squat beside Aurelia, assessing Ben. "I must have overdone it. We spent a few hours at the National Gallery."

"A few hours? You managed to keep him interested in art for all that time?"

"Yes, finally dusting off that art history degree I've never used," she laughed. "You should have seen us—I had a crew of mummies with toddlers following me by the end."

"Really? You know, I'm not surprised, actually. It's your solicitor skills coming back to you—commanding an audience. And that voice! I'm sure you had them all under your spell."

"Maybe so." Kali shrugged.

"Can I get you something?"

"Tea would be lovely, thanks."

Kali pulled off her coat and draped it over the back of the pram. Ben's eyes began drooping and soon closed.

"Ah, well, best laid plans. Gives us time to chat uninterrupted, at least."

Kali followed Aurelia into the back room, where Aurelia began making their tea. Remembering her aunt's note from the last time she'd made tea for a visitor, she caught her quivering lip between her teeth as tears threatened, but she managed to hold them in.

"I'm glad he's sleeping, actually," Kali said. "I wanted to stop in to see how you're doing?"

Kali was one of those people who always remembered her friends' birthdays and life events. Aurelia had known she would remember that it was the anniversary of her mother's death and was grateful for it.

"Oh, thanks. It was a hard day, but I'm doing okay." The tears that had been threatening escaped; sympathy always seemed to bring them on. "All evidence to the contrary." She managed to laugh as she wiped them away. "It'll only get easier, right?"

"It will, but it's still a slog to get through." Kali gave Aurelia a hug with a strength that was surprising given her size. "Did you see your dad or Antonia?"

"No, we decided we'd wait for Christmas since it's just around the corner."

"Well, you know I'm a phone call away, yes? I can always get someone to watch Ben if you want me to pop in for a chat or meet for a drink."

"You're very sweet," Aurelia said, giving Kali another hug.

The kettle clicked off and Aurelia put their mugs on a tray with a packet of biscuits, while Kali—who knew her way around the shop—brought an extra chair from the back room to sit beside Aurelia at the desk.

As Aurelia pushed papers around to make room for the tray, she spotted her copy of *Anna Karenina*. Setting it aside, she found herself wanting to share her new discovery with Kali, but Aurelia was once again held back by the fear that her friend would, appropriately, question her well-being. She still hadn't told Antonia and had forgotten to ask Cuff whether she'd ever be able to bring in other people at midnight so they could meet the characters.

"How's it going? Are you all moved in upstairs?"

"Mmm..." Aurelia thought of the boxes that still littered the flat. "Getting there."

"And how are things going down here in the shop?"

Aurelia wanted to laugh as she thought of the possible responses to that question but settled on what had become her usual: "The shop's been fine. I'm slowly getting used to it all."

"I remember the first day I came in here with you."

"When was that?" Aurelia asked, scrunching up her face as she tried to remember.

"It was Marigold's birthday and you wanted to drop off a present between classes, so I tagged along."

"That's right! Aunt Marigold wound up giving you a copy of something—what was it?"

"*Ivanhoe*!"

"Yes! Because you told her you had pretended to read it in school—"

"—and she said it was a crime to have skipped reading it and she expected me back in two weeks' time 'for tea and a discussion of the merits of the book,'" Kali finished, mimicking Marigold's bossy tone.

"I still can't believe you read it."

"I was scared not to! But I'm glad I did. I wouldn't have been able to come back and face her otherwise, and then I would've missed out on getting to know her."

"She liked you—especially because she knew you liked it here."

"I can't believe it's yours now, Aurelia," Kali said with awe. "I know you must miss her, but how lucky that she left this place to you."

"Yeah, that's started to sink in these past few days." Aurelia smiled. "At first it was a hassle, but now I'm seeing the upside."

"You could find some real inspiration for your writing here, what with all the different customers coming in and out. Plus, there must be quiet moments during the day when you can write?"

"I'm just focused on the shop for now," Aurelia said, trying not to wince at yet another reminder of her ongoing inability to put words to paper. "I swapped out the books on the Recommended Reads table this week, and I'm thinking of changing the displays in the front windows."

"Good for you, taking charge of the place! I'll have to come back next week and see how it looks."

Ben slept soundly as they continued chatting, waking just as Kali stood up to say they should be getting home. He blinked his sleepy, confused eyes first at Kali, then at Aurelia.

"You missed teatime, lovey—did you have a good nap?" Kali asked.

Ben continued his drowsy assessment of them.

"Here, Ben—take a biscuit for the road," Aurelia offered, pulling one loose from the packet and bending down to place it in his warm, damp hand. She kissed his cheek and he gave her a shy, sweet smile in return.

The rest of the day went by in a blur. Between frequent yawns and her anticipation of another conversation with Vronsky that night, Aurelia felt as though five o'clock took ages to come round. When at last the mantel clock struck the hour, she eagerly closed the shop and went upstairs to make a quick dinner and unpack some more boxes before settling down for a nap. Without closing her eyes for a bit, she didn't know if she could make it until midnight, never mind dawn. Although it took what felt like hours to fall asleep—*What if she didn't wake up in time to see them? What if they didn't appear tonight?*—she eventually drifted off.

18

At the first notes of her alarm, Aurelia practically fell out of bed in her eagerness to get moving. It was eleven thirty, so she had a few minutes to fully wake herself up before going downstairs to greet everyone. She picked another outfit that seemed appropriate for a nineteenth-century gathering—a deep blue velvet dress that swept past her knees, along with her mother's old pearl drop earrings.

When she opened the door from her flat into the shop, the only sound she heard was the ticking of the mantel clock. Fezz slipped out beside her just before she closed the door, then settled himself in a corner of the window seat. Aurelia stepped down the spiral staircase and went into the back room to make coffee, then sat at her desk with her chair positioned so that she could swivel her head to mind both the mantel clock and the Recommended Reads table. The minutes seemed to crawl along: five minutes until midnight, four, three, two, one...

The moment the clock began to strike the hour, Aurelia spun in her chair, her eyes almost aching with the strain of staring at the table and its stacks of books. She didn't have long to wait; soon enough, mists began rising from each book, whorls of words twisting across the whiteness. The figures slowly formed and, finally, each character appeared before her.

Rachel and Marianne were the first to spot Aurelia and they rushed to her side, trying to grasp her hand before remembering it was impossible.

"Aurelia!"

"Here you are!"

"We were worried—"

"We feared something had happened to you!"

Aurelia noticed Vronsky keeping his distance from the circle around her but was so caught up in Marianne and Rachel's anxious greeting that she didn't have a chance to wave hello to him.

"I'm alright! I'm sorry—I took a nap last night and meant to wake up by midnight, but I slept straight through."

"Our late nights must be wearing on you, dear," Marmee said, concern etched in her features.

"I'm fine. Really! But I was disappointed to miss seeing you."

"I surmised you had prior commitments," said Sergeant Cuff confidently. "One cannot spend all one's days running a shop and one's nights talking to its extraordinary inhabitants."

"Extraordinary? I suppose we are, but I am uncertain as to whether I should like to be described as such when I feel rather ordinary," Vronsky said with a slight smile as he appeared at Aurelia's side. His mood seemed muted, a contrast to the rest of the characters gathered around her.

"I am sorry for the manner in which we parted," he said quietly. "We have no control, you see. When first light appears, we are bound to return to our books."

"I understand," she said, nodding to reassure him. "Sergeant Cuff told me, but I'd forgotten."

Just then, Marianne, Elinor, and Rachel caught her attention, leaving Vronsky to speak with Sergeant Cuff.

"Aurelia, is it true you attended university?" Rachel burst out, incredulous. "Laurie said he thought he overhead as much but we could not believe it unless we heard from you directly."

"I am certain Laurie never meant to eavesdrop," Elinor told Aurelia. "Only, it is quite difficult to maintain a confidential conversation in the shop."

"I'm sure he didn't mean to—I don't mind."

"Is it true, then?" pressed Rachel.

"It is. I have a degree from University College London."

"A degree! Not just a course?" Marianne asked, incredulous.

"Lots of courses, actually," Aurelia said, laughing as she thought of the countless lectures she'd attended.

"Is it altogether normal for a woman to attend university during your time?" Elinor seemed concerned, as though Aurelia had done something scandalous.

"It is, yeah. I'd say most universities have a student body that's about half and half, men and women."

Marianne, Elinor, and Rachel looked at each other, then at Aurelia, their faces masks of amazement. Marigold hadn't gone to university, and while Aurelia wasn't sure about her great-great aunt and great aunt she assumed—given the characters' reactions—that they hadn't either. She hesitated, not wanting to shock the characters too thoroughly.

"We can also vote."

"Marigold did mention that, but I never quite believed her," Rachel said, her voice hushed in wonder. "Will we get to vote in an election?"

Aurelia did a few quick calculations in her head, then said, "I'm sorry, I don't think you will. Your daughters and granddaughters, though..."

She trailed off, seeing their disappointment.

"I suppose there is some comfort in knowing that future generations of women will vote, even if we are not amongst them," Rachel said diplomatically.

Laurie—who'd been speaking with Marmee, Cuff, and Vronsky—walked over to join their circle.

"Did I hear talk of women's suffrage? I seem to remember Jo saying she wanted to join the movement. We'll ask Marmee. She might have even gone to a meeting herself," Laurie said as he led the women over to her.

Marmee confirmed Laurie's guess and then listened as the others told her about Aurelia's degree. When Rachel and Marianne stepped aside to ask Laurie about his time at university, Marmee and Aurelia were left to talk amongst themselves.

"Tell me, what did you study, Aurelia?" Marmee asked.

"English literature, and then later I went back for a graduate degree in creative writing."

"Did you? My Jo would have loved that. What is your specialty? Novels? Poetry?"

"Well, I was working on the start of a novel, but I don't write much anymore."

Aurelia was about to change the subject, but Marmee pressed, "Why is that?"

"Oh... There are a few reasons, but mostly I just don't have the time. I've been busy with the shop."

"And the other reasons?"

Aurelia barely managed to hold in a sigh, but much as she'd rather talk about almost anything else, she couldn't be rude to Marmee.

"My mother died about a year ago, and Aunt Marigold died three months ago. I just haven't wanted to write since then."

"I'm very sorry," Marmee said, reaching out a hand as though to touch Aurelia's arm. "My family has suffered some difficult losses as well and I understand how terrible it can be. But I have no doubt you'll find a way to write again, just as my Jo did."

Aurelia's first instinct was to disagree and say she might never write again, but she was saved from making any dramatic declarations when Laurie and the others drew Marmee back into their conversation.

Vronsky, seeming to sense an opening, caught Aurelia's eye and lifted his brows, as though asking her to join him. They climbed up the spiral staircase to the window seat, where Fezz lifted his head and eyed them before resuming his nap. As they sat down, she dove right into her first question, as though no time had passed since he'd disappeared at dawn earlier that day.

"I was just talking to the others about university. Before, you mentioned that it wasn't really an option for Russian women in your time. But still, you must know some intelligent women who could have done well at university or in business if they'd had the chance?"

Vronsky took his time responding, his voice a near whisper when he spoke.

"I knew one very intelligent woman. I suppose, having read my novel, you know all about her."

Aurelia winced at the realization that he was thinking of Anna and instantly felt guilty for dredging up his worst memories.

"I do. I'm very sorry for your loss, Alexei."

"My loss... The pain of it is still quite deep."

"That's right—your novel ends just a few months after she died, doesn't it? It must still feel very raw."

"It is and yet, as each evening here progresses it feels more remote, as if it happened many years ago and I am reflecting back upon it. At times it has been a relief to be here and to have that distance, while at others I am filled with guilt not to feel her loss as intensely as I should."

"I know that exact feeling. My mother passed not long ago, and you've heard about my aunt."

She felt her eyes fill with tears and she willed them not to fall.

"I'm sorry. It's still difficult to talk about them without feeling sad. I keep hoping the sadness will be replaced by something else," she confided. "Someday, I want to be able to appreciate the fact that I had them in my life without always focusing on the fact that I don't have them here anymore."

Aurelia paused. She hadn't put those thoughts into words before and was surprised at how easily they came to her now.

"Maybe time will do the same for you?" she suggested.

"It is something to hope for, yes."

They were quiet, each collecting themselves.

"Please," Vronsky said after a moment. "Ask your question again and I will try for a better answer."

"My question... What were we talking about—university?"

He nodded.

"Right, I was asking if you know any women in your time who would have wanted to go to university?"

"I know a number of intelligent women, as you say, but it is difficult to imagine them as scholars. Perhaps because many of the scholars I know are great bores. How can I picture women in that world when I am used to seeing them glittering in ballrooms or arranging pleasant dinners with good company?" Vronsky smiled, as though he thought his answer would please her.

"Some of us have more interesting things to do than wander around glittering for other people's entertainment," Aurelia said, struggling to keep the sharpness from her voice even as she grew embarrassed for having dressed up before joining the characters. "I loved being a student. I spent my days reading, researching, and writing about all of you."

"Did you?" Vronsky asked with an amused laugh. "I suppose reading novels might be a suitable pursuit for a woman," he added in a conciliatory tone.

The fact that Vronsky was from a different time than her own was hard to keep in mind as Aurelia's blood simmered to hear him write off her hard work. Who was he to decide what women were capable of doing?

"I could just as easily have studied medicine or mathematics. Women in my time are physicians, solicitors, you name it. My mother was a Classics professor."

Vronsky shook his head and smiled, clearly struggling to decide whether Aurelia was pulling his leg.

"That may be so," he said at last, "yet I simply cannot imagine the women I know being interested in such things."

"Maybe if you actually asked one of them what they want to do or be, you could rely on more than just your imagination." Aurelia stared him down, daring him to challenge her.

"What is there to ask? No one would hire a female physician, let alone a female mathematician."

"That's something for you to look forward to, then, Alexei," she announced with a mischievous smile. "One day you'll have a female doctor who will stitch you up just as well as any man."

Vronsky stood abruptly.

"That is a scandalous proposal. This modern world you speak of sounds like... pure fiction—something out of one of your ridiculous novels."

"Well, certainly not yours," she couldn't help retorting.

Vronsky made a sharp, short bow and walked stiffly to the spiral staircase, descending rapidly. Aurelia stood and caught sight of him striding into the back of the shop, where he turned from the others and pretended to inspect a bookshelf.

How had they gone from bonding over their shared losses to being cross with one another, and so quickly? His narrow-mindedness was almost comical—so much for him not wanting to be left behind by modern times. But mostly, she was disappointed to discover that one of her favorite characters from one of her favorite novels was, in fact, quite different than she'd imagined.

From below, Marmee caught her eye. Aurelia attempted a smile but was sure it must have come off as a frown instead. Marmee excused herself from her conversation and climbed the spiral staircase.

"You remind me so much of my Jo," she said as Aurelia met her at the top of the stairs. "You are both very passionate about your beliefs."

"You heard us, then?"

Marmee lifted her shoulders and Aurelia nodded, realizing how their raised voices must have carried across the small shop.

"I've never had a conversation like that in my life," Aurelia said, shaking her head. "I can pretty much take for granted that people in my time are on the same page about these things."

"Think how fortunate you are, then, to live in a time when that is so."

Aurelia looked down at Vronsky, who continued to stand with his back to the others, unwilling to join in their conversations. She felt a pang of guilt, but only a small one.

"I usually tell my girls not to let the sun go down on their anger, but in this case," Marmee said as she looked to the mezzanine's darkened window, "perhaps it might be wise to gather your thoughts before revisiting the subject with Count Vronsky."

"Yes, best leave it for tonight." Aurelia sighed.

Marmee went back downstairs, and Aurelia moved to rest her hands on the mezzanine railing, watching Marmee's progress as she joined the others. Going from page to reality, Aurelia was finding it hard to remember that each character was a product of his or her time. But if she was going to spend her evenings with them, she'd have to do a better job of it. She scrunched up her nose as she thought again of Vronsky—could she really sit through another evening of his condescension?

Stifling a huge yawn, Aurelia decided to return to the flat instead of joining the others downstairs. She wondered if it would be rude to leave, but when another giant yawn threatened she knew that a good night's sleep—what was left of it, anyway—was in order. She waved to Elinor and motioned to the flat door. Elinor nodded and waved back. Aurelia opened the door, letting the waiting Fezz in and up the stairs, then looked out over the shop, seeing the characters talking, laughing, *being*. In spite of her argument with Vronsky, Aurelia was smiling to herself as she climbed the stairs to bed.

19

Pushing herself to focus on trying to patch things up with Vronsky, the next day Aurelia took notes during breaks from helping customers, writing out points to raise with him. As she scribbled, her emotions cycled between calm determination and heated irritation.

When Mrs. Smith appeared at the shop door just before noon, it took Aurelia some effort to drop her lingering annoyance. She stood up from her desk and said hello in the friendliest tone she could muster. Mrs. Smith strode over to Aurelia, displaying her usual rush of energy and shortage of time to spare. As usual, Alfie was trotting alongside her.

"Ready for another book so soon?"

"Yes," Mrs. Smith said brusquely. "You mentioned you had a recommendation for me—a mystery I haven't read."

"Oh, yes—it's here, actually."

Aurelia led her to the table at the front, where *The Moonstone* sat with her other selections, but then hesitated, unsure whether she should remove the book from the table. There was another copy there, she told herself. Shouldn't that be enough to bring Rachel and Sergeant Cuff into the shop again? Aurelia picked one up and handed it to Mrs. Smith but made a mental note to order a few more copies.

"I'm surprised Marigold never recommended this. It was one of her favorites."

"She did recommend it. I was just never all that interested in reading it."

Mrs. Smith peered down at the back cover.

"Yes, fine. I'll take it," she said, handing the book to Aurelia. "I'm tired of re-reading my Agatha Christies. I may as well try something new."

Aurelia felt a burst of pride in having swayed Mrs. Smith with one of her recommendations but tried to keep from looking self-satisfied. She could just imagine her changing her mind if it seemed Aurelia was too pleased with herself.

Mrs. Smith began following Aurelia to the register before stopping as she caught sight of the other titles on the table. "*Anna Karenina*? I never bothered with that one since everyone seems to know how it ends. Not much of a mystery, is it?"

"It's one of my favorites," Aurelia said automatically.

She paused then, looking at the cover and struggling to keep in the burst of frustration that surfaced as she thought about Vronsky.

"You know, to be honest, I've been rethinking that. I mean, Count Vronsky is so pompous and set in his ways. Tolstoy describes him as loving all things new and modern, but his thinking is completely backward."

"Sounds as if you've met a Vronsky or two yourself," Mrs. Smith said, pursing her lips in a conspiratorial smile.

Aurelia's eyes widened, almost believing that Mrs. Smith might have guessed her secret.

"Come to that," Mrs. Smith continued, "throw a stick in this city and you're bound to hit one."

Aurelia let out a laugh of relief; clearly she was talking about real-life men, not the fictional one Aurelia had in mind.

"I'd best stop throwing sticks, then," she said, still laughing as she led Mrs. Smith to the desk to ring up the sale.

Mrs. Smith paid for her copy and stuffed it into her handbag, then thanked Aurelia as she strode toward the door and pushed it open. Alfie dashed over and managed to squeeze himself through just before it closed behind her.

Aurelia shook her head, still smiling at the fact that she'd managed to break through Mrs. Smith's cool exterior, all thanks to her argument with Count Vronsky. She watched Mrs. Smith and Alfie walk through the square, then her eyes fell to the displays in the front windows. It had felt good to have Mrs. Smith take her up on a book recommendation. Maybe it was finally time to update the window displays and give other customers something new to see as well.

When her father appeared at five o'clock, Aurelia gave him a puzzled look—*what was Dad doing here?*—before she remembered.

"Oh, dinner!"

"Forgotten me, then?" her father teased.

"I did for a minute—it's been busy here."

She put the book she was holding in the window display and turned to give him a hug. "How was the train?"

"Fine, fine. Same as ever."

"All your errands in town done, then?"

"Yes, all ticked off the list. You don't mind an early dinner, do you?"

"Not at all." Aurelia spotted the overnight bag in his hand. "Should I make up the guest bed for you?"

Her heart sank a little, thinking that with her father visiting she might not have a chance to sneak away and see the characters.

"No, thanks, darling. I promised Edward I'd stay with him. I'll leave my bag here, if I can, while we're at dinner?"

Her father and Edward had taught at the same university. Edward was divorced and had been a good friend to him over the past year.

"Of course." Aurelia took the bag and tucked it behind her desk. "Let me just run up to the flat and make myself presentable."

An hour later, as their waiter brought dinner to the table, Aurelia had run out of small talk and found herself thinking back to the night—and nights—before. She grew quiet, which her father couldn't fail to notice since she was normally a chatterbox.

"Something on your mind?"

"Me? No. Well... Yes."

"Let's have it."

"It's nothing, really."

Her father gave her his patented 'out with it' look.

Aurelia thought through how best to say what was on her mind since she couldn't exactly tell her father *Count Vronsky annoyed me last night* or *I've been having chats with a man from the nineteenth century.*

"There's this... customer, an older man," she began. "I've had a bit of an argument with him."

"Is he bothering you?" Her father's protective instinct jumped in and he set down his fork.

"Oh, no—not at all. It's just that we've had a disagreement and I can't figure out how to... well, how to convince him that he's wrong."

"Give it time. I'm sure your stubbornness will wear him down," her father said, chuckling.

"I am *not* stubborn," Aurelia insisted.

"You see the problem?" her father asked, tenting his fingers in a professorial pose.

She rolled her eyes at him but couldn't hide her smile.

"Alright, I'll give you 'strong-willed.'"

"I'll take it. You get that from your mother, by the way."

"I know."

They were both at risk of growing misty-eyed, so they focused on their food for a moment.

"Is he a regular customer, or someone you won't have to worry about seeing again?" her father eventually asked.

"Who? Oh, right. I'd say he's become a regular."

Although she supposed she could try taking his book off the table, that seemed like a petty way to avoid him. Not to mention the other characters likely wouldn't appreciate thinking she'd pull their books off the table any time they said something that might annoy her. No, she'd just have to try to get Vronsky to see reason—or avoid him so she could keep chatting with the others.

"Aurelia? Have I lost you?"

She shook her head, returning to the present. "Sorry, I was just thinking of something else. Someone else."

"Someone I know?"

She blushed.

"No, no one you know." *Just a few characters that've been materializing in the shop*, she added to herself.

"Really? Someone new, then?"

The sudden memory of her date with Oliver turned her cheeks redder still.

"Oh, Dad, not like that. Not a boyfriend. Just... some new friends."

"Well, I'm glad to hear you're out meeting people again." Her father turned serious. "I do worry about you, Aurelia. It's a lot of pressure on you to run the shop, and living and working in the same spot can be very isolating."

Aurelia heard echoes of conversations she'd been having with Antonia.

"I don't want you to worry, Dad. It's fine—I'm getting used to it all." She paused as she realized that was finally true. "I'm actually starting to enjoy it," she said with a smile.

20

Returning home that night, Aurelia was afraid to nap, thinking she might miss her alarm again. But her father had commented on her frequent yawning, and she had to admit she might not be very good company without getting a few hours' sleep. She still wasn't sure whether or how to attempt mending fences with Vronsky, but she'd just have to wing it. She set her alarm, turned out the lights, and was asleep in no time.

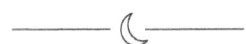

Aurelia woke to her alarm at eleven thirty through sheer force of will. After changing her clothes and downing a cup of coffee, she stood near her desk as the clock began striking twelve. She held her breath until the first mist appeared above the books on the table and exhaled in relief as the characters arrived in front of her, one by one.

They said their hellos, though she noticed Vronsky kept himself apart. That wasn't exactly out of character for him, but she guessed he was likely just as unsure as she was about how to move past last night's argument.

Eventually, the crowd around her thinned and he stepped forward.

"I was afraid you might choose to sleep through yet another visit this evening, after our... disagreement."

Aurelia narrowed her eyes—*had Count Vronsky just made a joke?* The tentative smile he gave her confirmed it.

"I definitely considered it," she said with a laugh.

His smile grew wider and he nodded before turning to the others.

"I know we are all eager for Aurelia's company, but might I monopolize her attention for a brief time?" He turned back to Aurelia and added, "With your permission?"

"Of course."

Marmee nodded her encouragement as Aurelia followed Vronsky up the spiral staircase.

"Thank you for giving me a moment to speak with you, Aurelia," Vronsky began once they were settled on the window seat. "I want to apologize for my anger when last we spoke. It was ungentlemanly and I hope I did not cause offense."

"No, you didn't. I'm sorry too. I know I raised some new ideas—maybe I should have given you a little more time to get used to them."

Aurelia took a breath, prepared to launch into some of the talking points she'd been thinking through earlier that day, but Vronsky beat her to it.

"After you departed last night, I had the opportunity to speak with some of the ladies in the shop." He gestured below, where the others were gathered. "Several of them, Marmee and Rachel, are from a period of time near enough to my own. They may not be Russian, but they understand many of the circumstances and perspectives of my time."

She couldn't tell where this conversation was going but saw that Vronsky was working hard to get through it.

"I learned from them that, as you suggested, they were not happy with the limited choices available to them. Marmee said she felt raising her daughters was exceptionally important work, but once they were grown, she said she often felt an occupation—outside her home—might have been appealing."

His expression, sincere until now, showed some uneasiness as he went on.

"She also expressed the opinion that having a vote in political matters would be of interest to her, as she feels her husband cannot adequately speak for her."

Aurelia tried not to smile, thinking how much it cost Vronsky to say those words. He paused again, and she decided he might need a life ring.

"And Rachel? What did she have to say?"

"She indicated that she would like to run her own business, as you do, or at least run her own affairs. She expressed frustration when, after her mother's passing, she had not been allowed to 'take the reins,' as she put it, and manage her own finances and living arrangements."

"I knew that must have annoyed her!" Aurelia cut in.

"I find that if, as Marmee suggested, I put myself in their position, I can understand that not having choices about my actions would be frustrating indeed. In fact..." He hesitated. "It has led me to wonder about Anna, and her options. Rather, her limited options, as you have described them." Another pause. "I wonder what her life might have been if she had been free to make the many choices that were made for her by others... including myself."

Aurelia heard guilt and anxiety in Vronsky's voice. How many times must he have asked himself what he could have done to change Anna's path, to make her happy? Aurelia's years of reading and re-reading the novel, her reflections on its themes and characters, flooded her mind. She'd often wished she could reassure the Vronsky in those pages that he wasn't to blame for Anna's death, and now she had the rare opportunity to tell him in person.

"What I understand of Anna is that she was a product of society," Aurelia began slowly. "She knew how to shine at social gatherings, how to dress to the best effect, how to enter a room and make all eyes turn to her."

Vronsky looked across the mezzanine, as though he were picturing Anna as Aurelia described her.

"When that was stripped away because people cast her out over her relationship with you, she had nothing left."

"You say she had nothing left—she had me."

"Exactly, but *only* you. She'd lost her friends and her son, and then you were all she had. Today, a woman can get a divorce and uproot her life. She can choose a career over marriage or have both without being cut from her circle of friends. Anna didn't have those options."

Aurelia was warming up to her literary analysis but had to remind herself that she wasn't writing a thesis paper; this was a discussion about someone Vronsky had known and loved, someone who'd been very real to him.

"Without society and her marriage, without the things she'd been raised to be, she was left to put all her energy into you and it destroyed her. You had an exterior life but Anna was trapped at home, waiting for you."

"That does not paint a very flattering portrait of me," he said, growing visibly upset. "I have always known that her position, her fall, was my fault. I acknowledged that to her countless times. Now there is even more to be ashamed of, it seems."

"No, Alexei, I'm sorry—that's not what I meant. It wasn't her fault or yours. No one could blame you for what happened to Anna. She loved you, very deeply. But her choice to be with you, and her pride, tied you two together in an impossible future. Anna was a captive of her time, but so were you."

Aurelia broke off, seeing Vronsky open his mouth as if to speak, but he stayed silent and she continued.

"Her limited choices affected you too, didn't they? If she'd been free to get a divorce and stay in society, think what a difference that would have made for you and your life together. But fate—or Tolstoy—pitched you both into a battle you could never win, no matter what you did."

Vronsky turned away and took in a deep breath. Aurelia thought of her mother's words all those years ago—the indelible mark of his loss—and could only guess at what he was feeling. He nodded, once. Sensing that he needed time alone, she retreated to the top of the spiral staircase and looked back to see him stand and turn toward the window. She couldn't tell whether he was gazing at the square outside or at his own reflection, but either way, he was deep in thought.

Aurelia spent the rest of the evening downstairs, talking with the others. Occasionally, she would look up to the mezzanine to see Vronsky standing and staring out the window or sitting on the window seat. Even though she enjoyed her other conversations, her mind kept drifting back to him and Anna. She worried that all she'd done was give him cold comfort, since he couldn't change Anna's death, not to mention the social barriers that had made them so unhappy.

When dawn arrived, Aurelia said her goodbyes to the characters as they disappeared back into their novels. Watching Vronsky disappear into *Anna Karenina*, she felt terrible knowing that he was slipping right back into the grief and heartache that awaited him at the end of his novel.

21

The next day was quiet in the shop, giving Aurelia time to think back over her night with the characters. Once again she saw Vronsky looking out the window, again she saw how tortured he was by memories of Anna and her misery, and again she saw him disappearing into his novel at first light—pulled back to his tragic ending by some invisible thread.

It felt heartless to watch him return, knowing what he would face and yet being powerless to help him. She found herself thinking about fate, about being carried along by unseen forces. As their author, Tolstoy had dictated Vronsky's and Anna's fates; they were subject to his creativity. Aurelia knew that authors manipulated their characters at will, but it was amazing to see first-hand how that impacted a character who felt as human as anyone she'd met in the 'real' world. She wondered: if Vronsky could change anything about his life and the decisions he made (or was made to make by Tolstoy), what would he choose?

That night, as she greeted the other characters, Aurelia noticed that Vronsky was reserved and quiet. Eventually, he warmed up and began talking with the others, and Aurelia realized it wasn't the first evening that he'd needed time to match everyone's cheerful mood. She guessed it must take some work to shake off the weight of the emotions he was carrying at the end of his book before he could laugh and socialize with the group. Those first weeks and months after her mother's and then Aunt Marigold's death had been brutal—she couldn't imagine how Vronsky managed to live in that dark place day after day.

After an hour or two of chatting with the other characters, Aurelia and Vronsky were once again sitting on the window seat, this time with Rachel and Marianne. When she asked her question, though, his answer wasn't as satisfying as she'd hoped.

"It is a pointless exercise. Tolstoy wrote my life as he did, therefore why consider the impossible?"

"But for argument's sake," she said, addressing all three of the characters now. "If your life had been completely up to you, would you change anything that happened?"

"I think not, Aurelia," Rachel said pensively. "I would not deign to consider myself a better judge—with only my own perspective on the world and the lives of those around me—of what ought or ought not to occur."

"I would change things—certainly I would," Marianne said with conviction. "I would never have given my heart to Willoughby and would have immediately left my heart open to Colonel Brandon."

"Would you really, though? Was it not loving and losing Willoughby that helped you to open your heart to Colonel Brandon?" Rachel asked. "Your first instinct was to reject him—it therefore took time and experience to appreciate who he is."

Aurelia smiled to hear that Rachel and Marianne had swapped stories about their old romances.

"I suppose that is true," Marianne conceded. "It does seem hard, however, to have to go through the difficult hours and days to arrive at the pleasant ones."

"It is a reflection of life, is it not? We cannot appreciate the good without experiencing the alternative," said Rachel.

"I would change nothing," Vronsky said suddenly. "If I changed one thing, it might have prevented me from meeting and loving Anna as I did. What if Tolstoy had chosen someone else to love her, and I was left to simply observe all that happened to her? This I could not tolerate."

He took a moment to steady himself before continuing.

"I have experienced great unhappiness, that is true, and it could have been avoided if I had never loved Anna. But I have also experienced great happiness—to be loved so completely by a woman such as her."

Marianne's eyes brimmed with tears as she said, "That is something to be grateful for amid your sorrows."

"As I said, I do feel that changing one aspect of my life might unbalance the rest and change aspects I was quite happy to have lived through. But perhaps—" Vronsky paused and then shook his head, chasing away a thought.

"Please, Count Vronsky, do share with us," said Rachel.

"Yes, amongst friends we may build our castles in the sky," added Marianne.

"Perhaps, then, I would ask Tolstoy to give me something to hope for in the future. At my novel's end, I am traveling to join a war in Serbia. But after the war, what then? I have no hint of what will come in my life, or whether I will ever find joy again."

"That sounds dreadful," said Marianne in horror. "No hope but war? I at least am married and happily settled in my new home with my husband. I do not know whether we will have children or live long and happy lives, but all evidence suggests that we are not wrong to hope for a bright future."

"Me as well," echoed Rachel. "I have married my dearest love and we, too, are hopeful for a full and happy life together. More and more I see that this Mr. Tolstoy has done you a disservice, Alexei. I would take up a correspondence with him immediately and demand he write you a new ending."

"Well... unfortunately, Tolstoy died many years ago," Aurelia said, hating to be the wet blanket to their enthusiasm. "A new ending seems unlikely."

Their faces fell in disappointment, though Vronsky seemed unmoved. But then Marianne sat up and reached out to grasp his arm.

"We could imagine a better future for you, Alexei, could we not?" she asked excitedly. "Let us dream of one that might satisfy your wish for hope!"

"What good is imagining something that may never be?" Vronsky countered.

"What good is imagining the worst?" Rachel returned. "Our imaginings may not be possible, but likewise your dreariest visions for your future may not come to pass."

Vronsky looked to Aurelia for support, but she raised her eyebrows as if to ask, *Why not?*

"Alright, then. I shall promise to consider the possibilities. Will that satisfy you?"

Marianne stood, linking her arm in Rachel's. "For now. But only for now! Come, Rachel, let us walk and consider how we might improve upon whatever he devises." The two women stepped away, heads bent toward each other as they began a lap around the mezzanine.

Vronsky smiled indulgently as he watched them talking, but Aurelia saw how quickly his smile faded.

"What happened to considering the possibilities?" she asked softly.

"Any future I imagine must take place without Anna. It is difficult to conceive of finding contentment in a life without her."

"There must be some kind of future that could bring a little bit of joy into your life?" She thought for a moment, then asked brightly, "What about horses?"

Vronsky let loose a loud guffaw. "Horses? What about them?"

"You like horses and racing. What about a future where, after the war, you raise prize-winning horses?"

He grew thoughtful. "I do enjoy a good thoroughbred."

"There—you see? There's your hope. I mean, I think we can do better than just horses, but at least it's a start."

Aurelia noticed Sergeant Cuff peering up at her from the shop below, a playful smile lighting his face.

"Would you excuse me for a minute? I think Sergeant Cuff wants to speak with me."

"Certainly. I shall remain here and continue thinking of horses," Vronsky teased.

At the bottom of the spiral staircase, Aurelia found Sergeant Cuff waiting for her.

"You look like you have a secret."

"Do I?" he demurred.

"Is this a secret you're willing to share, or one you plan to dangle until I guess it?"

"I will continue to dangle it but shall give you one hint: you are coming closer to answering the question we discussed those few nights ago."

"Am I?"

Aurelia had forgotten about his mysterious response to her question about why Vronsky was the only character who'd appeared from his novel.

"Let me see if I can guess... It must have something to do with my conversation with Count Vronsky just now?"

"It does, miss."

She squinted her eyes, as if trying to see the answer.

"We were talking about the future, about possibilities."

Sergeant Cuff gave an encouraging nod.

"Marianne and Rachel asked him to imagine a happy future for himself, something to give him hope."

"A happy future? Indeed." Cuff smiled.

"But what does that have to do with Count Vronsky being here alone?"

"You are coming closer, but not quite there yet, I see. Steady on, miss. It will become clear soon enough."

Aurelia's exasperated sigh did nothing to shake Cuff's apparent resolve to make her unravel the mystery on her own.

22

I t was a Sunday and the shop was closed, giving Aurelia a free day to do as she pleased. The day before had been busy with Saturday shoppers, and she'd spent another night with the characters, listening in as Marianne and Rachel shared their ideas for Vronsky's future. Although she usually spent Sundays running errands or meeting up with friends, she was at home reading through her battered copy of *Anna Karenina* and trying to come up with a few ideas of her own for what Vronsky could do in his imagined future.

When her phone rang just past one o'clock, it gave her a start.

"I'm very busy," she said importantly, knowing it would be Antonia.

"Apparently! I haven't heard from you in days. What've you been up to?"

"Um, the shop's been a bit hectic," Aurelia invented quickly. It wasn't an outright lie; she had been busy in the shop, only more so at night than during opening hours.

"Well, I hope you did something last night? Or Friday? Kick up your heels a bit?"

"I did, actually," Aurelia said as she tried and failed to hold back a yawn.

"Wild party? Rave?"

"Dinner with Dad."

"Not exactly what I had in mind. Has David been harassing you about that guy—what's his name again?"

Aurelia had filled her sister in on the date, but only after threatening to withhold details because of Antonia's role in arranging it with David.

"Oliver."

"That's a good name."

"It is," Aurelia agreed, momentarily sidetracked by the observation. "And David hasn't been too bad—only some mild prodding about trying for a second date."

She paused, debating whether to tell her about Oliver's visit to the shop before quickly deciding she was already keeping the characters from her sister and didn't want another secret she'd have to remember to keep.

"He stopped by the shop a few days ago."

"David?"

"No, Oliver."

"Did he, now?" Antonia's voice went up dramatically, clearly happy to have a scoop.

"He did and don't you dare tell David."

"He came by to tell you he's desperate for a second date and to give him another chance, didn't he?"

"Mm—not quite," Aurelia mumbled, embarrassed by how very different his message had been.

"You said he's cute, right?"

Aurelia thought back to that smile of his—the few he'd given her that lit up his face—and had to admit, "Yeah, he is."

"Well, did you ask him to go out again?"

Embarrassment doubled as memories of Oliver's visit came back in full force—how he'd come by just to tell her he wasn't interested in her, how he'd paused as if he'd wanted to kiss her again but then quickly changed his mind. Those were details she didn't feel guilty about hiding from her sister.

"No, he's not my type. He's cute, but sort of... buttoned up. He's also hung up on an ex-girlfriend. Oh! *And* he hates classic literature."

"He's out then," Antonia said with a laugh.

Aurelia was so focused on trying not to think about how Oliver's visit to the shop had felt like a rollercoaster ride with its unpredictable highs and lows that she forgot to hold back yet another yawn.

"Why're you so tired?" Antonia asked.

"I haven't been sleeping well."

"What's been going on there, Aurelia?" Antonia asked, her tone quickly shifting to concern. "First burglars, then ghosts—are you alright?"

"Oh, no, nothing's going on," Aurelia said quickly. "I was just overtired before, but I'm catching up on sleep."

"Are you still hearing things at night?"

Aurelia hated to lie to her sister—again—but didn't think she had a choice.

"No. Nope. All quiet here. I'm really settling in. I've been unpacking and getting things sorted in the flat and organizing the shop."

"Okay..." Antonia said, sounding unconvinced. "But it sounds like you're spending all your time there—aside from this failed date, when was the last time you actually left the building?"

"I go out! I leave the building. I told you—I went out for dinner with Dad."

"Hmm," Antonia intoned critically. "Why don't you meet someone for dinner tonight—a Sunday roast with friends?"

Looking around her flat longingly—she'd wanted to spend the day and evening researching and thinking—Aurelia decided it wouldn't hurt to leave for a few hours.

"Fine. I'll find something to do."

"Relia..."

"I will, I promise."

Deftly switching the subject to her niece and nephews, Aurelia managed to fend off Antonia's disapproval for the rest of their call.

Once they'd rung off, Aurelia had to decide which of her friends might be up for a last-minute plan as she knew Antonia would call the next day for a full report on where she'd gone. Kali usually went to her parents' house in Essex for Sunday dinners, but David and James might be up for a visit, so she gave David a call.

"What are you up to?"

"I'm plotting my next culinary masterpiece," he said matter-of-factly.

Aurelia hesitated. As a history buff, David had recently started a food blog where he detailed his attempts to make recipes from different historical periods. He was a fantastic cook, but some of the strange dishes—tested frequently on Aurelia and James—weren't all that appetizing.

"Antonia is harassing me about not getting out enough. I was going to ask to crash your Sunday roast, but now I think I might try my luck facing her wrath instead of one of your medieval experiments."

"Tonight's recipe is really just beef stew, so you're probably safer with me."

"No strange secret ingredients? Hair of calf? Essence of pork liver?"

"Not this time, I promise. James has already reviewed and approved it. The recipe makes enough for an army, so you'd actually be doing me a favor if you came by. Oh..."

He trailed off, prompting Aurelia to ask, "What?"

"Nothing. Never mind."

They made a plan for Aurelia to stop by at seven o'clock so she could keep him company while he cooked, since James had been banned from the kitchen after 'ruining' one too many of David's experiments by 'helping.'

Having been in the same spot on her sofa for over an hour, Aurelia uncurled herself to go and make another cup of tea. Passing the bookshelves on the wall, she slowed as she caught sight of the rows of notebooks she'd unpacked and lined up there. She ran a finger along them and pulled out a notebook she had bought just before her mother became ill. Flipping it open, she saw that it was still blank inside—not a single pen or pencil dot marked its pages.

She carried the notebook to the kitchen, made tea, hunted down a pen, and then sat on the living room floor with the coffee table serving as a desk. Sipping her tea, her mind traveled back to her conversations with the characters, their plan to dream up a future for Vronsky, and what she imagined might make him happy.

23

Aurelia had started by writing a few sentences, but soon enough she'd filled pages and pages of her notebook. She'd been so swept away by her writing that she thought her watch was broken when she looked down to see that it was a quarter past six. She jolted up, muscles cramped from sitting for so long, and dashed to feed Fezz, change into something presentable, and eat enough to tide her over in case David's promised beef stew turned out to be inedible.

When she arrived at their flat just after seven o'clock, James greeted her at the door. He had a few inches on Aurelia but was only slightly taller than David and had auburn hair with a few freckles across his nose and cheeks. She hugged him in between taking off her coat and shoes, so it took her a minute to notice that he was carefully avoiding eye contact.

Putting a hand to his arm, she asked, "Everything alright?"

"Yes, yup." He nodded quickly.

Aurelia wasn't convinced and was about to ask him again when he offered her the glass of wine he'd been holding.

"You'll need this," he said, leading her toward the kitchen while still avoiding eye contact. "David's in there mumbling about the humors being out of balance."

"If I hear him mention 'black bile' again, I'm going home," Aurelia declared, pretending to turn back for the door.

"Don't you dare!" James laughed, visibly relaxing. "We've got to stick together."

With the glass of wine in hand, Aurelia took a large sip and then followed James through the hallway which, like much of the flat, was decorated with items David had brought back from his many visits to Kenya, where most of his extended family still lived.

James ushered Aurelia into the kitchen, then backed away dramatically, true to his word not to interfere in David's cookery. The kitchen was blessedly filled with the lovely scent of sautéing onions, mushrooms, and garlic.

"It smells amazing in here," Aurelia said as she pulled out a stool from the kitchen island.

"Don't sound so surprised," David said threateningly as he brandished a wooden spoon at her. "Is that what you're wearing?" he added, staring her up and down.

"Yes, clearly it is," she said, tugging self-consciously at her top before pulling a face at him. "Were you expecting me to put on my medieval finest for ye olde beef stew?"

"Very funny," he said dismissively, though she caught him eyeing her again. "So, why's Antonia bothering you?"

"She thinks I'm housebound."

"Are you?"

"Not really. I mean, maybe a little. I've just been very... engaged in what's happening in the shop these days."

"And what's happening in the shop these days?"

Aurelia considered what she could share from the past week—toting up another lie she'd have to tell a friend.

"Hmm... Well, I've been making some overdue changes," she said, thinking back to her conversation with Mark and the improvements she'd made. "It's sort of nice to finally feel like it's mine, not just like I'm watching over it for Aunt Marigold."

Her face fell and she was about to correct herself when David spoke up.

"I know. You'd rather it was still Marigold's." He reached across the counter and squeezed her hand. "It's okay. It's yours now and it's good that you're starting to feel more at home there."

Anxious not to be led into a discussion where she might make a mistake and share something about what had been happening in the shop after hours, she asked David what he was making for dinner. He launched into an explanation of the history of the recipe, making her smile as she imagined him standing in front of his students, enthusiastically describing some pivotal moment in history. She was so distracted she didn't fully register that the doorbell had rung, especially since David chose that moment to change the subject.

"I really want you to give Oliver another try."

"David," she said, shaking her head in confusion at the shift in topic from historic recipes to Oliver. "Go back to stirring. We weren't talking about him."

"No, but we're talking about him now." David lowered his voice as he continued. "I think you two would really hit it off if you gave him another chance."

Just like with Antonia, she was too humiliated to tell him about Oliver's appearance at the shop—to fill him in on how Oliver had visited just to let her know that he had zero feelings for her whatsoever. But maybe if she was more firm than usual, she thought, David might get the message and stop his meddling.

"Please accept the fact that Oliver and I are never going to happen and stop pushing," she insisted, her voice rising as she tried for a very stern tone.

David's eyes flew to the doorway and back to Aurelia, widening dramatically before he said, "Oliver, welcome! Come in, let me get you a glass of wine."

Aurelia's back stiffened and she froze. *The doorbell*, she remembered suddenly. *Oh, please tell me that wasn't* actually *Oliver arriving.* That thought was quickly followed by, *How loud was I just now?*

With a sinking heart, she knew she'd been loud enough for her voice to carry down the hall. She was afraid to turn around and confirm that Oliver was there, that he'd just heard every word she'd said and how she'd said it. And what had she said, exactly? It was only seconds ago, but she barely remembered, though she was certain it had been something harsh since she'd wanted to discourage David. She winced and slowly turned to see that, yes, Oliver was standing just inside the kitchen, with James next to him and David handing him a glass of wine.

Oliver took a quick sip and Aurelia stood, preparing to apologize.

"It looks like they've tricked us both into another date," he said, giving her a slow smile. "But I hear David's a good cook, so at least we'll get a meal out of it this time."

Aurelia could have kissed him for trying to diffuse the awkward situation, then felt herself beginning to blush at the thought.

"I'm so sorry," she said, her hand resting over her heart. "David is... relentless? Persistent? Annoying?" she offered.

David moved back to the stove and pulled a face that only she could see before waving his spoon again.

"Go off to the living room and drink your wine. Dinner should be ready soon and I'll get it done faster without you in here distracting me."

Aurelia inhaled, tamping down her annoyance at being sent away with Oliver. Still, she obeyed, knowing she had to make up for her outburst. James led the way down the hall, making theirs an odd little parade of awkward adults bearing wine glasses.

24

O nce they were settled in the living room, everyone seemed to relax. Maybe it was because she and Oliver were both on their best behavior after what had happened in the kitchen, or maybe it was having James there as a buffer.

Dinner was more of the same—easy conversation and even laughter as they all enjoyed David's excellent cooking and the wine that James kept pouring liberally. By the time David insisted that Aurelia and Oliver relax while he and James cleared the dishes, she managed to take it in stride that he was flagrantly trying to get them alone together.

"No, we're fine," David insisted as she and Oliver stood to help. "You two can chat. Oliver, did you know Aurelia is a writer?"

David disappeared with a pile of plates in hand, leaving them with his all-too-obvious conversational prompt.

"You're a writer?" Oliver dutifully asked.

"I am. Sort of. I haven't been writing lately, though."

"Ah. There's a routine to it, isn't there? A habit you can fall out of, but also back into—when you're ready?"

Aurelia tilted her head, thinking both about what he'd said and how he'd said it. He hadn't asked why or pushed for a reason; he'd just accepted that sometimes writers don't write.

"There is—that's true. I guess I'm out of the habit for right now."

"When you're writing, what is it you love about it? What makes you keep coming back to it?"

Aurelia was surprised to see he looked like he really wanted to know. These were good questions—not the surface-level chatter of their date—so she took a moment to come up with a good answer.

"Hmm... I love when I've been trying to work out a problem—how to handle a scene with a certain character, or what needs to happen next in the plot—and I have that moment, that flash of 'that's it!' when I know I've figured it out."

Oliver nodded. There was more that she loved, and he was clearly giving her space to keep going—so she did.

"I love when I think a story is finished and then days, or weeks—sometimes even a year later—I see something new. And it might be little or big, but it's some new way of understanding what should happen, like the clouds have rolled away and I'm seeing everything more clearly than before."

She'd been looking away, formulating her thoughts, but she looked back and saw he was still listening. She hazarded one more example.

"And I love when I'm first working out an idea, just letting it work its way through my brain while I'm on a walk, just sitting with a cup of tea, or listening to music. That patience, that waiting—slowly finding the pieces and putting them together."

Earlier in the day, she'd started to get that feeling as she'd worked out ideas for Vronsky. It was just a bit of fun, but it had been exactly like that—as though something bigger was coming and she was just laying the groundwork, getting her mind ready as it gathered up the pieces.

She felt a little shy after sharing, so she spoke up before Oliver could ask her more.

"What about you? What do you love about editing?"

He raised his eyebrows as he thought for a moment, then said, "I never much liked writing in school. I wanted everything perfect in the first go and didn't like that it never was."

Aurelia gave a small laugh of recognition; she'd prefer if her writing was perfect the first time she put pen to paper too.

"But somehow," he continued, "friends started giving me their papers and essays to revise, and word started to spread that I was good at it. And I liked that—it was easier to see possibility in someone else's writing. I liked shaping it and feeling like I was helping them chisel away what wasn't working and get to the best parts underneath."

"And now?" Aurelia asked, her voice soft after listening to his thoughtful answer. "You feel the same?"

"I do. Where James and I work, it's a great little press, but we turn things around pretty quickly—about a year to publication—so I don't get to spend as much time with my authors. I'd like to find a place where I'm there at the start, helping work through early drafts, not just final drafts. And a bigger shop will have more money to bring in more authors, which means I'd have more choice in who to work with too."

He'd said something similar on their date, only now it seemed less like an overly ambitious slam against where he worked and more of a reasonable goal for his career. Had she been too judgmental then, or was he being more forthcoming now?

There was a pause as they both sipped their wine, and Aurelia thought she should apologize again for what he'd overheard earlier, to explain why she'd sounded so angry, but the moment seemed too far away now. She started thinking of what else she'd like to know about him, but just as she was about to ask him to tell her about his favorite authors—the modern ones he liked more than her classics—David and James finally joined them.

Their conversation had felt so honest yet so easy that she'd almost forgotten everything that had come before, like David pushing them together and Oliver coming to the shop to tell her not to get the wrong idea. And sitting here, she'd almost done just that—started getting ideas about him and her. Chastened by her realization, Aurelia started to thank David for dinner as if to end the evening, but he shushed her and pushed her and Oliver into the living room for coffee and dessert, insisting the night wasn't over yet. Soon they were all chatting again, and she fell back into that comfort she'd felt moments ago, with Oliver.

Eventually, long after dessert was finished and their coffee mugs were empty, Oliver pulled himself up from the sofa and thanked David and James for a lovely evening. Aurelia stood as well, and they all walked to the door. As she put on her coat, she saw that the hall clock showed it was nearly half past eleven.

"It's not really that late, is it?" she asked.

"It is," David said with a satisfied smile.

Aurelia glared at him as she made a mental note to give him an earful the next time they talked.

She and Oliver stepped outside and Aurelia remembered the last time they'd said goodbye, and the time before that. The kiss, and then that moment—it *had* been a moment, hadn't it?—at the shop door as he'd said goodbye. Her stomach betrayed her by giving a little jump at the idea, despite what she'd told David.

"My car is just over there. Do you want a lift home?" Oliver offered.

Aurelia could only imagine how awkward *that* goodbye would be. She had a vision of him pulling up in his car and spotting the characters milling about inside the shop. She wasn't sure it was even possible for anyone to see them from outside but decided not to risk it.

"No—no, I'm fine. It's not far. But thank you," she said, nodding her head decisively in the hope that he wouldn't insist.

"If you're sure?"

"I am, thanks."

Aurelia started her walk home, not wanting to be left standing there, watching as he drove away. She was attracted to him, sure, but it was obviously just some physical chemistry at work. *He told you he's not interested*, she reminded herself, *and he now knows you're not interested either*. It was fine; she wasn't ready for a relationship, with him or anyone. At least they seemed to be on their way to being able to sit in a room together without all the unease of a first date, which would come in handy since—as Oliver had so cleverly foreseen—they were likely to see each other again given their mutual friends' insistence on throwing them together.

Her thoughts of Oliver drifted away as she began walking faster and faster in her excitement to get back to the shop. She was looking forward to sharing her notes with Vronsky and seeing what he thought about her ideas for his future. At the door, she wondered if she'd be able to see everyone through the gaps in the blinds, but she saw only the books and shelves, illuminated by light from the streetlamps coming through the uncovered window on the mezzanine.

Frowning, she unlocked the door, stepped in, and locked it behind her. She slowly turned to face the shop but saw only the rows of books and heard only the soft ticking of the mantel clock. Aurelia walked over to check the hour; it was just after midnight, and past time for the characters to appear. She stood still, looking around and hoping something might happen.

Fezz made his way down the spiral staircase, then began twirling himself around her ankles. She picked him up and pressed her ear to his side, feeling the vibrations of his purring. Pulling her head back, she stared into his eyes.

"Where are they, Fezz?"

His only response was to rub his cheek against her nose.

25

After a restless night's sleep, Aurelia awoke no closer to figuring out why the characters hadn't appeared the night before. She'd gone upstairs to change for bed, then had come back down and popped her head through the door to the shop to see if they'd arrived: no. She woke up twice before dawn to try again, but still, no one had appeared.

It was a slow morning in the shop, punctuated by Mark's weekly visit, giving Aurelia time to review her notes and continue writing out possibilities for Vronsky's future. She tried to put thoughts of something going wrong, of not being able to see the characters again, from her mind. It helped remembering that Cuff had told her not to doubt that it could, and would, all happen again. In fact, she was sure Cuff would have an explanation, if only she could be patient enough to get through the hours until midnight to find out what it was.

By four thirty, when no one had darkened the door of the shop for over an hour, Aurelia decided she might as well close early and get a head start on her evening nap.

Waking at eleven thirty wasn't difficult—she practically leapt out of bed—but keeping her emotions in check until midnight was a challenge. Why hadn't the characters appeared last night? Would they appear again tonight? By the time she got downstairs to wait out the last two minutes before midnight, she was chewing her lip and shifting from foot to foot as she stood by her desk. Midnight finally arrived and she let out a breath of relief as she saw the mists rising from the books on the table.

When the characters were in solid form (or as solid as they could be) Marmee and Elinor approached Aurelia. The others, however, nodded and smiled at her before nonchalantly walking around to chat with one another. Vronsky, as usual, stood apart, collecting himself as he gazed around the shop, a sad smile playing across his face as he nodded hello to the others.

"What happened? Where were you last night?" Aurelia burst out.

"Weren't we here?" Marmee asked, her face mirroring the worry in Aurelia's tone.

"No, I was late coming home. It was after midnight."

Marmee's eyebrows unbound themselves and rose upwards in surprise.

"Oh, it's alright. People—women—in my time often stay out late," Aurelia explained.

"Hmm," Marmee mused in slight disapproval. "Go on, then."

"Well, when I came into the shop you weren't here. I waited, and checked a few times, but none of you came."

Sergeant Cuff had sidled over to the small group around her.

"You say you entered the building after midnight?"

"Yes—again, that's perfectly normal in my time," Aurelia said defensively.

"Ah, that explains it then," Cuff said cryptically as he turned away from them.

"What does it explain, sir?" Elinor asked.

"It explains why we did not appear." Cuff began to turn away again, but at the sight of many mouths opening with more questions, he stopped. "In my experience, there are two occasions when we will not appear in the shop. One occurred last night." He paused, but impatient faces urged him on, and he continued. "We cannot appear when the shop owner is not in the building at midnight. Entering the building after the hour inhibits our arrival."

"Interesting," Aurelia said, relieved to know that what had happened wasn't a fluke but just a bit of the shop's unique magic.

"I was not aware of a lapse in time," noted Vronsky as he approached their circle.

"I failed to feel it myself," Elinor agreed.

"You mentioned there's another time when you can't appear?" Aurelia asked.

"Quite so. The second occasion is when someone else, someone other than the owner, is in the shop."

Aurelia's face fell. She'd guessed it was true, but knowing she'd never be able to share the experience with her sister or friends felt like a real blow. How could she tell them about the characters when she'd never be able to prove it was all real?

"We cannot appear if someone else is here?" Vronsky asked.

His voice brought Aurelia back to the moment, and she looked to Sergeant Cuff for his answer.

"Correct," he confirmed with a nod.

"Well, that's hardly likely to happen, is it, Aurelia?" Elinor asked, confident of the answer. "Who would be in the shop late at night other than you?"

Aurelia composed herself, trying hard not to blush.

"Yes, good point," she managed to say. "I'm sure that's very unlikely."

She was secretly grateful to know that the characters couldn't detect gaps in time when she wasn't in the building or when someone else might be there with her, since it would avoid some awkward conversations. Aurelia might have a boyfriend come through the shop to spend the night at the flat, or she might stay at a boyfriend's. Either way, the characters wouldn't be there to witness her very modern dating habits. But, given the state of her romantic life, she reminded herself, there wasn't much to observe anyway.

Marmee and Elinor moved off to the front of the shop with Cuff, who continued discussing his theories. Aurelia began to follow them but stopped when she noticed someone reaching out to catch her attention. It was Rachel, who was arm in arm with Marianne.

"We hoped to engage Alexei in conversation," Rachel said with an arch smile.

"Let us see what future he has conjured!" Marianne added excitedly.

"We have been concocting our own adventures for him and would like to see how his ideas compare."

They walked over to Vronsky, who had begun talking with Laurie about their experiences traveling through Italy. Both men bowed to the women as they approached.

"We arrive with a plot afoot," Marianne began.

"Yes, we are ready to share our visions for the life you might lead after your novel ends," Rachel continued.

"Oh! Is Vronsky featured in a sequel?" Laurie seemed eager to join the ladies' fun, likely recognizing his friends, the March sisters, in Rachel and Marianne's scheming. "I myself am in a sequel—two, in fact."

"You know about *Little Men* and *Jo's Boys*?" Aurelia asked in wonder.

"Yes, Cristobel told me about them."

"And... did she tell you anything about what happens?"

Aurelia wasn't sure whether Laurie and Marmee were aware that some of the March family didn't survive the sequels.

"No, she insisted it wouldn't do to know all that would happen. She only told me enough so that I would know I had a fulfilling life ahead of me. She quoted one line from *Jo's Boys* about me and Amy, and said that should give me peace of mind: 'Life had been a kind of poem to them since they married...'"

Laurie smiled, seeming to find comfort in what Cristobel had shared. Aurelia, too, smiled to think of the great-great aunt she'd never met.

"And you have a sequel, Count Vronsky?" Laurie asked again.

"I do not, and sadly my novel ends at a most unfortunate period in my life."

His smile dimmed and Aurelia thought again of the strain he must feel, held forever in the limbo of his grief at the end of *Anna Karenina*.

"We have been working on a project for Count Vronsky," Rachel said. "We thought that imagining his future could give him some comfort, just as you said your sequels have done for you."

"Rachel and I are quite happy with our endings, as our authors gave us some hint of what our futures might hold," Marianne explained. "Sergeant Cuff is happy with his, and Marmee is happy with hers as well. Only Alexei seems to have been left to face a troubling future."

Something clicked in Aurelia's mind. Only Vronsky was unhappy with his ending and where it left him; only Vronsky had appeared alone from his novel. She looked around the room and saw Sergeant Cuff smiling at her. His eyes sparkled in amusement and she knew she'd figured out his mystery at last. She smiled back, but then frowned as she realized she wasn't sure what it all meant. They were trying to help Vronsky think of a better future, but once they'd helped him, what then? Would he come out of the book with another character? Could just dreaming about a new life really make a difference for him?

The others in Aurelia's circle noticed her distraction, and Rachel reached out again as if to touch her arm.

"Are you quite alright, Aurelia? Has Sergeant Cuff been troubling you?" She nodded in Cuff's direction and gave him a sly smile, which he returned.

"I was just lost in thought for a moment," Aurelia said.

"Speaking of old Cuff, I had best rescue Marmee from another of his monologues on roses," Laurie said, nodding in farewell.

Marianne suggested they move upstairs to the window seat, so Rachel, Vronsky, and Aurelia followed her up the spiral staircase. They shared their ideas and though Vronsky tried to look interested, something seemed to hold him back. Aurelia found herself watching him, wondering again and again about Cuff's hints.

26

Aurelia sat at her desk the following day, writing in her notebook in between visits from customers. She decided to take a lunch break so that when Antonia called to check in on her later, she could truthfully say she'd left the building at least once since dinner at David and James's place.

As she ate at a favorite spot, sitting at a counter overlooking a small park, she kept thinking back to Laurie's words—'I myself am in a sequel.' Aurelia guessed that Cristobel hadn't told Laurie much about his sequels because she hadn't wanted to worry him with any difficult truths about his future. Overall, he would lead a good and happy life, but it wouldn't seem fair to tell him about the challenging times that were ahead of him. Aurelia had to admit that she wouldn't have wanted to know about the events of the past year; it was hard enough living through it all without having to dread what was coming in advance.

But Vronsky had already lived through what might be the most difficult time of his life. True, if Tolstoy were alive, he might write a future for Vronsky that was as dark and tragic as what had happened to him in *Anna Karenina*. But what if Tolstoy wasn't the one to write Vronsky's sequel? What if someone who knew Vronsky could help him write a new ending to his life? Then he'd be able to control what happened to him and create his own future. It would be like Rachel's and Marianne's castles in the sky on a larger scale—not just to imagine Vronsky's future but to write it.

A waitress came by to clear Aurelia's dishes, bringing her back to reality. A new story for Vronsky, but who would be the author? *It's one thing to jot down thoughts about his future in my notebook*, Aurelia told herself, *but another to actually write a sequel*. She dismissed the idea, feeling anxious that it had come to her so easily.

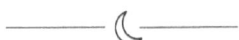

That night, Marianne and Rachel once again wanted to discuss plans for Vronsky's imagined future.

"What has you all so eager?" Marmee asked as she came over to join them.

"We've been thinking of ideas for Alexei," said Rachel.

"Yes, something for him to look forward to since his novel ends so cruelly," Marianne said.

"Laurie told us about your sequels, and how it cheered him to know his life would be a happy one," Rachel continued.

"And we wanted to do the same for Alexei."

Aurelia held in a laugh as she listened to Rachel and Marianne; their conversations were practically synchronized.

Marmee looked to Aurelia, her gaze steady and piercing, and Aurelia's good humor ebbed away.

"I think that's a wonderful way to put Aurelia's writing skills to use. I'm sure Count Vronsky will appreciate your efforts."

Aurelia's eyes widened in disbelief. *What was Marmee doing?*

"You're a writer, Aurelia?" Marianne asked excitedly.

"Then you shall write his sequel!" Rachel declared, as though it were settled.

"No, I'm not sure that's such a good idea," Aurelia said, shaking her head rapidly. "I haven't written anything in a long time—"

"What better way to rediscover your talents?" Marmee asked. "Here we have Count Vronsky in need of some hope, and you are uniquely able to provide him with it."

Aurelia stared at Marmee, unable to hide the exasperation that began bubbling up. She'd told Marmee she couldn't write anymore, so why was Marmee volunteering her?

Vronsky, hearing his name, walked over.

"What's this?" he asked.

"It's nothing—" Aurelia began.

"Aurelia is a writer and she is going to write a sequel for you!" Marianne exclaimed.

"Now you won't just have to imagine what happens next in your life. She can make it happen," Rachel added.

Vronsky considered this, his brow furrowed.

"But whether we write it or imagine it, what is the difference?" Vronsky asked. "You cannot mean to publish it, can you?"

"No!" Aurelia replied with a start.

She felt absolute terror at the idea of publishing something like this. It seemed like sacrilege just thinking about writing a sequel to Tolstoy's masterpiece, but to present it to the world was a few steps further over that line.

"No, we hadn't talked about publishing anything. I... I'm not even sure I can write it," she added.

"I'm certain you can," Marmee said determinedly.

Aurelia looked around the shop in a panic, as if she might spot an escape hatch. Instead, she caught sight of Sergeant Cuff, who was lurking nearby. He made his way into the center of their little group.

"A sequel! Yes, that just might do it," he said.

"Do *what*?" she asked, her voice betraying her anxiety with just those two words.

"Night after night you have observed that the books you have laid on the table there"—he gestured to the front of the shop—"release characters into the shop. Write this story you propose and try putting it on the table. If this experiment succeeds, then Count Vronsky or someone else from your new story will appear and confirm that he is, at last, happy with his ending. Furthermore, I suspect the next time you leave a copy of his first novel on the table, he will not appear. Instead, two characters who are satisfied with their ending will appear in his place."

"Thank you, Sergeant Cuff," Marmee said, looking pleased with herself.

Cuff gave a dramatic bow, as if he were on stage taking his applause at the end of a performance.

For a moment, Aurelia's anxiety took a backseat to her curiosity. Earlier that day, she hadn't taken the idea this far. Was it possible that writing a sequel could, as Cuff believed, *really* change Vronsky's future?

She and Vronsky exchanged glances. He looked doubtful, but Aurelia could tell he hadn't completely dismissed the idea. She waited for his verdict. It was up to him, now—if he wanted to do it, she'd have to agree. How could she refuse when it might release him from his constant state of grief?

Vronsky took a deep breath, then let it out in an expressive sigh.

"I am dubious as to the outcome, but I am intrigued by the process. I would like to see what Aurelia would write of my future. Therefore I shall leave myself in her hands."

He turned to Aurelia. Though she was still overwhelmed at the idea of writing again—and writing something so unique and important—she was also honored by his decision to trust her with a project that could, if Cuff was right, change the course of his life.

She took a moment to collect herself, then held out her hand, as if to shake his. Vronsky let out a laugh, moved his hand next to hers, and they pretended to shake in agreement.

27

News of Vronsky's sequel quickly spread amongst the characters. They wanted to know what Aurelia planned to write, whether she would tell Vronsky or keep it a secret, and whether her writing would keep her away at night. Without giving it much thought, Aurelia told them that she would write at night so that Vronsky could have a say in shaping his own future. When someone asked how she planned to start, she realized she already had, really; her ideas were scribbled throughout her notebook. It was just like she'd told Oliver—she'd been letting the pieces of Vronsky's new story come to her and now, apparently, it was time to put them together.

Throughout the next day, Aurelia's mood shifted from excitement to nervousness and back again. It was a huge project to take on, but there was no way for her to back out now.

Just before midnight, as she walked through the living room in search of her notebook, Aurelia passed the coffee table with its collection of her copies of each of the novels from the Recommended Reads table. She paused when she spotted *Anna Karenina*. It was a dog-eared paperback that looked like it'd been through the wars; she'd read it at least three times and it was her favorite edition. She grabbed it along with her notebook, which was partially hidden under Fezz on the sofa, and brought them downstairs.

Once the characters had appeared and said their hellos, they left Aurelia and Vronsky to their work. Aurelia's nervousness doubled as she felt many eyes watching her expectantly, but Vronsky's eagerness brought her back to the task at hand. She took a breath and reminded herself: *you can do this.*

As Vronsky finished a conversation with Laurie, Aurelia sat down at her desk and began flipping through her copy of *Anna Karenina* to find his final scene. She thought it would be helpful to start by reminding herself what, exactly, had happened to him at the end of his novel.

She didn't notice that he was standing behind her until she heard his sharp intake of breath.

"What is *that*?" he asked, scandalized.

Aurelia held it up, flipping to the front cover to show him.

"It's a copy of your novel."

"*That* is my book? What on earth have you done to it?"

"I've read it!"

"Reading involves turning pages, perusing each word. This looks like you dropped it into a lake, let a dog masticate it, and then threw it across a room."

He reached out as if to touch the book, then pulled his hand back as if he were afraid of being contaminated by it. She was starting to feel self-conscious. It really was looking worse for wear, but wasn't that a sign of a much-loved book?

"Well... I've read it a few times. And I like carrying a book in my bag or reading it over a meal or a cup of tea."

"Yes, I believe I see evidence of tea." He pointed to a dark stain along the bottom edge of the book. "And was a lake involved in this?" He pointed to a chunk of pages toward the front of the book that was rippled and raised.

"No, not a lake—just a bathtub."

Vronsky quirked an eyebrow. "I generally prefer reading a newspaper in the bath for that very reason. It preserves one's books should there be an accidental slip of the hand."

"I'll have to remember that," Aurelia said drily as she continued paging through the book.

Vronsky thrust out his hand again, pointing to the tops of the pages.

"What have you done there? Why have you folded the corners of those pages?"

"I do that when there's a phrase or a description I like. Let me see."

Aurelia paused on one of the dog-eared pages and scanned it.

"Here it is. This is about Levin. 'He became aware of something new in his soul, and took pleasure in testing this new thing, without yet knowing what it was.'" Aurelia looked up. "Isn't that beautiful?"

Vronsky wrinkled his nose in distaste. "Levin is an odd figure. I find it difficult to imagine him doing anything one might describe as 'beautiful.'"

"He's a wonderful character—or person," Aurelia corrected herself. "He's shy and unsure of himself in social situations—very unlike you—but he's got a big heart."

"Perhaps. I have only met him a few times, though I did like him a bit better when I met him in Moscow at the club."

"You might like him more if you spent more time with him. He's interested in improving the land and the lives of the laborers, and he loves Kitty very much."

"I know he married her—does he really love her, then?"

His curiosity confused her until she remembered that, unlike readers of his book, Vronsky didn't know anything about Levin's inner life.

"The novel is half his and Kitty's story, and half yours and Anna's. I thought you might know about his chapters, but... Do you not know the whole story?"

"I know what happened to me—that seems to me to *be* the whole story. Are you telling me that Tolstoy wasted half the book on Levin?"

"'Wasted' isn't a fair description," Aurelia said peevishly. She liked Levin, even if she, too, thought was a little foolish at times. "Levin's story balances yours. Your stories are like two different sides of a coin."

"Hmm... Perhaps he would be a good foil for me. We are rather opposite ends of a spectrum." He gave her a stern look and added, "I am on the upper end of the spectrum, obviously."

"Oh yes, obviously." Aurelia gave him a teasing smile, which Vronsky returned.

"Then I would like to read my book. I should like to know what makes Levin so fascinating."

Vronsky walked closer to the book and reached for it, forgetting that his hand would, as it did then, pass through it.

"That is inconvenient," he mused. "Well, then, you must read it to me, since I cannot hold the book. Or perhaps you might simply turn the pages and I can read it myself."

He looked at her expectantly, as if she would help him to start reading immediately.

"I... I don't think we have time for that tonight, Alexei."

She bit the inside of her cheek, hoping he'd accept her dodge. There were passages he would undoubtedly find difficult, particularly toward the end, when Anna spun into depression and jealousy. Some things might help—moments of Anna loving him and thinking fondly of him—but others might break him.

"I've set us off course. Where were we?" Aurelia said as she flipped through the pages of the book again and found the last chapter where Vronsky made an appearance. "Okay, here it is. You were on a train, heading off to fight in the Serbian War, which"—she flipped to the very last pages of the book—"based on an endnote, took place around 1876. Does that ring a bell?"

"Yes, that is right."

"So: what do you remember?"

Aurelia held her breath, hoping her attempt to distract him would work.

"I am traveling with my mother, and we are surrounded by volunteer infantrymen and well-wishers. I remember speaking with Sergey Ivanovich on the platform before continuing on my journey."

She let out a relieved breath. Looking at the final pages, she saw that he had a heartfelt conversation with Ivanovich, where he reflected on having lost Anna just two months earlier. Seeming to sense her thoughts, or perhaps just recalling the events from his own memory, Vronsky grew still.

"It is a trying time for me."

Aurelia waited a beat in respectful silence before asking, "And you don't remember actually fighting in the war?"

He thought for a moment and then shook his head.

"I remember seeing the countryside rushing past the windows of our train, and nothing more."

"Right, then. I've been thinking," Aurelia said as she opened her notebook and began flipping through its pages. "What if there's a problem with your train? What if you never make it to Serbia and instead you go somewhere else?"

"I do not understand. What do you mean by 'somewhere else'?"

"What if your train stops in... I don't know... Budapest, and you decide to just live there for a while, start over with a new life?"

"What kind of life would it be if I had run from my obligations to my country, to my men? How could I fail to serve with my army in a time of need?"

"We're writing you a new story—we can make your life whatever you want it to be. Why put you at the frontlines of a war?"

Vronsky stiffened at her words.

"I could never disregard my duty. I studied at the Corps and trained as a cavalryman. I have soldiers waiting for me to lead them into battle—I would not abandon them to 'start over' and live a life of frivolity whilst they put themselves in harm's way."

Aurelia remembered how devoted Vronsky had been to the men who served under him and to his career in the army. She respected his patriotism, but still, she'd grown fond of him and—despite the fact that she'd be writing his story and could keep him safe—she hoped he'd reconsider.

"War is a terrible thing, Alexei. You'd see your friends killed, or injured and suffering... No one would think less of you if you didn't want to experience that. Don't you want to consider some alternatives?"

"There are no alternatives," he said tightly. "Ask me again in a week or a month or a year, and my resolve will not waver."

"Alright," she said at last, giving a sigh. "You go to Serbia. I'll need to research how long the war lasted since I'm not well-versed in the Serbian War of 1876."

She tried to keep the sarcasm in her voice to a minimum, but it wasn't easy.

"Just for tonight, then, let's start after the war. What would be the first thing you'd want to do?"

"I would want to tend to my men, ensure they were properly cared for and their wounds were treated." His face suddenly brightened. "Anna and I built a magnificent hospital near my home. Perhaps I could accompany them there?"

"Would you really want to go back to Russia?"

Aurelia was caught off guard. She'd thought he would want to get a fresh start somewhere else, far from memories of Anna or awkward conversations with friends who'd known about their relationship.

"It is my home," he said simply.

"Think big, Vronsky," Aurelia teased him. "This is your chance to do anything, go anywhere, be anything! Well, you don't have any medical training, so we couldn't write that you're suddenly performing surgeries. But if you want to go to medical school, we could write it."

Vronsky made a face. "Surgery is not in my line."

"For now, then, let's say you return to Russia. You bring your men to your hospital, make sure they get the treatment they need, and then?" She put down her pen and began paging through her notebook again. "What about Italy?"

"What about Italy?" Vronsky asked blankly.

"You liked Italy, didn't you? You and Anna lived there for a few months and you seemed to like painting and living the artistic life there."

"I did enjoy Italy. Next you'll suggest I raise a stable of racehorses there," he said with a laugh.

"Alexei, you can do anything you like! Just imagine it and I'll write it."

28

Aurelia and Vronsky spent the rest of the evening throwing out ideas that grew more and more wild as the hours wore on. At one point, she suggested he tour with a troupe of Russian circus performers as their ringmaster. Vronsky laughed so hard he snorted, which sent Aurelia into a fit of laughter. A reproving look from Cuff made it almost impossible for her to pull herself together, though she eventually caught her breath and put on her best serious face. She and Vronsky agreed to get back to outlining real possibilities for his future the following evening.

In spite of her ongoing fatigue from late nights in the shop, Aurelia was in a delightful mood the next day. The shop was getting busy as the holidays were now only a few weeks away and she felt invigorated by all the activity. In between helping customers, she pulled out Aunt Marigold's old holiday decorations and set about making the shop more festive. Her spirits wobbled a bit as she remembered decorating the shop with her aunt just last year, but she soldiered on. She even ran out to a local florist and bought garlands to string around the mezzanine railing and the front windows, which she'd always thought would look pretty set against the books and the shop's woodwork.

Hours passed easily that day, and by the time her head settled onto her pillow for her now regular early-evening nap, she fell asleep almost instantly.

That night, the characters complimented her on the decorations, and she was pleasantly surprised by how good it felt to have made yet another improvement in the shop. *My shop*, she corrected herself, and she liked how right it sounded.

Soon, she and Vronsky were at her desk, ready to begin writing. *This is it*, she told herself. *Preparation over, time to start putting pen to paper.*

She'd taken the extra chair out of the back room for Vronsky and put it next to hers at the desk. Her notebook was getting too jumbled to read, with notes that jumped across periods of time and were sometimes just a collection of words that, in the moment, had made sense but now were indecipherable. Deciding it would be easier to start fresh, Aurelia opened a desk drawer and pulled out a stack of loose-leaf paper.

"This'll do," she said matter-of-factly.

She grabbed a pen from a mug full of assorted pens and pencils and drew a squiggle on the paper to confirm it actually worked.

"Right—paper: check. Pen: check."

She pulled her chair to an open corner of her desk, sat down, and set the paper in front of her. Holding her pen in position, she looked up to see Vronsky, who'd been silently observing her with his brows drawn together in a question mark.

"Are you ready?" Aurelia asked.

"I believe the better question is, are you?" he countered.

"Yes," she said, holding up the pen and pointing to the stack of paper.

"These are the instruments that will catalog the rest of my life?"

He cocked his eyebrow so quickly that Aurelia had to stifle a laugh as she imagined it shooting off his head.

"Well, they may not be a feathered quill and parchment, but they'll do the job."

"We do not write with feathered quills in my time," he said witheringly, but with a hint of a smile at her jab. "But a silver or gold writing implement would seem much more auspicious for the occasion."

"As it happens, I'm fresh out of silver and gold pens," Aurelia said, once again trying not to laugh. "But I promise this will capture your story just as well. In any case, this is just a starting point. Once we've got a few chapters, I'll start typing up the finished product."

"*Typing?*"

Aurelia had spoken without thinking, but now realized that using her laptop in the shop at night might require more explanation than the characters could handle. Her eyes caught on the slightly battered typewriter that had been on the desk for as long as she'd been coming into the shop and she thought it just might work.

"Yes, hang on," she said as she moved papers and stacks of books around her desk to pull the typewriter closer.

"Have you seen or heard of a typewriter before?"

Vronsky took a few steps forward and dropped down to inspect it at close range.

"A typewriter... I have heard of such a machine but never seen one," he said, his voice rising with excitement.

Aurelia remembered that he and Anna had owned the latest and best of everything. He had a natural curiosity for innovation.

"Here, I'll show you how it works."

She took a blank page from her stack and fed it into the back of the typewriter. After turning the knob to advance the wheel until the paper was under the guide, she set her hands over the keys and paused as she tried to think of something to type. Once an idea came to her, she began typing, the keys clacking away as she went.

Vronsky read aloud over her shoulder: "'Count... Alexei... Vronsky... is... a... Russian... aristocrat.' Ha! Just like that! Much faster than a pen!"

"It can be. But a pen and paper are still better for some things, like writing out our first ideas."

"But you'll use this—you will type my story when it is finished?"

"Sure. Then we can use the typed manuscript for the experiment." Aurelia leaned in to inspect the faded ink of her typewritten words. "I'll just have to get some new ink ribbons now that we'll be pressing this thing back into service."

"Wonderful. Very modern indeed." Vronsky nodded his approval. Then, seeming to recall himself, he said, "I suppose we ought to begin if we are to have something worth typing. Do you agree?"

"I do," Aurelia said with a smile. She, too, was ready at last.

"Well, then, where shall we start?"

29

Over the next three weeks, Aurelia and Vronsky developed a routine: they wrote together at night; Aurelia edited their draft during quiet moments in the day; and then they reviewed the draft the following night before beginning to write again. A few times now she'd remembered how Oliver had described writing as just that—a routine—and she'd smiled to think she was finally back in it.

The shop took up most of her time as the holidays approached, giving her only spare minutes to write and edit during the day and driving her to make the most of her writing time with Vronsky at night. A few times some of her regular customers, like Sophie and Mark, had caught her scribbling away and asked what she was working on, but Aurelia wasn't yet ready to tell them about her project. It was all part of the compounding secret of her new double life.

Keeping her writing a secret from her customers was easier than keeping it from David. She found herself telling him about it on a cold Sunday morning when they met for coffee and a long walk around Hampstead Heath. David was waiting for her at the Tube station on the high street, wearing a hat she remembered Aunt Marigold knitting for him. Aurelia smiled at the sight of it, which marked the first time in a long time that she didn't feel like crying over stirred-up memories.

David filled Aurelia in on school, the never-ending renovation of the guest bathroom at his and James's flat, and the progress he was making on his cooking blog. He then turned expectantly to Aurelia, waiting for her to fill him in on what had been keeping her busy. She told him that the shop was in full swing with holiday shoppers, and then paused. What else could she tell him? She looked over and saw his frown, knowing that he, like Antonia, was probably worrying that she was keeping too much to herself at the shop. In a spark of inspiration, she shared the one part of her new secret life that she could.

"I've also started writing again."

"You have? Really?"

The eagerness in David's voice made her break into a grin.

"I really have."

"Finally!" he exclaimed, stopping in the middle of the gravel path where they'd been walking. "Was it all of my bullying that did it?"

"I'll let you believe that, sure."

"What are you working on, then? Your novel?"

"No—well, it's *a* novel, but not the one I was working on before." She let 'before' hang there, knowing David would understand. "It's something new."

"I'm *so* proud of you," he said as he gave her a hug. "You've been sitting on your talent for much too long." He held her at arm's length and looked her full in the eyes. "We're out for a walk, you're writing again—you're finally back."

She felt the all-too-familiar pricking of tears in her eyes and gave David a nudge.

"I've kept it together all day, and now you've blown it," she joked with a sniffle.

"Well, I can't help being excited for you," he said, hugging her again. "When can I read it? What about James? Oh, maybe he can publish it!"

"Hang on! I'm just happy to be writing again," Aurelia said, laughing. "I don't think it's going to turn into something I could publish, but it just feels good to know I can still do it."

"I knew you could," David said sincerely.

"I love you, but if you make me cry..." she threatened.

"Okay, okay," he said, taking her arm in his and continuing down the path. "Why don't I tell you all about the lamprey pie I made last night?"

"That sounds horrendous, but in the interest of me not weeping, let's hear it."

Then, kissing his cheek, she added softly, "Thank you."

30

A few days later, as Aurelia sat at her desk working on Vronsky's story, David called. Her mind was caught up in the section she'd been editing, otherwise she might have been more suspicious about his insistence that she join him and James out for dinner that very night.

"It's our last chance to see each other before the holidays," he pleaded.

Looking up from her desk, her eyes scanned the shop. She was sure she could get back before midnight, so she agreed to meet them at eight.

By the time eight o'clock rolled around, Aurelia was running late. She knew David and James wouldn't mind even though she had no excuse—she didn't exactly have a difficult commute home from work each day. Scanning the room as she walked into the restaurant, she spotted David and waved to him as she wound her way through the crowded space. Once she was just a few tables away from them, however, Aurelia drew up short when she noticed someone else at their table: Oliver. He was talking to James and didn't see her, which was fortunate as her forehead was drawn together in a frown. *Had David honestly done it again—blindsided her into another night out with Oliver?* She felt immediately embarrassed, worried that Oliver might think she'd asked David to do it, as if Oliver's rejection weeks ago hadn't gotten through to her.

"Aurelia, you're late! We've all been waiting for you."

David's voice had a false cheer to it. She bit down both a tart response and her instinct to flee and turned to James and Oliver, who had stood to greet her.

"Hi, James," she said, kissing his cheek and staring daggers at him.

James slid his eyes toward David, a clear sign that this was all David's doing, and she squeezed James's arm in solidarity.

"You remember Oliver?" David asked innocently.

"Of course I do," Aurelia said, plastering a smile on her face. "Good to see you again."

"You too," Oliver said, adding, "Don't tell me... You're surprised to see me?"

Aurelia looked at him and saw that his lips were working to keep from laughing. She let out a laugh of her own then, relieved he'd recognized David's plotting. When Oliver's laughter joined hers, she felt that fluttery feeling—the one she hadn't felt since the last time she'd seen him.

"What?" David asked. "What's funny? Have you two got inside jokes already?" he added hopefully.

Aurelia pointedly ignored him and moved to the only empty chair which, by David's design she was sure, was next to Oliver. As she took her seat, she couldn't help but notice that Oliver was once again wearing a jacket and an oxford shirt with just one button undone. He didn't seem to do casual. She started adjusting her hair but an instant later scolded herself for caring. This wasn't a date, regardless of David's desperate intentions and the fact that Oliver looked as good as she'd remembered. He smiled at her as he caught her looking and she felt that flutter in her stomach materializing again. She smiled back, but then tried to play it off by looking around the restaurant, hoping he might think her eyes had just happened to land on him even though she suspected he was smarter than that.

"I thought it'd be nice if we all got together," David explained, "seeing as how we'll be off on our separate ways for the holidays."

She hadn't seen Oliver in weeks and likely wouldn't have seen him ever again, holidays or no, if David hadn't kept forcing them together, but she decided to wait for a private opportunity to correct him. As it happened, it didn't take long. Oliver excused himself to go to the restroom once they'd ordered.

Aurelia and David stared each other down as Oliver walked away.

"This was all David," James said as soon as Oliver was out of earshot.

"I gathered as much," Aurelia said coolly.

"I'm sorry, I am, but... Okay, I'm not," David admitted. "You're writing again and the shop's doing well. I just want to see you get your love life back in order too." Aurelia glared at him, and he added, "You're my best friend and I want you to be happy."

That took the edge off her irritation at him and she gave a dramatic sigh. She wasn't any less annoyed by his incessant matchmaking, but it was hard to be too angry with him when she knew his heart was in the right place.

"But I told you I wasn't interested in Oliver," Aurelia reminded him.

She was about to add that Oliver had made it perfectly clear he wasn't interested in her either, but the memory of his visit to the shop still stung.

"Maybe so, but he practically begged me to invite you tonight!"

"Well, if I remember correctly, and I do," James interjected, "his exact words were, 'Is Aurelia coming along?'"

"*Begged?*" Aurelia said, looking back at David with a raised eyebrow.

"Alright," David conceded, "but when I said I could ask you, he said 'Sure.'"

He spread his hands out, as though Oliver's eagerness to see her again was obvious. Aurelia rolled her eyes at him. She was certain that Oliver had simply asked after her out of politeness. He clearly didn't know David well enough yet to realize he was capable of making a mountain out of the tiniest speck of sand.

David leaned toward her, his tone softening as he said, "I just think you two are right for each other. And maybe you both need a little push to realize it."

"Oh, David. I love you, I do, but..." Aurelia trailed off as she spotted Oliver walking back toward the table.

"Oliver," David prompted as soon as he'd taken his seat. "Did Aurelia tell you? She's writing again and working on something new."

"Are you?" Oliver asked.

"Yes—yeah," she said, self-conscious to be at the center of David's change of subject. Apparently, the pushing portion of the evening wasn't over yet.

"What are you writing?" Oliver asked.

"Um, it's a novel."

"Right up your alley, then," James told Oliver. "Oliver edits fiction," he added for Aurelia's benefit.

"Ah," she intoned, hoping against hope that single syllable would end the conversation.

Just then, David spotted a fellow teacher from his school and he and James excused themselves to go and say hello, leaving Aurelia and Oliver alone at the table.

"I'd be happy to read your book sometime, if you'd like. Give you some feedback," Oliver offered.

Her eyes widened at the idea of sharing her project. It was still early days and nowhere near ready to show people, least of all someone who edited books for a living.

"Don't worry," he said with a laugh. "No pressure here. I'm just glad to hear you're writing again."

She nodded at his kindness, then felt the compulsion to tell him more.

"I'm working on a sort of reimagining—thinking of what might happen to a character from another novel."

That hadn't been scary at all. In fact, it felt sort of nice to let him in on something that had been occupying most of her days and nights.

"Really? It's a fun concept—reworking an old story or taking a character and popping them into a new one. I could recommend some similar stories if that would be helpful?"

Aurelia felt her breathing go back to normal; she hadn't realized she'd been holding her breath. He hadn't laughed at her or demanded to know which novel she'd had the nerve to borrow from.

"Actually, that'd be great."

"Do you have any paper? I have a pen, but—" He broke off as he reached into his inside chest pocket, fiddling with something there. The restaurant was dimly lit, but she was certain she could see a faint blush rising up his cheeks. "Um, I have a pen," he repeated, drawing it out of his jacket carefully, as if worried something might fall out.

"I have a notebook," Aurelia offered, pulling one out of her bag and searching for a blank page before sliding it over to him.

She watched as he started writing out a few book titles and noticed his blush fade as he seemed to relax again. She wanted to ask if he was alright, but he'd already turned the notebook back to her.

"I'd start with these. I think they do a good job of playing with the old while making it feel new."

David and James came back to the table, and Oliver slipped his pen back into his pocket. Aurelia eyed the list, noticing Oliver's steady handwriting and how different it was from her messy scrawl, before closing the notebook and putting it back into her bag.

"Thank you."

She nodded to him, and they exchanged smiles before David and James pulled them back into a conversation.

When they'd finished eating, David—wisely sensing an obligation—paid the bill. As James, Aurelia, and Oliver got up to leave, David threw his hands out as if to stop them.

"James and I are going to head home, but you two should feel free to stay. Maybe you can get another drink here or somewhere else?" he suggested.

Aurelia had had enough of David's meddling for one evening. She made a face at him and then, afraid Oliver might have noticed, quickly tried to shift her expression into a look of disappointment.

"Actually, I have to get home as well," she said.

"Yeah, I'd better get going," Oliver agreed.

"In that case, you're both heading in the same direction, so you can walk together," David said, looking very smug.

Seeing no way out of it, Aurelia exchanged goodbyes with David and James, and then she and Oliver started toward the nearest Tube station.

"I'm debating whether to call David tomorrow to shout at him for not giving up on us, or to ignore him for a few days and see if that cures him," Aurelia quipped.

Oliver was quiet for a moment, then said, "I didn't mind seeing you again, but I'm sorry if it upset you."

She felt instantly guilty, realizing she'd probably made it seem as though spending another evening in his company had been miserable when, she had to admit, it hadn't.

"Oh, no, I'm not upset! I mean, David is a total meddler and must be stopped, but no, it was fine!" She paused, then added, "He seemed to misinterpret something you'd said and thought you wanted to see me again, so I'm sorry for that. But now you've learned a valuable lesson: you should never utter my name in David's presence again."

She laughed and gave his side a gentle nudge with her elbow, but he only gave a soft exhale of a laugh in return.

They'd arrived at the entrance to the Tube and Aurelia took a few steps down the stairs that led underground before realizing Oliver was no longer beside her. She turned and saw he was still at street level, looking down at her.

"You said this was your line, right?" she asked.

He looked around and then back at Aurelia before saying, "It is, but... I think I'll walk a bit further."

She tried to read hurt or anger on his face, but it gave away nothing. Maybe he'd just had enough of being forced together, she decided.

"Goodnight, then," she said.

"Goodnight."

They both turned and went their separate ways.

As her train rattled homeward, Aurelia frowned, wondering if she'd hurt Oliver's feelings. But he'd made it clear he wasn't interested in her, not like that, so what was there to hurt? Her mind lingered for a moment on the attraction she'd felt again, on how the conversation had flowed once the awkwardness of the situation had passed. She put it down to having David and James there, reminding herself that they'd been with her the last time she'd seen Oliver, when things had also been pleasant and lovely. Conveniently, she swept over the conversations between just the two of them—about her writing and what books they were reading—and focused instead on all the reasons they were destined to be friends.

She made a mental note to remind David of those reasons ad nauseum until he'd accepted them.

31

The next day was Aurelia's last in London before she left for Yorkshire for the holidays, and the shop was hectic with people rushing in for last-minute presents and needing things gift-wrapped. The fuss provided a helpful distraction from yet another confusing encounter with Oliver. When she locked the door at five, she was so tired out from the day that she had to haul herself up to the flat for her evening nap.

Waking at eleven thirty, Aurelia was excited to see the characters but also disappointed to know it would be their last night together until she returned the following week. They'd become such a major part of her life in such a short time, each one occupying a different, unique role.

Rachel and Marianne kept Aurelia laughing. They were so eager to learn about her life, her university studies, anything from her time. She'd stopped dressing specially for their evenings in the shop, since Marianne and Rachel wanted to see her twenty-first century clothes and ask her what was in fashion. They were two strong-willed, intelligent women who might have done or been anything they set their minds to if only they'd been written a century or two later. Their joy and excitement were a welcome change after spending the past year struggling to see beyond her own grief.

Having read *Little Women* many times, Marmee was as familiar to her as any character could be. And yet, Aurelia hadn't counted on her being as demanding of Aurelia as she was of her own daughters. Aurelia felt the weight of Marmee's hopes and it drove her to want to impress Marmee, to write something she might think was as good as Jo's writing.

Elinor had become a steadfast friend. Though not as lighthearted as her sister, she was wise and thoughtful. Aurelia had noticed that Elinor was slowly opening up and sharing more and more of her thoughts and perspective, which Aurelia loved to hear.

Laurie still had his boyish interest in all things fun and adventurous. He often sat in on her writing sessions with Vronsky and offered suggestions for dramatic interludes. And although he couldn't possibly be interested in Sergeant Cuff's ongoing obsession with roses, Laurie never seemed to get tired of hearing him talk about them.

Cuff was altogether too pleased with himself for setting Aurelia and Vronsky off on their experiment, but Aurelia loved him for it.

He deserved to be pleased with himself after figuring out so many of the shop's secrets, but she often wondered if he were hiding any others up his sleeve.

And Vronsky—Aurelia couldn't categorize or label what he'd come to mean to her. He was a friend, a partner in this writing project of theirs, and a relentless agitator. He loved saying things that made her roll her eyes or sigh with exasperation, challenging her, annoying her, and making her evenings in the shop more fun than she could have imagined. He still carried that sadness with him at the start of each evening. It was a sadness she recognized, almost as though it were her own grief being reflected back at her. Yet his excitement over their project also mirrored her own, keeping her hopeful that she could help him move on, even if she hadn't yet found her own way to do the same.

A few days before her trip up to Yorkshire, Aurelia had prepared everyone for the fact that she'd be away from the shop, even though she knew they wouldn't recognize the break between her visits. Marianne had begged Aurelia to read to them from the draft of Vronsky's sequel as a Christmas present, and though Aurelia had tried to put her off, soon everyone in the shop had begun asking too. Once she'd given in, they'd decided that the night before she left would be the perfect time for it.

That night, there was a party atmosphere in the shop and Aurelia was caught up in it before remembering how different it was from last night's dinner. Everyone here knew exactly what she got up to at night; they knew all about her writing project and were about to get a preview of it. Somehow, a group of fictional characters now knew more about how she'd been spending her time than her friends and family. The realization made her frown, but she forced herself to shrug it off as she still believed that secrecy was her only option.

Later, when everyone grew quiet as her reading was about to start, Aurelia experienced a slight case of stage fright. She'd offered to turn the pages of their draft so that Vronsky could read it himself, but he'd insisted that Aurelia take center stage.

When she finished to a round of applause and cheers, the group started calling out suggestions for future chapters.

"A cottage is the thing, Count Vronsky," insisted Cuff. "A cottage with a rose garden in front."

"Take up the piano, Vronsky! I would have been a musician myself if I'd had the chance," was Laurie's offering.

"I do hope a circus is in your future. I know Aurelia was only teasing, but consider what a thrilling life that would be!" Marianne sounded ready to run away with the circus herself.

As the others continued to offer up suggestions, Marmee appeared at Aurelia's side, looking thoughtful.

"Moments like this make me regret more than ever our physical limitations," she said, reaching her hand to Aurelia's shoulder as if to touch it. "If I could, I would give you the warmest of embraces, but my words will have to suffice." She smiled. "I am very proud of you, Aurelia. You are using your talent in the service of others and giving much-needed comfort to your friend, Count Vronsky." Marmee paused. "I see so much of my Jo in you—my two novelists."

Aurelia thanked Marmee, her heart swelling as she smiled through tears of happiness and a little sadness too, wishing she could share this experience with her own mother.

Their celebration continued into the early hours of the morning. As dawn arrived, Aurelia and the characters gathered around the table to say their goodbyes before they were drawn away, back into their books, until her return.

32

When she started her drive to Yorkshire, Aurelia had been looking forward to spending time with Antonia and the kids. As the miles ticked on, however, she began thinking of holidays past with her mother and Aunt Marigold. Melancholy crept in, making her dread what she knew would be a constant awareness of their absence throughout the next week.

But when she stepped out of the car at her father's house, she was thrown out of her gloom at the sight of Antonia's huge grin.

"Wait until you see it." She laughed as she hugged Aurelia.

Her niece, Julia, joined them, followed by her nephews, Owen and Hugo. The children circled around Aurelia, talking over each other and shouting in their excitement, and it took her a moment to finally make out what they were saying.

"Granddad's a pirate!"

"Mummy says he's got buried treasure in the garden and I can dig around to find it!"

"What's this about?" Aurelia asked Antonia.

Then her father appeared, looking sheepish as he stepped out of the house with Antonia's husband, Max.

"Oh my god," Aurelia breathed as she spotted the gold hoop hanging out of his ear. "What did you *do*?"

He waited for a break in her laughter so that she could hear his answer.

"I had it done when I was in town on my last visit."

He rolled his eyes when that just set them laughing harder.

"Edward and I walked past a place and joked about getting one, and now here I am."

"Bit late for a mid-life crisis," Aurelia said as she gave him a hug. "Though I guess I'm glad you didn't go for a motorcycle or a mustache."

"I'll take it out," he said. "I don't know why I didn't do it before you lot arrived, saved myself the trouble."

"Don't you dare!" Antonia insisted. "You'll break the kids' hearts. And it's growing on me."

"I only wish you'd told us sooner. I would have gotten you some earrings for Christmas so you could swap them out," Aurelia said, attempting to keep a straight face.

"There's always his birthday," Antonia added, also trying to pull a serious face.

"Go ahead, enjoy yourselves," their father said good-naturedly.

Antonia and Aurelia laughed again as everyone began helping to empty her bags from the car. Aurelia brought Fezz's carrier into the house and set him free. He'd sat through the ride in stoic silence, insulted at the ignominy of being locked away for a few hours. He was used to the house after many visits with Aunt Marigold over the years, though he was, as ever, wary of the children and their desperate desire to befriend, chase, and pet him.

Soon they were all settled in the house, with a fire blazing in the fireplace and the children moving from adult to adult, enjoying the attention and holiday atmosphere.

The first few days in Yorkshire were a blur of visiting with her father's friends, spending time with Antonia and her family, managing the children's excitement about Christmas, and stemming the inevitable tide of disappointment once the holiday had passed. As Aurelia had predicted, there were difficult moments when the gaping hole of her mother's and Marigold's absences were particularly painful. But being with her father and Antonia helped, as they either joined in or pulled each other out of those holes as needed.

They'd passed the milestones of the first anniversary of her mother's death and now the second Christmas and were finding their way as this new version of their family.

33

E ven with the holiday activity in Yorkshire, Aurelia found it difficult to keep from thinking about her shop and her new group of friends. Some moments she felt restless in her longing to be with them again, while in other moments she felt anxious about taking so many days off from writing, afraid that she might fall back into a bout of writer's block like the one she'd been stuck in before meeting the characters.

Once Christmas had passed and there was less to distract her, Antonia began needling her about her moodiness. Aurelia tried to put her off but knew there was no getting past Antonia's skills of detection—she could rival Sergeant Cuff. During an afternoon ramble through the neighboring fields with their father's dogs leading the way, Antonia started in again.

"I don't know why you won't tell me what's got you all out of sorts, Aurelia," she said with genuine concern in her voice. "If it's something good, why won't you tell me? And if it's something bad, have out with it and maybe I can help."

"There's nothing wrong, Tonia—don't worry! No, it's just… Now that I've started writing again, I want to get back to it. I love seeing all of you, but it's been too hard to write here."

And, she didn't add, Vronsky wasn't there to share his thoughts on what should happen next in his story, so Aurelia hadn't made any progress at all.

"And?" Antonia asked.

"And what?"

"There's something else—this isn't just Aurelia on a writing tear. There's something else going on with you."

Aurelia sighed. She'd been rumbled. She should have guessed she would be.

"Nothing else is happening," she lied waspishly.

"Is it that Oliver guy? You keep telling me you don't like him, but do you?"

Aurelia had filled Antonia in on both of David's surprise dinner set-ups, and even Antonia agreed he'd taken his meddling too far.

"No! I've told you a million times there's nothing there."

"He kept your bookmark, though. You said he had it when he came to the shop—that seems like something."

"Yes, and that 'something' is that he hadn't been through his pockets since our date," Aurelia said dismissively. "Anyway, that was weeks ago. He's probably tossed it in the bin by now."

"Well, something else is going on. You can keep pretending it's not, but I can tell—you've been different."

Am I really acting strangely? Aurelia wondered. She'd grown close with the characters over the past few weeks, looked forward to spending time with them, and was counting down the days until she'd be back at home. She hadn't felt excited to be part of a community like this since her writing classes at university.

"Are you going to share what's going on in there?" Antonia asked, her tone softening.

"Okay... There is something else."

Aurelia's mind desperately raced through the options of what she could plausibly tell her sister.

"It's just that I've... I've joined a writing group."

The idea had popped into her head, and it seemed like the easiest way through—a half-truth that amounted to something close to reality.

"Oh." Antonia sounded disappointed by the lack of intrigue. "Well, that's great."

"We've become really close, all of us. I see them almost every night after work and we've been sharing ideas." The half-truths were coming faster and faster.

"Then I'm glad," Antonia declared. "It's good you're getting out and meeting people again. You know I hate thinking of you being cooped up in the shop."

Aurelia didn't correct Antonia, in spite of the stab of guilt she felt at her deception.

"Shall we head back?" she suggested.

Antonia nodded and turned, and Aurelia linked her arm through her sister's and called for the dogs to stop splashing in a puddle of muddy water. On the walk back, she sensed her sister stealing glances at her, but she kept up a flow of chatter to keep from giving Antonia an opening for more questions.

Her break in Yorkshire seemed to come to a rapid close. Fezz reluctantly climbed back into his carrier for the drive home, and the family tearfully said their farewells. Aurelia's father chivvied her into her car, warning her of traffic if she didn't get on the road. It was hardest saying goodbye to him, but she knew he had friends and company nearby. With a last smile and wave, Aurelia put her car in gear and started the drive home to London.

Once she was on the motorway and in the traffic her father had predicted, her mind went directly to her shop and the characters that would be waiting for her there. Did she really seem different, as Antonia had said? It was hard not to be with everything she'd experienced over the past few weeks. It was also hard to think about getting out of the shop despite her promises to her father, Antonia, and herself to do just that. But what could be the harm in spending time with characters that had become as real to her as David, Kali, and her other friends?

As traffic continued to crawl southward, Aurelia slowly let go of her worries and focused instead on the fact that each mile was bringing her closer to the friends she'd be seeing again at midnight.

34

A urelia's first night home was filled with happy chatter as she caught up with each of the characters and told them about her holiday and her family. By the following day, she'd fallen back into her schedule of working in the shop during the day, napping in the early evenings, and spending her nights with the characters. She and Vronsky came up with ideas at night, and she wrote them out and added detail, dialogue, and descriptions during the day. The relief of falling back into a writing routine drove her to keep going, so that she wouldn't fall back out of it again.

———— ☾ ————

Weeks passed and suddenly it was February. Aurelia and Vronsky were working quickly now, motivated by their plan to get a copy of the manuscript ready for their experiment. Other characters often joined their writing sessions, adding ideas about what Vronsky ought to do, or where he ought to go. And as the characters disappeared back into their books at dawn each morning, it was less jarring now that Aurelia knew Vronsky was getting closer to disappearing into his new story.

With Aurelia spending so much time writing and editing, she was spending less time with her friends outside of the shop. David had started bringing her samples of his cooking experiments just to get a chance to see her each week. Most of them were edible and kept her fed through the many hours of writing she was putting in each day and night.

Fortunately, it was easy to keep up with Antonia and her father by phone since they didn't live close enough for regular visits. Antonia always made sure to ask Aurelia for updates on her 'writing group' and, although Aurelia felt guilty each time the lie resurfaced, she just couldn't tell Antonia about the true cast of characters that were helping her to write each night. As much as Aurelia wanted to share it all with her sister, she knew that she would doubt Antonia's sanity if their roles were reversed. She didn't want to put her sister in such a terrible position when she knew what she was experiencing was perfectly harmless.

Her friends, however, couldn't be put off indefinitely with phone calls and quick visits. Kali arrived in the shop at lunchtime one afternoon, just as Aurelia was hitting her stride on a section of the sequel that had Vronsky settling into his new life in Paris after deciding he'd had enough of Italy.

"It's non-negotiable, love. I insist you come to lunch with me, for my own sake as well as yours."

"Now?" Aurelia dragged her attention away from the typewriter. "Couldn't we go tomorrow?"

"No, afraid not. Come on, get your coat." Kali held the front door open, letting in the cold air and forcing Aurelia to her feet.

Once they were out the door and sitting down to lunch, Aurelia didn't mind the break after all. It was fun to socialize with a non-fictional friend who she could hug and who was willing to share dessert with her.

"How're you here without Ben?" she asked. "Is he with Tom's parents today?"

"No, I've found someone who can watch him for a few hours each week. I've been working on something."

"I thought you weren't going back to work?"

"I'm not—not back to my old job, anyway. Do you remember a while back, I told you about going through the National Gallery and those mums following me for my art talk with Ben?"

"Yes, right. I remember."

"It got me thinking, so I posted on one of the mummy groups I follow and offered to do tours for mums with toddlers. Mad as it sounds, people actually signed up."

"*Mad?*" Aurelia scoffed. "You're great with kids and you love art—this sounds perfect! Have you started already, then?"

"My first one's tomorrow! I just spent a few hours back at the National Gallery, plotting my tour. I'm thinking I could expand it, do different themes each week or tours at different museums, if people are interested."

"That's brilliant—you can make your own hours and you love talking about art. You have to stop by and tell me how it goes, okay?"

"I will, if I can manage to get you away from your typewriter again," Kali laughed.

"I know, I'm sorry. I've just been 'in the zone.' I'm plowing along and it's nearly finished now."

"Oh, that's fantastic! Are you going to send it round to publishers? Is that how it works?"

"No. No, this is just a sort of... passion project," Aurelia said, feeling her heart race at the idea. "More of an experiment than something I want to publish."

"Don't be silly. You're spending all this time on it—you should really try and get it published."

"I'm just enjoying myself for now," Aurelia insisted.

Yet the truth was, ever since David had mentioned it a few months back, she'd also begun to wonder whether she might publish Vronsky's new story. But she couldn't decide if he'd be open to the idea since the story was so personal—and was there really a market for a sequel to *Anna Karenina*? She could picture the reviews now: '*height of hubris to attempt to take up Tolstoy's pen...*'; '*should have left readers to imagine their own ending for Count Vronsky...*'

As a fan of the novel, she didn't think she'd like to read someone else's version of what happened to the characters from *Anna Karenina*, so why would anyone want to read hers? But she wanted people to experience Vronsky's own version of his life, even if they could never know it was truly *his* version.

———— ☾ ————

That night, after she and Vronsky had reviewed the pages she'd typed up earlier in the day, Aurelia cleared her throat.

"Alexei, I've been thinking about something."

"Yes?" He was standing, leaning casually against her desk even though he was in full dress uniform.

"We've talked about using a manuscript, just these typed pages, for the experiment," she said, gesturing to their pile of chapters. "But I've been wondering what you might think of trying to publish your sequel—having it bound and printed into an actual book."

Vronsky nodded thoughtfully before answering.

"I have been thinking the same. We could try, but we cannot be certain that leaving these pages on the table will be sufficient to call me forth from my sequel. From what we have witnessed, we appear from books, not manuscripts."

"Right—it might work with what we've got, but we can't be sure. And if it didn't work and I put your old book back on the table, you might not come out again."

"That is true, and I shouldn't like being absent as you attempted to find a solution. But in addition to the question of the manuscript form," Vronsky continued as he straightened to his full height, "we must also consider the time and effort you have invested in this project. Others should have the opportunity to read the beautiful chapters you have created."

"Oh, thank you," Aurelia said, feeling a little self-conscious about his compliment. "But... I should tell you, if we publish, I doubt if we could put your name down as a co-author."

Aurelia could just imagine the puzzled looks of publishers and readers who wouldn't understand why a fictional character was being credited for helping to write a book.

"The chapters may reflect our shared ideas, but you brought those ideas to life in a way I never could have done. It is just as well that your name alone should grace the cover of my sequel." Vronsky wrinkled his nose, adding, "Publication was never an ambition of mine. I leave that to scholars and writers like you."

They held each other's gaze for a moment, on the brink of yet another experiment.

"Well: publication. I can't guarantee that I can find a publisher—"

She stopped, realizing Vronsky might not appreciate hearing that the audience for his story could be small enough to keep publishers from banging down her door, and changed tack.

"I've never published a book before, so they may not want to meet with me."

"I see. I know a handful of men who own publishing houses in Petersburg and Moscow, but that does nothing to avail us here."

"Actually, I know someone in publishing," Aurelia said, surprised she hadn't thought of James before now. "My friend works for a small press. I'll call him tomorrow."

And just like that, it was settled.

35

By noon the next day, the shop had grown quiet, giving Aurelia a free moment to call James.

"Is everything alright?" he asked once the receptionist had put Aurelia through.

"Yes, everything's fine. How are you?"

"But... You never call me at work—you always text or call my mobile."

"Well, this is a work-related call, since I'm calling about the book I've been writing."

"Ah, the mystery project. How's it going?"

"Really well! I'm almost finished with the first draft and starting to think about what to do with it. Would you be willing to give it a read?"

"Sure," James said eagerly, then added, "Well, actually, I don't think I should."

"Oh, right. Okay. I understand—I'm sure you're busy." Aurelia suspected she hadn't managed to hide the disappointment from her voice.

"No, it's just that I don't edit fiction very often. But Oliver does."

"Oliver?"

"Mm-hmm," James said, his smirk evident even over the phone.

"James, please! I thought David was the devious one, not you."

"What?" he asked innocently. "Oliver *does* edit fiction."

"I'm serious—I really want to talk to someone about my book," Aurelia pleaded.

"I'm telling you, Oliver's your man."

"No, he isn't. You and David have made a valiant effort, but he's *not* my man."

"Fine—he's your editor, then."

"Isn't there anyone else? I know you say it's a publishing closet, but there must be other editors tucked away in there."

Her mind swam through visions of how awkward it would be to work with Oliver when their mutual friends were constantly trying to get them together. But then she remembered how supportive he'd been at dinner back in December, and how the books he'd recommended had actually been very helpful.

"There are but, kidding aside," James said, dropping his teasing tone, "I think you two would work well together."

Aurelia let out a heavy sigh. He wasn't giving her any other options, and she didn't exactly have a wealth of friends in publishing. The goal was to get the book published for Vronsky, she reminded herself. Couldn't she push through her own feelings to help him? And Oliver *had* offered to read a draft, even if she'd been terrified of the idea back when she was working on the early chapters.

"Do you honestly think he's a good fit for my writing?" she asked.

"I do—he has a great eye for fiction," James said excitedly, sensing she was giving in. "Lately he's been working on a manuscript that came in at nearly a thousand pages. Everyone's been raving about how much he's done to help the author edit it down into something really beautiful."

"Okay, then," she said with another sigh, just for show. "Let's give it a try. Should I ring him? I might still have his card somewhere."

"I'll stop by his office now and get a lunch date on his calendar."

"I mean it, this isn't another set-up—"

"'Date' as in a meeting. Don't be so tetchy. I'll get a lunch *appointment* on his calendar and ring you with the day and time. I assume your schedule is open?"

"You know it is," Aurelia said. She dropped her salty tone and added, "James, I really do appreciate your help."

"Oh, you're going to have lots to thank me for!"

Sighs and eye rolls escaped Aurelia throughout the rest of the day as she thought back over her call with James. What would he tell Oliver? Would Oliver think she'd been pining over him all this time and was desperate to see him again?

A brief call from James just before closing confirmed lunch with Oliver for noon the next day at a bistro that was a short walk from the shop. Apparently, his schedule was just as open as hers.

Even though their lunch was not a date (as Aurelia kept reminding herself the following morning), she couldn't help but worry over what to wear. If she overdid it, Oliver might think she was trying too hard, but if she wore her usual work attire, he might wonder why she hadn't tried harder to impress given that this was a writer's equivalent of a job interview. She felt silly to be facing the same dilemma, only slightly different, as she had before their first date. In the end, she settled on a navy blazer, white t-shirt, and jeans, which seemed to send a mixed message that matched her mood.

When she walked into the bistro, Aurelia scanned the tables and spotted him. He hadn't seen her yet and she caught a look of boredom, and perhaps annoyance, troubling his face. Almost the same expression he'd worn on their date: *excellent*. Determined to win him over, she put a smile on her face.

"Hi, Oliver," she said as she reached the table.

"Aurelia. Hi."

He half-stood and shook her hand, and her mind stuck on that handshake. It felt formal given that they'd met a handful of times before. Telling herself to ignore it, Aurelia sat opposite him, her smile flattening as she tried to calm her nerves. She noticed that he was wearing an oxford shirt again, one button undone at the neck, this time in white with a dark grey jacket. No, it was too hard to ignore the icy chill radiating from him.

"It's good to see you again," she said at last. "Without David's maneuvering, for once."

"You too," he said, smiling though there wasn't much warmth to it. "Well. James said you wanted me to look at the book you've been working on."

Straight to business, then.

"Yes, I'm almost done with the first draft—the one I was working on when I saw you last—and I'd like to get it published."

"I'm sure you would," Oliver said, barely suppressing a laugh.

Aurelia bobbed her head, acknowledging that getting published generally took a bit of work.

"Right, I know. But this isn't just a hobby or a one-off thing," she said, deciding to level with him. "I have a master's from Goldsmiths and I've had a few short stories published."

She hated to boast, but right now it seemed necessary. Hadn't they left things on friendly terms? But then her face warmed as she remembered the look she'd given David at the end of that dinner months ago—had Oliver seen? It wasn't until this very moment that she remembered it, but maybe it was fresh in his mind now that she was calling in a favor.

"If you want to give me your draft, I can take a look," he said. "Let you know whether it's something we'd be interested in."

"Oh."

Aurelia was instantly thrown off her high horse.

"I didn't bring a copy with me, which seems stupid now, but I can drop it at your office after lunch, if that's alright?"

"Sure," he said, nodding.

They looked at each other, then shifted their eyes around the restaurant.

"I haven't been here in ages, but it's one of my favorite spots," Aurelia finally managed to say. "Did James suggest it?"

"No, I did. I remembered your shop was in the area." He paused before adding, "It's one of my favorites too."

Oliver smiled, then, one his genuine smiles that reached his eyes, and she was startled to find that the flutter she'd felt around him before was now a full-on tugging sensation. She was given a helpful distraction from that thought when the waiter came to take their order.

As soon as he'd gone, Oliver asked, "Why don't you tell me about your book? What's it about?"

Aurelia took a deep breath.

"Well, it's not finished yet. Nearly done, but not quite there yet. I mean, it's really just an early draft. I'm still working through—"

"Get to it."

"Sorry?"

"You're stalling—tell me the story. I'm going to read it eventually, anyway."

He was right: she *was* stalling. The story meant so much to her that it was hard to finally let it out into the world, but if she wanted to get the book published, that's just what she'd have to do.

"You said before it was a retelling, or a reimagining of an older story?" he prompted her.

She looked at him and saw he'd softened a little, as if he understood her hesitation. She wanted to linger over the fact that he'd remembered what she'd said about her book but reminded herself that this was business and she needed to press on.

She nodded. "*Anna Karenina*. Tolstoy's novel?"

Oliver let out a soft laugh. "Yeah, I've heard of it."

"Right," Aurelia said, shaking her head as if to clear her thoughts. "Well, it's set after the end of the novel, and it follows Alexei—Count Vronsky—after Anna's death."

"Uplifting." His eyebrows went up again.

"He had such a tragic ending in the novel, and we thought—*I* thought—it would be interesting to see his life afterwards, to get a better sense of what happened to him and what he made of his life after losing Anna."

"Maybe... But why *Anna Karenina*? What about a novel from Swift or Fielding, something less dreary?"

Aurelia steeled herself, insisting, "Vronsky is who I've chosen and Vronsky's is the book I'm writing."

"Alright, then." Oliver gazed at her appraisingly. "What happens to Vronsky?"

"He fights for Serbia against the Ottomans. I don't know if you remember, but he was heading off to fight there at the end of the novel."

"Sure. Wasn't he on a train with a bunch of other soldiers?"

Aurelia was impressed; his recall of the novel was better than hers. Or at least, better than it had been before she'd started this project.

"Yes, exactly. So he fights in Serbia, is there for two years, then returns to Russia to bring his wounded men back to the hospital he and Anna built at his estate."

"Alright. What then?"

"He wraps up his affairs in Russia, then goes to Italy for a year to get his bearings."

"He and Anna lived there for a while, didn't they? Wouldn't it be too painful for him to go back there?"

"Yes, but those memories will follow him anywhere—he can't escape having lost her."

Aurelia and Vronsky had been through the same conversation, only she'd been arguing Oliver's side at the time.

"It's a chance for him to get grounded after the war, after not having time to really consider a future and what he might like to make of it," Aurelia continued. "He's left Russia, left behind friends and family, so it's a big leap for him. He needs the year in Italy to rediscover what he loves about life—like painting, going out, and being social. After two years at war we—I—thought he needed a chance to recuperate. He was raised as a soldier but even so, as mundane as it sounds, he needed a holiday."

Aurelia caught herself talking about Vronsky as if she'd just been chatting with him. Which, of course, she had, but she needed to rein herself in if she didn't want to scare Oliver off.

"At least, that's my approach," she added.

"He goes to Italy, lets loose, and then?"

"Then he moves to France for what we—I—think will be a permanent change of address. He speaks French fluently and it's close enough to the Russian society he's used to, but a little less rigid, especially since he'll be an outsider. He can make a start on a new life there."

"Hang on," Oliver interrupted, sounding irritated, "is there a co-author I should meet?"

"Sorry?"

"You keep saying 'we.' Are you cowriting this with someone? Is there a ghost writer or something? I don't usually go in for that sort of thing. I want to work directly with my authors."

Oliver put down his knife and fork and stared at Aurelia from across the table. It seemed as if the entire restaurant fell silent as she readied a response.

"No. No, there's no ghost writer—no co-writer—just me."

She was panicking, thinking quickly how to cover her mistake.

"I get a bit carried away when I'm writing. It's going to sound ridiculous, but sometimes I feel like..."

She realized there was nothing for it—she might as well go all in.

"I feel like I'm in conversation with my characters. Like they're guiding me through the story."

She looked down and pushed the last few bites of lunch around her plate with her fork, waiting for Oliver to politely—or not so politely—decide against working together.

"One of those, eh? I've worked with your type before."

He smiled, teasing her, and she gave a smile in return.

"Do you think you could work with one again?"

"Let's see your pages first. You've given me the bare bones of a story. I need to see the innards and flesh before I can decide if there's some life there."

"'Innards and flesh'? You're lucky I have an iron stomach," Aurelia said as the waiter arrived with a dessert menu. "Otherwise you would've put me off dessert and I'd never have forgiven you."

36

Over dessert, Oliver discussed his editing process and style, and explained how the small company managed its authors and publication schedule. Aurelia tried to focus but she was distracted by the fact that it might really happen—the book might actually get published. As they left the restaurant, he offered to walk her back to the shop to get a copy of her book, rather than wait for her to bring it round to his office.

Aurelia kept wanting to bring up their date or David and James's meddling and make a joke about it just to get it out in the open, but Oliver was so stoic she wasn't sure if bringing it up would help ease any lingering tension between them or just add to it. After a few minutes, she was glad she'd decided against it because she rediscovered that his reserve almost entirely melted when they talked about books. He reminded her that he preferred more modern authors, from David Mitchell to Kazuo Ishiguro, and teased her again about the fact that her bookshop only sold books by authors born before 1900.

"Are you trying to drive customers away? Hard copy books by obscure authors?"

"They're hardly obscure! Well, most of them, anyway."

She unlocked the door to the shop, and he stepped in behind her, quiet as he once again took in the shelves and silence. It was almost a moment of reverence and she gave him a chance to enjoy it before speaking up again.

"I've got the chapters just here," she said, walking toward her desk and taking off her coat. "Can I get you coffee? Tea?"

"Sure, why not—I'll have tea."

Aurelia tossed her coat on the desk and went to the back room to turn on the kettle. When she came out, he was standing at the Recommended Reads table, looking over her selections.

"What's this, then? Books of the month or something?"

"More of a 'staff picks' table."

"Does anyone else work here?"

"No. So just my picks, then," Aurelia laughed.

"*Anna Karenina*—not surprising." He looked up at her with that teasing smile of his. "But why the rest? Seems a bit of a jumble."

"Not really... There are a few themes that could tie them together. Disappointed in love, but happy in love by book's end?"

She went into the back room at the sound of the kettle switching off.

He followed, stopping at her desk and calling after her, "And Vronsky?"

"Well, no—obviously he wasn't happy in love by book's end," she answered as she made their tea. "Levin was, though—eventually."

After a minute, she brought out two mugs and offered him one. Oliver took a sip and cast his eyes around the shop.

"Shall we go upstairs?" he asked. "I'd like to see the rest of the place."

He walked to the spiral staircase without waiting for an answer and Aurelia followed. Once at the top, he walked straight toward the window seat and sat down, then looked expectantly at her.

Aurelia hesitated, then walked to the window seat and sat at what seemed like a respectful distance. But then she realized that the space she'd left was much too large. She stood up to move closer to him, then felt that might send the wrong message, and sat back down again. But, of course, the problem remained—they were still miles apart. After another awkward moment, she kicked off her shoes, pulled her legs up and sat cross-legged on the seat, turning toward him. No way to explain away or rescue the moment; she'd looked like an idiot. When she looked up, shaking her head at herself, he had both eyebrows fully up, and a smile threatening to turn into an all out laugh at her expense.

"Just never mind," she scolded, though a smile crept at the corners of her mouth.

Oliver let his laughter escape, and she couldn't help laughing too.

"You're comfortable, then?" he asked.

"I am. And you?"

"Very comfortable."

He took a sip of his tea and gave her a moment to collect herself. Once she'd taken a sip from her own mug, he ventured a question.

"You mentioned before that the shop's been in your family?"

"Mm-hmm. My great-great aunt, Cristobel, opened the shop in 1919. Then her niece, Lucy, took it over when Cristobel died in 1945."

"Tough time to run a bookshop," Oliver said, shaking his head.

"I know. Lucy was a star keeping it going. She ran the shop until she retired, and then my aunt, Marigold, took it over. Marigold was young, in her twenties, and really into the London music scene. I have some of her old concert posters on the walls upstairs." Aurelia pointed at the door to her flat.

"Upstairs? Is that part of the shop too?"

"No, I live upstairs—there's a flat. Marigold lived there until she died. That's when I took over."

Oliver looked toward the door and Aurelia had a panicked moment of feeling as though she ought to offer to show him upstairs. But she resisted the urge to be polite, knowing that if he took her up on the offer it would only double her discomfort.

Oliver turned his gaze back to her.

"Were you and your aunt close?"

"Yeah, we were really close. I worked here with her on and off over the years. I sort of knew I'd be the one to take it over."

"Why's that?"

"You're a man of many questions, Oliver," Aurelia laughed, hoping to change the subject before she got weepy discussing Aunt Marigold.

"I am," he said, smiling as he looked down at the mug in his hands. "My ex-girlfriend used to say that conversations with me felt more like interviews," he added, a little abashed. "I can drum up some small talk if you'd prefer?"

Aurelia wasn't sure she'd ever seen him looking so self-conscious, and she smiled reassuringly.

"No, it's fine. You asked why I thought I'd take over the shop?"

He nodded.

"Well, Cristobel, Lucy, and Marigold never married and didn't have any children. My sister, Antonia, is married with three kids and lives in Paris. And me—I love books, and I've loved this shop ever since I first stepped inside when I was little. It took some getting used to, but it really feels like mine now."

"Does that mean you can never marry or have children? Is that the curse of the shop?"

He said it with a smile, clearly intending it as a joke, but Aurelia bristled. She'd never thought of that possibility—as if there might be a requirement that she stay single in order to run the shop. She knew Marigold had dated on and off over the years, and while it was true that her great aunts hadn't married, Aurelia didn't think that meant they'd never dated or were lifelong spinsters.

"No, of course not," she insisted, ignoring her own uncertainty. "And there's no curse—I can do whatever I like. It just seems to be a pattern, that the women who run the shop are independent."

There was a strained pause, which Aurelia broke by jumping up from her seat.

"I promised you pages, didn't I? I'll run and get them for you," she said.

He stood slowly, seemingly aware that he'd hit a nerve.

"Sure."

Aurelia felt flustered. She was angry and self-conscious at the same time. Something about his questions made her feel as if the life that her aunts, and now she, had chosen was something sad and lonely.

She slipped her shoes back on and led him to the spiral staircase, flouncing down at double speed with Oliver following at a normal pace behind her. The chapters were held fast under a book on her desk, and she pulled them free and bound them together with a large clip she found in a desk drawer.

When she turned to hand them to Oliver, she was surprised to find him standing just behind her, an apologetic look on his face. It reminded her of their first date—when she'd turned around in the hotel lobby to find him standing right behind her, waiting for her. Only now, that confident, slightly bored man had shifted into someone who wasn't quite sure how to right whatever had gone wrong. Aurelia's frustration melted into guilt for being so short-tempered.

"Thanks for lunch," she said, giving him a smile. "And thanks for agreeing to read my book."

"Thank you for trusting me with your book," he replied, inclining his head toward her.

His gesture was so much like Vronsky's that Aurelia had to hold in the laugh that bubbled up at the resemblance.

"I'll be in touch after I've read your pages," Oliver said as they walked to the door.

Once he was across the street from the shop, he turned back and waved to Aurelia just as he had after his first visit. She stood in the doorway and waved back at him, her eyes moving to his hand, which was holding her only copy of Vronsky's story. Her heart gave a lurch as she realized it was now well and truly out of her hands.

37

B efore arranging to meet with Oliver, Aurelia had decided not
to tell Vronsky. She wanted to wait until she could tell him
she'd found a publisher, rather than get his hopes up for nothing if
she had to pitch his story to a few different ones.

But in the nights that followed her lunch with Oliver, it was
difficult to keep it from Vronsky. Her mood shifted constantly as she
thought about Oliver's questions, how he'd challenged her about
her subject matter, and the possibility that he might decide he didn't
want to work with her at all. A few times, Vronsky asked if she was
alright but instead of answering she just asked what he wanted to
happen next in his story.

And in the days that followed her lunch with Oliver, Aurelia
found it almost impossible not to wonder what he'd have to say
about what she'd written. The exception was a Monday visit from

Mark that led to a new discovery about Aunt Marigold and the shop. The visit started as his visits always did: Aurelia had tea waiting for him, they said their hellos, and then Mark began his wander. But this time, when he passed the Recommended Reads table, Mark stopped to look at the books on display.

"You've had these out since before Christmas, haven't you?" he asked.

Aurelia had been looking out the window, wondering if Oliver would call that day to discuss the book, and Mark's voice brought her back to the shop.

"Hmm?"

"These books, they've been here for a few months?"

"Oh, yes, I suppose they have."

She'd planned to swap them once a month, just as Marigold had, but after discovering that the table could release each book's characters, she couldn't bring herself to do it. She liked everyone too much to change their books, and still worried that if she took away or added books to the table something might go wrong—so that she might not be able to see any characters at all. Besides, they were all looking forward to finding out whether the experiment with Vronsky's sequel would work.

"She sometimes kept books out for a few months too," Mark said, smiling. "I once asked her why and she said, 'The characters feel like family. I couldn't bear to put them back on the shelves.' I always thought that was rather fanciful for Marigold. It stuck with me."

"I can see why."

Aurelia smiled as yet another piece of evidence slipped into place to confirm that her aunt knew what the table could do, even if she'd never mentioned it.

"Although Marigold still has you beat. She had *The Three Musketeers* on the table for the longest time. I lost count after about two years."

"*Two years?* Really?"

"Mm-hmm. She said it was a favorite, but one day it was gone. I asked her why, but she wouldn't talk about it for the longest time. Eventually she told me, 'It just doesn't do to live in fiction.' She sounded so sad..." He trailed off, apparently lost in the memory.

Aurelia gaped at Mark. What could have happened? Had Marigold gotten into an argument with a character?

He was looking expectantly at her but the only thing she could think to say was, "That must have been before I started working here."

"Oh, it was ages ago—not long after she took over the shop. After that she sometimes left books out for a few months, but never as long as *The Three Musketeers.*"

Mark had given Aurelia a solid distraction from waiting for Oliver's call, but it left her with questions she was afraid she'd never get answers to. She decided to ask Marmee or Sergeant Cuff about it that night since they'd both visited the shop during Marigold's time and might know what had happened. But her preoccupation with Marigold and the *Musketeers* mystery was cut short when Oliver called just before she closed the shop at five o'clock that evening.

"You've got to show me this typewriter the next time I'm in the shop," he said instead of 'hello.' "I haven't had an author submit typewritten pages to me since... well, I think ever."

Aurelia was confused for a second before she realized it was Oliver on the line.

"Oh! So... you've read it?"

"I have. Should we meet to go over my notes? It might be better to do it in person."

Better in person—like a breakup? Was he going to tell her it was unpublishable?

"Yes, okay. Um, should I come to your office?"

"No, I've been stuck here all day. Why don't I come to you at the shop. Are you free now?"

She couldn't tell him that she needed to nap so she could be alert at midnight to meet with a cast of characters, so she choked out a 'yes' and he promised to meet her in half an hour.

The minutes passed in an anxious silence as Aurelia paced around the shop, inventing various good and bad messages Oliver might be coming to deliver.

When he arrived, she noticed that he was more upbeat than she'd ever seen him. He stripped off his coat and dropped his messenger bag onto her desk. Aurelia eyed the bag warily, thinking her manuscript was likely inside. She offered him coffee or tea, but he said was ready to get right to it.

Aurelia cleared a space on her desk and watched as Oliver sat in Vronsky's chair and then pulled her manuscript out of his bag. It was covered with flags, dog-ears, and red pen marks, and her jaw was ready to drop at the sight of it.

"I've read through it a few times, and I think it has promise. I've made some initial notes here and we can talk through those later," he said, placing his hand on the manuscript. "But there are some bigger issues we should focus on at this stage. I'd like to see what you do with my notes—some authors think they want to be published until they realize they'll have to edit their work. But if you're open to making these changes—which *will* make it a better piece—then I think we'll be on the road to something worth publishing."

There were compliments in there but her mind had filtered them out so that all she really heard was that, without his edits, her book would be unpublishable. She ground her teeth and bit down her ire.

"Okay." Aurelia was preparing to add to this, but Oliver took it as an invitation to dive into his notes.

"Let's not waste time on little things like moving paragraphs around or deleting them outright. I've noted those changes on the manuscript itself and you can work on those on your own."

Aurelia's eyes widened.

"I want to focus on the bigger picture. First, this is plodding. It takes you almost a hundred pages to get him to France and that's where the real story is."

"But it took him a few years to get there—"

"But *you* don't need to spend years getting him there. Just summarize, something like: 'His time in Russia was occupied with tying up loose ends and checking in on his men. It wasn't long before he was on a train for Italy.' You get the idea."

Her cheeks started burning with the effort of holding in her anger. She knew it was well out of proportion to the situation, but she couldn't help it.

"Yes, I get the idea," she said, her voice a simmering warning that Oliver clearly didn't recognize.

"Then there's his time in Italy. Frankly, it's a little boring. He's sitting around painting and thinking through his plans for the future. I'm yawning just talking about it, let alone reading pages and pages about it."

Aurelia was barely processing his words; she was too focused on whether she should reach over and flick his ear with her finger or kick him in the shin. He was ripping her manuscript to shreds with no regard for the fact that she'd worked so hard on it.

"But I think the biggest issue for me is the lack of any love interest."

The rising color instantly drained from her face.

"Love interest," she repeated flatly.

Aurelia was in shock. The thought of a love interest honestly hadn't occurred to her. Vronsky had never mentioned it, nor had the other characters—everyone knew how devoted he'd been to Anna. It seemed completely heartless to think of suggesting that he write himself into a new love affair when he was still in mourning.

Her silence finally seemed to register with Oliver.

"It might seem like a lot to tackle, but these are all minor changes in the grand scheme. These changes are going to give this"—he gestured to the manuscript—"muscle."

He sounded excited and energized by his notes and the project, the complete opposite of Aurelia's feelings of disappointment and frustration. All her hard work, all these months of writing with Vronsky, and she still had so much further to go before they'd actually be able to publish it. Maybe she wasn't the right person to write this book. Maybe she was too close to Vronsky, to *Anna Karenina*, to write something that anyone other than her would want to read. Maybe it was too soon and she needed more time to process all that had happened in the past year. And Vronsky—she'd have to tell him about Oliver now. But would he want her to find another publisher after hearing Oliver's notes?

She'd had her work critiqued and edited plenty of times before, but this felt so much more personal.

"Aurelia? You look stricken."

He was leaning toward her, eyebrows furrowed as his eyes ran over her face and caught sight of her hands, which were clenched around the arms of her chair.

"I feel stricken," she said with a hint of a laugh as she repeated his old-fashioned expression.

"I know editing's a rough process, but you'll weather it, I'm sure."

"And if I don't make these edits, you won't publish it?"

"If you want to push back, you should. Though there may be a point where I don't feel confident about moving forward without certain changes."

Aurelia nodded.

"You should take some time to think about my notes—the ones we've discussed and the ones I've marked on the draft. What do you need, a few days?"

She nodded again.

"Today's Monday…" he said thoughtfully. "My week's a bit crazy with meetings and a production deadline. I might be able to do lunch on Friday, but it would be tight. Maybe dinner then?"

"Dinner," she said vaguely, trying to keep up with the conversation while her mind was still on his edits.

Oliver seemed to take that as an answer, so he continued. "Great, we can talk through what you do and don't want to change, then see where we are. In the meantime, I'll have my office send over a contract. We're a small outfit, so the advance will be small. Is that an issue for you?"

Aurelia's mind was spinning as she tried to process making revisions, talking to Vronsky about Oliver's notes, reviewing a contract, and having dinner with Oliver. How wonderful—they'd have the span of an entire meal to discuss what he didn't like about her book. But, she reminded herself, as of right now, he was her only option.

"No, that's fine. I just want to get it published."

Oliver stood and walked himself to the door.

"I'll give you a call with a place and time. See you Friday."

Aurelia followed him. She watched absentmindedly as he walked out of the shop, crossed the street, and turned to wave at her before continuing through the square. It's possible she waved back, but she couldn't be sure. She locked the door and walked back to her desk, eyeing the battered manuscript before piling a few papers and books on top. It was still under there, but somehow, she felt better having it out of sight.

Walking toward the spiral staircase to head upstairs for her nap, she paused with her foot on the first step before looking back at her desk with a sigh. There was no way she'd be able to sleep without seeing the full extent of his notes. She turned back and excavated the manuscript, then went upstairs to start sorting through them.

38

"So, you and Oliver met to discuss your book. How goes it?" James asked her over lunch the next day.

Aurelia had woken up that morning with a headache and the idea that it might be worth checking in with James to get his take on Oliver and his many notes.

She'd eventually read through all his suggestions and had to admit that most of them were pretty good. Even so, she couldn't decide if he just wanted something he could put his name to, whether or not it would be anything like her writing style. She'd decided to wait before diving into the edits with Vronsky so that she could feel James out on what to do next.

"Um, it's going," Aurelia said uncertainly.

"Lots of edits?" he asked wickedly.

"Yes!" she exclaimed.

"Annoyingly excited about tearing apart your work?"

"Yes!"

"That's Oliver to a T," James laughed. "How are you holding up?"

"Just alright, honestly. Some of his edits are really good. But the quantity is... a lot. And some of the notes..."

"He's very enthusiastic about his work, especially when he sees something he likes," James explained. "This is just his process. But you should speak up if—*when*—you disagree," he added with a laugh. "I'm not worried about you speaking your mind, it's more whether Oliver gives you a chance to get a word in before you run screaming from the room."

"I have no problem pushing back, especially now that I've gotten over the shock of his delivery." She paused. "But he's good, James? He'll make the book better? Not just... something that will sell?"

"He's great, Aurelia," James said soberly. "I've seen him do fantastic work. Actually, you should read some of the things he's edited. Have you heard of Marie Hanson? He worked on her latest book and it's been very well-received."

"Her name's familiar, but no—I haven't read anything of hers."

"Well, you should take a look. It still has Marie's distinctive style, but I recognize Oliver's hand and know he helped make it better."

They finished their lunch and, after thanking James for the pep talk, Aurelia stopped by a small bookshop on the way back to her own. She'd been a regular there since her university days, picking up newer books that weren't stocked in her shop. The owner, an older man, had become a friend since she took over from Marigold and had helped her find her footing as a business owner. His shop was newer than hers but still had the aura of an independent bookseller's that made Aurelia feel as though she were home. After catching up with the owner, she found and bought the book James had mentioned, then went back to her own shop.

She'd hoped for a quiet afternoon to get through it, but customers kept her busy. When five o'clock rolled around, she closed up and went to her flat to make a quick dinner and read a chapter or two before her nap.

James was right—the book *was* good. Aurelia became so absorbed in the story that she got through dinner and two cups of tea before realizing it was nearly ten o'clock and she'd missed her window for a long nap. With a sigh, she looked from her book to the stairs that led to the shop. She wanted to finish the book and give herself time to think about whether she should move forward with Oliver or look for someone new. And maybe, she thought guiltily, it might even be nice to get a normal night's sleep. The characters would wonder where she was but they'd agreed a few weeks ago, after she'd missed her alarm two nights in a row, not to worry if she didn't come down.

Aurelia put her nose back in the book and fell asleep just before midnight, waking up at eight o'clock the next morning with the book spread open next to her and the bedside lamp still on. As she shook off sleep, she realized she must have drifted off while reading. It used to be a fairly common thing, but she hadn't had much time to read for fun lately.

Turning out the light, she wandered into the kitchen to make tea and finish the last few pages of the book. It held up; from start to finish, it was a wonderful read. When she reached the end, she re-read the last paragraph, not quite ready to put it down just yet.

Just as James had predicted, Aurelia now felt better about letting Oliver take on her own book, even with his exuberant edits and notes. She also had to remind herself that, while she wanted to feel some ownership over the novel since it would be the first book of hers to be published, the goal was to have something to put on the table so that Vronsky's future would no longer be an endless train ride of grief. Writing the story had been a group effort, she reasoned, so why should editing it be any different?

39

Vronsky didn't seem to appreciate that finding a willing publisher was a stroke of luck. When Aurelia told him about Oliver later that night, he took it as a matter of course that someone wanted to publish his life story.

After reading through Oliver's notes on her own, Aurelia had made a plan to tell Vronsky about him and to introduce his notes one at a time. She would get a read on Vronsky's reaction to each one before she moved on to the next. Then, if he approved of Oliver's major suggestions, they could start flipping through the manuscript to review his other notes. Aurelia almost laughed when she realized she'd landed on the same approach Oliver had used with her.

Once she and Vronsky were sitting at her desk, she shared Oliver's first note, about how long it took to get him from Russia, to Italy, and then to France.

Vronsky listened carefully, then said, "It may have been important for you and I to understand exactly what happened, but readers may prefer a condensed account of my travels. The real focus, as we know now, will be my life in France, therefore I agree with this Oliver. Let us cut to the chase, as they say."

"I guess that's true. Readers don't necessarily need to know every step you took to get to France."

She frowned, confused by her sudden agreement with feedback that, when she'd first heard it, had been hard to take.

"Precisely. You have the meat of the thing—I'll leave you to trim the fat." Vronsky waved a hand dismissively.

He was using Oliver's metaphors, which made Aurelia think how much more efficient it would be if only Oliver and Vronsky could sit down to talk about the manuscript without her.

"Alright, I'll work on cutting it down tomorrow," she said.

"What other notes did this publisher have to offer?" Vronsky asked as he settled deeper into his chair.

"He thinks your stay in Italy is too boring," Aurelia said, deciding to take the gloves off now.

"Well, I am not visiting casinos or bordellos, but those are hardly palatable pastimes for our readership."

Aurelia couldn't help letting off a snort at the word 'bordellos' and he narrowed his eyes in mock disapproval.

"If you are trimming the fat to get me to France, perhaps that will cure some of his boredom, eh?"

"Sure, I'll try to keep only the most exciting bits of your time in Italy."

She couldn't hide her sarcasm but at least resisted the urge to mention that wouldn't leave them with much since painting and visiting stables wasn't exactly the stuff of high drama.

"We've made quick work of his notes, haven't we?"

Vronsky sat up, looking satisfied with himself. Now was the moment to raise the prospect of writing a love interest for him, but Aurelia felt her throat tighten. She didn't want to hurt Vronsky and knew it would upset him, but she had to admit that her own feelings were at play too.

As a reader, she felt invested in his relationship with Anna. It was one thing to want him to move on and build a new life for himself, but another to imagine him running off with a new woman after losing her. Her mother's words came back to her once again: *a love that powerful is written in indelible ink.* For Aurelia, her mother's death felt just like that. It was a loss that would stay with her forever, written in indelible ink across the pages of her own life. If Aurelia was still dealing with her own loss, could Vronsky really be ready to move on from his?

"Alexei, he did have some other notes," she said after a moment.

"Yes?"

Aurelia pulled the manuscript out from a desk drawer, deciding that she might be able to build up to the major edit that hung in the air between them if they started with some of the minor ones. She pushed aside the scattered papers and books on her desk to make room for the manuscript, and Vronsky watched as she ran her thumb along an edge and flipped through it. His eyes widened as he took in the red marks that crisscrossed the pages.

"He has a lot to say, this Oliver fellow," Vronsky observed.

"Oh, yes. He does indeed," Aurelia said ruefully.

They spent the rest of the evening working their way through the manuscript, debating over which edits to make and which to reject. By the time dawn arrived, they'd spent so much time working on minor changes that Aurelia had completely forgotten to raise that lingering, most significant one.

40

L ater that morning, Aurelia pulled out her laptop and started typing up a clean, new draft. With the amount of edits she was likely to get from Oliver in future, she couldn't be bothered retyping entire pages on the typewriter, so she'd just have to hide her laptop away before the characters arrived each night. She smiled thinking that Oliver wouldn't be able to make fun of her about typewritten pages the next time they saw each other.

A publication contract arrived in her inbox that afternoon, just as Oliver had promised, so Aurelia called Kali and asked if she'd be willing to dust off her solicitor's skills and review it for her. Kali stopped by to look at it after one of her art tours, giving the two friends an excuse to catch up over tea. Before she left, Kali spent a few minutes going over the contract and said it had her stamp of approval. Aurelia was exhilarated to be one step closer to making

Oliver's commitment to publish the book official, but that feeling was matched by worry over having to ask Vronsky whether he'd let her add a romantic storyline.

Back at her desk after her visit with Kali, Aurelia called Antonia. She still hadn't told her what she was writing about and thought—as she had a contract to publish it—now was the time. Aurelia dialed and barely registered a single ring before Antonia answered.

"Usually I beat you to it, but this time you did," Antonia began.

"What were *you* calling about?"

"Owen's finally told us what he wants for his birthday next week and I need help figuring out how not to break his heart when we don't get it for him."

"What is it—a life-sized robot or something?"

"Worse. A dog."

"Oh dear. I'll start thinking of excuses for you."

"Let me know once you've got a few—Max and I haven't come up with any good ones yet. Anyway, why're you calling?"

"I have news."

"Do I need to sit down?"

"No, I think you're safe standing." Aurelia paused for dramatic effect. "I've got a contract to publish my book."

"A *what*?"

"A contract. James's company is going to publish my book."

"Aurelia! Have you already finished writing it?"

"Well, no," she conceded. "But I'm pretty far along now."

"Has James read it? Does he know what it's about and I don't?"

"Not yet, but I figured it's time I told you."

"High time. You've been closeted away with that writing group and refusing to say a word."

Every time Antonia mentioned the 'writing group,' it took Aurelia a moment to remember the little lie she'd told her back at Christmas.

"You can keep scolding me about it or I can tell you," Aurelia said, feigning her threat.

Antonia was silent in response.

"I'm writing a sequel to *Anna Karenina*."

Antonia remained silent, but now there was a different quality to her silence.

"Okay, I know that sounds ridiculous, but I'm writing about what happens to Count Vronsky after the novel ends. I just sort of... got into his head a bit and feel like I can imagine what he'd want to do and where he'd go next."

Not too far from the truth, Aurelia reassured herself.

"And James is going to publish it, but he hasn't even read it yet?"

"His company is going to publish it. I've been meeting with one of their editors, Oliver."

"Oliver... Not *that* Oliver?"

Of course she would remember him, Aurelia thought, rolling her eyes.

"Yes, *that* Oliver, but this is strictly professional."

"Alright," Antonia said suspiciously.

"Actually, he's given me a mass of edits. They're mostly good, but there's one I just don't know if I can make."

"What is it?"

"He wants me to write a love interest for Vronsky."

"So?"

"I don't think I can do it. Mum used to say Vronsky would never get over Anna—that he would love her forever."

"That was Mum's view of things, though. He's a fictional character and you're a writer, you can do whatever you like."

Hadn't Aurelia given Vronsky that very advice? Now it was her turn to be silent.

"If you think he should fall in love with someone else, then write it. Don't let something Mum probably said in passing hold you back."

"She didn't say it in passing, though. She really felt it."

"But what do *you* feel?"

Aurelia paused, thinking the thoughts that had been running through her mind since her meeting with Oliver. She wanted to believe that Vronsky could fall in love again, for his sake, but she was afraid to ask him to consider it, afraid to push him down a path he didn't want to travel. She'd been pushed and prodded for months now—taking over the shop, writing Vronsky's sequel, going out with Oliver and now working with him. As it happened, she was happy with how things had turned out, but would Vronsky feel the same about her pushing and prodding him?

"I'm not sure," Aurelia finally admitted.

"What does your writing group think?"

"My writing group? Um... I haven't asked them."

"Well, are you seeing them tonight?"

As the characters arrived that night, Aurelia made sure to stand closest to the spot where Elinor usually appeared and then, once she'd greeted everyone, Aurelia asked her if they could speak privately. Catching Vronsky's eye—and his raised eyebrows when she didn't meet him at her desk—Aurelia signaled that she needed a minute.

Elinor followed Aurelia to the window seat on the mezzanine and, though she couldn't hide her look of interest, she patiently waited for Aurelia to start.

"I need some good advice tonight and I think you're the best person for the job."

"I shall do my best, Aurelia, though whether my advice is good may depend upon the topic."

"You know how I've met with an editor, Oliver, and he's given me notes and suggestions for Alexei's book?"

"Yes, I recall your mention of Mr. Oliver."

"Oh, just 'Oliver' is fine," Aurelia said, trying not to laugh at the thought of calling him 'Mr. Oliver' the next time she saw him. "One of his suggestions is about Alexei's... romantic prospects. Oliver thinks the story needs a romance between Alexei and another character."

"I see," Elinor said carefully. "You have not, I presume, raised this suggestion with Count Vronsky?"

"No, not yet. I haven't been able to think of a way to bring it up without upsetting him. And, if I'm honest, it's hard for me to picture him setting off into the sunset with someone other than Anna. I've read their book so many times... It feels wrong, like I'd be canceling out his heartbreak and forcing him to love someone else."

"I agree the suggestion is liable to upset him. But you did begin this project with the hope that he might find happiness in being able to choose his own future."

"We did, yes," Aurelia groaned, catching onto Elinor's meaning. "And here I am, selfishly trying to manipulate that future."

"No, I do not think selfishness is at the root of your reluctance. But I believe you overstate what a new romance might mean for his love of Anna. I do not think it would cancel out his heartache, as you say. I have seen my own sister become the object of love for a man whose heart was deeply bruised. Having heard Colonel Brandon's story, I would not have thought it possible for him to love again, yet I have witnessed the earnest love he feels for Marianne and know it to be true. I am certain you could help Count Vronsky devise a love story that would do honor to Anna without erasing her memory."

"Then I guess it's just a matter of finding a way to ask him. I don't suppose you fancy doing it?" Aurelia asked.

"Oh, no. As it is your project, I think it far better coming from you," Elinor said with a wry smile.

Aurelia laughed grimly just as Rachel and Marianne arrived to join them.

She tried to shake loose her thoughts and chat with them but eventually had to admit that she was too preoccupied to stay in the shop. She asked Elinor and the others to make her excuses to Vronsky so that she could escape to her flat for the night. What she needed was time to think on her own, a good night's sleep, and a fresh start in the morning.

41

When she came down to the shop the next day, Aurelia realized she'd lost a night of editing the manuscript and was due to see Oliver for dinner within hours. She'd been dragging her feet about talking to Vronsky and hoped Oliver might not mention the love interest again. The shop was relatively quiet, giving her time to finish typing out the revised chapters on her laptop. Keeping busy helped to occupy her mind, but since she was writing about Vronsky she couldn't help but think about the conversation that she knew they'd need to have, and soon.

———— ☾ ————

When Oliver arrived at the restaurant, he was buoyant and full of energy, as though he were actually looking forward to seeing her, rather than facing another dreary work assignment.

His buoyancy seemed to deflate slightly when Aurelia slid the manuscript across the table.

"Is this a new draft?" he asked, pulling it toward him.

"It is. Well, a new draft for the first half of the book—I'm still working on the rest."

"You've revised the first half already?"

His disbelief was making her feel very full of herself, so she said, "Of course," as casually as she could.

"I take it you didn't work in many of my edits, then."

"I did. They're there. Well, most—not all. I shortened the beginning, made Italy more fun for you," she said, her eyes narrowing as she ribbed him. "Overall, I think you'll be happy."

"But are *you* happy?"

He seemed to genuinely care about her answer to that question, which made Aurelia drop her teasing tone.

"I wasn't at first. It's always hard to get edits on something you care about. But I agreed with most of them once I had a chance to work them out and see what they might mean for the story."

He gave a smile that warmed his eyes, and she smiled in return, telling herself to ignore the tugging feeling in her stomach. The moment passed, and he was back to his edits.

"What about the love interest? Does Vronsky have a mademoiselle waiting for him in France now?"

The stomach tug instantly vanished at the casual way he'd referred to Vronsky's love life.

"No. No, I haven't gotten to that note yet. I'm not sure about...
Well, I'm not even sure how to address it."

"Aurelia, his is one of the greatest love stories in literature. As a
reader I would find it hard to believe that, even after the tragic loss
of Anna, he would never love or be with another woman ever again.
Fine if it's not the love of his life like Anna was, but can you really
not see him having feelings for another woman again—*ever*?"

After last night's conversation with Elinor, Aurelia had to
admit—at least to herself—that she, too, found it hard to believe he
would never love again, even if that love were only half of what he'd
felt for Anna. She looked up to see Oliver studying her face, trying
to puzzle out her silence.

"You alright?"

"I am, yeah," she said, nodding. "I'm going to think about the
love interest. I can't promise anything, but I'll see what I can do."

"Okay," said Oliver, nodding his head decisively. "You know,
you can take your time with the next round of edits—there's no
rush."

"Actually, there is a bit of a rush. I know the contract you sent
said the book would come out next year, but I'm hoping we could
get it into print a bit sooner."

Oliver's eyebrows went up.

"How much sooner? A year is tight as it is, even for a small press
like ours. And you're only on an early draft."

"I was hoping to have it published in a few months?"

Oliver had taken a sip of water and began spluttering as if it had
gone down the wrong way. He coughed, holding up his finger as he
tried to recover.

"Sorry! I didn't mean to shock you. But you did say you liked working with early drafts."

"I did say that." He paused to clear his throat again. "But I also said I wanted more time to work on those drafts, not less."

"Oh, right." She'd definitely forgotten that part. "It's just... It's important to me to get this book out as soon as I can. It means something to me, to have it out in the world. And now you've seen that I can work quickly. I don't want to push you, but... If we could try for a publication date this year—maybe in autumn?—I promise I'll put in the time to get it all done."

He regarded her, giving no sign of what was going through his mind. She wanted to keep making her case but thought it best to give him a moment to think.

"I'll have to get the lead editor to approve it, but I'm willing to put in the time if you are."

"Really? That would be brilliant! Thank you!"

"I'll take a look at your changes this weekend, and I'll work on getting notes back to you early next week," he promised.

"Excellent. Okay."

Relief shot through her and she sat back in her chair, limbs feeling like jelly after the tension she'd been holding. Oliver, meanwhile, stared down at the table and then took a sip of his wine, seeming out of his element now they were done discussing edits to her book. Aurelia decided to help him out by setting him back on familiar ground.

"I just read Marie Hanson's book, the one you edited."

"Did you?" he asked.

"Yes, James mentioned it, so I picked up a copy. It's a gorgeous book, Oliver."

"I'll tell Marie you think so. She was lovely to work with—I pointed her in a direction and off she flew."

"You make her sound like a labrador."

"Fair enough," he said with a laugh. "I just meant we found a good working rhythm."

For some reason, Aurelia felt annoyed to think of him 'finding a rhythm' with another writer. *Another female writer*, she admitted to herself. She gave her head a little shake, trying to work loose the thought.

Oliver squinted at her and Aurelia knew she needed to keep the conversation going or risk him asking once again if she was quite alright.

"Do you keep in touch with Marie now that the book is finished?"

"I do. In fact, I'm a regular at hers for bridge," he said with a hint of a smile.

"Bridge? As in the card game?" Aurelia left *at hers* unsaid.

"My granddad taught me how to play, and when Marie found out I knew how... Well, you need a group for bridge, so she and her husband invited me to join."

Aurelia caught at the word 'husband' and felt a wave of humiliation wash over her. She knew only too well that Oliver didn't want to date her, but she'd still allowed herself to feel jealous thinking he had a romantic relationship with poor Marie Hanson.

"Well, that's good. I'm glad your authors aren't keeping you too busy to have fun. I'll try to do the same, even with my tight deadline," she added with a self-deprecating smile.

Oliver grew serious, then said, "I tend to get very wrapped up in my work. It's hard to make time for fun—for dating—when I'm knee-deep in an edit. But I'm ready to find that work-life balance thing everyone keeps talking about, to find someone worth making time for."

He said this earnestly, looking directly into Aurelia's eyes in a way that made that tug in her stomach feel slightly uncomfortable. His meaning seemed clear—that he'd like to make time for *her*—but that couldn't be right. Hadn't he told her, a few times now, that he wasn't interested in her?

"Do you think we could skip dessert tonight?" she asked suddenly.

Oliver sat back, taking in yet another of her rapid mood shifts.

"Working on all of your edits this week has tired me out," she added with a small smile—the best she could do when she felt so at sea. "Oh, here," she added, taking the signed contract from her bag and handing it to him.

"We're going to work together? It's official, then?"

"It is."

They left the restaurant and, despite his offer to walk her home, Aurelia insisted she needed the air and was fine on her own.

42

Although she knew she'd be tired the next day, Aurelia didn't bother attempting to nap before midnight that night. She was home by nine thirty and decided to give in to her rushing thoughts and try sorting them out. Sitting on the squishy armchair in her flat, she sipped tea and worked through those thoughts one by one.

Most insistent were her thoughts about Oliver. She was still getting to know him, really, but she couldn't deny she was attracted to him. No matter how many times she told herself she wasn't interested, the fluttering sensation that had become a full-on tug every time he flashed one of his best smiles was a sure sign of it. But while he said he was trying to make time in his life for a relationship, that didn't mean he wanted one with her. And she didn't have much time for a relationship herself—not when she was working so hard to finish Vronsky's story.

It wasn't just that. There was the fact that she hadn't dated anyone since her mother died. She'd lost two people she'd loved too quickly. Keeping her circle of loved ones small felt safer, better than finding someone new she might love and one day lose. And there was the fact that, as these thoughts were swirling in her head, she was very conscious of each passing minute bringing her closer to midnight and the characters she was about to see. The word *characters* alone made the impossibility of starting something new with Oliver—with anyone, for that matter—all the more obvious. She'd managed to hide her secret life at the shop from everyone else, but hiding it from a boyfriend would invite the sort of chaos she'd been trying so hard to avoid after losing her mother and Marigold. And, still and always, there was the lingering sadness waiting at the edge of her feelings, threatening to break through.

Working on Vronsky's story had made her feel as though she could take control of the spinning threads of fate. The idea that she could write him a story that would change his life for the better gave her a purpose, made her feel as though despite everything she'd lost, she could still reach out and hold onto something solid.

As she sat in her living room, Aurelia thought again that something 'better' for Vronsky might mean helping him to open up to loving someone new. It wasn't fair not to share Oliver's note, and her own belief now, that his sequel wouldn't be complete without giving him a chance to find love again. Even if she was in no position to move on with her own life, she at least owed Vronsky a choice in his. It would be a difficult conversation but as his friend, as someone

who wanted the very best for him, she could help him see that he
didn't have to choose a future without love.

When the clock struck midnight that night, Aurelia was downstairs,
standing at her desk as her visitors appeared from their books. She
watched Vronsky struggling to smile and greet the others as he
fought through the emotions he always brought with him from the
end of his novel. After saying her hellos to everyone, Aurelia asked
him if they could talk privately, up at the window seat.

"Are you feeling better?" he asked once they were settled.

"Better?"

"Elinor informed us that you were afflicted with a headache last
night."

"Oh! A headache... Yes, I did have one last night and that's why
I left early," she improvised quickly. "But I'm better now."

"Shall we resume our project tonight, or would you prefer a
respite in order to recuperate?"

"Actually, there's something I wanted to talk to you about. You
remember I was meeting with Oliver tonight?"

"Did that engagement take place this evening?"

"Yes. We met for dinner and I gave him the revisions."

"You met him alone? At a restaurant?"

Oh great, thought Aurelia, *here we go.*

"In my time, women don't need a chaperone to have dinner
alone with a man," she said with a smirk. "My honor is very much
intact."

Vronsky snorted out a laugh.

"At dinner we talked about one edit that I hadn't mentioned to you before, something he'd asked me to consider when I saw him earlier this week. I'm sorry I didn't tell you. I just... I wasn't sure how to talk to you about it."

"Yes?"

"He asked—he suggested—that the story would be more interesting if we wrote a love interest for you."

"A what?"

"A love interest. A romantic storyline."

Vronsky was silent, watching her.

"He thinks the story would be better with one, and after thinking about it... I agree with him."

Vronsky continued to stare at her, his eyes hardening as he took in her words.

"Alexei, how can we write your life story without love?" Aurelia reasoned.

"My life has not been without love," he said, iron in his voice.

"No, of course not—not in the past," she said, shaking her head at her careless mistake. "But what about your future? This whole project is about trying to help you find a happier ending. And what would that look like without love? Oliver is right—he reminded me that yours is one of the greatest love stories in literature. We can't write a future for you that leaves you alone when you deserve so much more."

"You say this was Oliver's idea. *He* insists?"

"He doesn't *insist*, but he thinks it would be a mistake not to write about you falling in love again. And I agree with him."

"What right does he have to dictate my life?" Vronsky's tone was heated, growing angrier by the moment.

"He's not dictating, he's just suggesting. He's an editor—he knows what makes a good story."

"You told me to 'think big,' but now you want me to think like a small-minded man I've never met? A man who dines at a restaurant *alone* with a woman?" Vronsky's voice rose with each word.

"I told you, that's completely normal in my time."

She was losing her footing now that he was gaining steam.

"Not in mine! You pushed me to write this, you cajoled me and now we have to change our story to suit this self-important—"

"Alexei—"

"No! I will not have it," he said, standing. "I am tired of rules, what I can and cannot do, who I can and cannot love, who will or will not allow it." His voice cracked and Aurelia knew he wasn't thinking about a new relationship now, but about his relationship with Anna, and everyone and everything that had conspired against them.

"But we could write whatever you want—we could create a woman that you love. You can decide what you want to say to her. You can decide that society adores her and welcomes you both."

Vronsky barely seemed to register what she was saying as he paced in front of her.

"Write what you like. With any luck, the experiment will work and I shall be free of this Oliver and this... this shop!"

Aurelia flinched at his words.

"Do you know, you went on and on about women having choices, yet you seem all too eager to write whatever *Oliver* tells you."

"That's not fair!" she said, leaping to her feet. "I'm not blindly following his orders. I've thought about what he has to say and I think he's right. He's a very talented editor. I've been impressed with his work and his suggestions—and so have you, for that matter!"

Vronsky's face fell.

"I see," he said softly. "This has nothing to do with me and my story. You have taken an interest in this Oliver."

"What? What do you mean?"

She felt her face shaping itself into a guilty expression against her will.

He looked at her incredulously but said nothing. Aurelia felt as if she were fighting with David, only David would have used any hint that she liked Oliver to try and force them together.

"There's nothing between me and Oliver. He made a suggestion and I agree with him, that's all. You have to know I would never push something on you just to please someone else."

"You promised me a new ending, my own ending, and now I have to watch as you allow this Oliver to warp my story to suit his own ends," Vronsky said, his voice quietly seething with anger.

He turned away from her to face the window just as Aurelia caught sight of Elinor, who was slowly making her way toward them.

"We heard your voices downstairs," she said cautiously. "I see you are in the grips of powerful emotions and wonder if there is anything we might do to ease your distress?"

"I'm alright. We're alright, thank you, Elinor." Aurelia tried to collect herself. "I'm sorry for making such a scene."

She looked down to the shop below and saw everyone quickly turn away.

Just as quickly, Vronsky stalked to the spiral staircase, barreled down it, and disappeared into a far corner of the shop. Aurelia opened her mouth to speak to him as he passed, but nothing came out. She sat back on the seat and stared out across the mezzanine.

Elinor sat next to her, a gentle presence at her side.

"I take it you raised Oliver's suggestion with Count Vronsky."

"I did."

"It seems it did not go well."

"It did not," Aurelia agreed.

"We knew it would be a painful subject to raise, but it is nonetheless difficult seeing him so very angry."

"Especially when I'm the one that's done it," Aurelia said. "I've brought back awful memories and here we were trying to help him move on from all that."

"He will remember your good efforts, I have no doubt. But for tonight, he must recover himself. I do believe he, too, has thought about finding love again, despite his protestations."

"Maybe... But now I'm afraid he'll refuse to consider it ever again."

"Give him time," Elinor said kindly.

They talked in hushed tones for a while longer, but Vronsky stayed in his self-imposed exile for the rest of the night.

43

Aurelia had a fitful sleep. Her recent conversations with Vronsky and Oliver played themselves over and over again in her mind. She finally got out of bed at half past seven, having tossed and turned for an hour. She took her time making breakfast, lingering over her coffee, and showering and dressing for the day, but eventually had to go downstairs to face the shop. Opening the door from the flat slowly, she half-expected to see everyone staring up at her from below. But, of course, it was well after sunrise and they were all safely back in their books.

By early afternoon, Aurelia had worked through her conversations with Vronsky and Oliver so many times that she was starting to blend them together in her mind. She hated the accusation that she was acting under Oliver's direction rather than in Vronsky's best interests. But she also had to admit that she did find Oliver intriguing. Vronsky hadn't been entirely wrong about that.

After spending so much time in her head, Aurelia needed to get out. She rarely closed the shop for longer than it took to get lunch or a coffee during business hours, but she had the sudden idea to take off the rest of the afternoon. The shop had been quiet after a rush earlier in the day, so she had no customers or urgent business that couldn't wait. Before she could change her mind, she walked to the door and locked it. Elated by her own daring, she stepped backward a few paces, looking out the windows and wondering what to do next. She began thinking about Antonia, Marigold, and her mother and father. Each of them would have told her to leave the shop for the day to get some air and perspective.

It wasn't long before Aurelia had grabbed her coat and bag and was out the door. Much as she'd grown to love running the shop, it felt liberating to have a day off. She walked around the city, spontaneously went to a movie after noticing that she was just in time for the opening credits, and then went for dinner at a new restaurant she hadn't tried before. But as she sat down to eat on her own, she realized that she could have called Kali or David to see if they were free, rather than spend the day by herself. She'd grown so used to being on her own in the evenings it hadn't even occurred to her to have company. And if she'd called, she suspected they might have told her off—and with good reason—for finally wanting to do something at night.

By the time Aurelia got home, it was just before midnight. She hesitated at the door to the shop, knowing that if she wasn't in by the time the clock struck the hour, she'd be able to avoid an awkward night of trying to clear the air with Vronsky. Her hesitation was short-lived, however, as she knew it would be better to face him rather than put it off another night.

Having gone upstairs to drop off her things, Aurelia was a few minutes late coming back down to the shop. As she walked through the door from the flat, she caught sight of Vronsky standing near the top of the spiral staircase and they each jumped in surprise at the sight of the other. It turned out to be the perfect way to break the tension between them. After laughing and taking a moment to recover, they walked over to the mezzanine railing and leaned against it, looking across the shop toward the square outside.

Aurelia started to speak, but Vronsky waved a hand and said, "Please, Aurelia, I have much to apologize for and wish to ease my conscience for my behavior toward you." He heaved a sigh and continued. "I spoke in anger last night, saying things that were only partly true, and in some cases saying things that lacked any truth whatsoever." He paused. "I do not wish to leave the shop. I do not wish to end this project we have begun." Another pause. "My only wish is that we may carry it out as *we* see best, absent the overtures of someone who does not know me or understand what I would make of my future."

After taking a moment to choose her words, Aurelia said, "If you're still interested in publishing your story, Alexei, then the editor"—she avoided mentioning Oliver by name—"will want us to make certain changes... certain revisions."

Vronsky's brow furrowed, and she rushed on, saying, "But I give you my word that I won't let him make any significant changes without asking you first."

"I shall assent to those terms," he agreed with a nod. "The first significant change I must reject is the prospect of writing myself into a love affair or a marriage. I understand it would serve as intriguing fodder for a reader, but I cannot allow myself to once again have my heart set upon the page for all to see." In a gentler tone he added, "I would find it difficult to set aside my love for Anna and consider a new 'love interest' as you say."

"I understand. I'll tell Oli—the editor—that I won't write you into a relationship. If he says he won't publish it... Well, then you and I can keep working on the book and we'll try to find someone else."

Aurelia knew it wouldn't be easy to find another publisher, and that even if she did, they'd likely raise the same concerns as Oliver, but she pressed on.

"I want to apologize too. I know I upset you last night and brought back painful memories. Please know that was never my intention."

Vronsky nodded solemnly, then asked, "I hope we may remain friends despite my rash words? I would regret losing such a devoted friend and ally."

"Absolutely. Should we go downstairs and start working on a new chapter?"

"In fact, I thought we might converse with our friends this evening. I fear my behavior last night made the shop an unpleasant destination for many and I should like to make amends."

A few hours later, Aurelia and Marianne were standing at the front of the shop talking to Elinor, who sat in the armchair that had recently been vacated by Fezz.

"He does seem more like himself this evening, does he not?" Elinor asked in a hushed tone.

Marianne and Aurelia turned their heads to look at Vronsky, who was across the shop speaking animatedly with Marmee.

"I know I ought not to speak of it, but I cannot help myself," Marianne began guiltily. "Did I hear correctly last night that Count Vronsky suggested you might have developed a regard for the publishing man, Oliver?"

"Oh," Aurelia said, blushing. "Yes, he did say that."

"And? Did his statement reach its mark?"

"Marianne!" Elinor chided.

"It is only that I should like to think Aurelia might find her own happiness in love, as we have found ours," Marianne said defensively. She turned back to Aurelia, adding, "What of this Oliver? What are his prospects?"

"His prospects?" The question made Aurelia feel like she'd been dropped into a conversation in Elinor and Marianne's novel, but she managed not to laugh. "Well, he works in publishing, as you know. He's very good—I read one of the books he edited."

"He is not a gentleman of leisure, then?" Elinor sounded slightly concerned.

"No, those come few and far between in my time."

"What of his mind, Aurelia? Is he an intelligent man?" Marianne asked.

"He is—he's very smart. And he's well-read, even if I don't like most of the books he reads."

Marianne nodded encouragingly.

"He gets carried away with his work," Aurelia continued, "and he seems to like me, but he can also be a bit closed off sometimes."

"You have cataloged his faults, but I warn you, your heart may betray you. I was categorically determined not to fall in love with my husband, but he proved himself to be worthy of my love twice over."

"I believe Marianne astonished herself and Colonel Brandon with her change of heart," Elinor added.

"Indeed. I am ashamed to think of the many times I scoffed at his attentions, only to now find myself seeking them out and cherishing each kind word and thoughtful gesture. Perhaps the same may be true of you and this Oliver?"

"Perhaps," Aurelia said uncertainly. She was growing self-conscious despite the fact that she'd thought about that very possibility herself.

Elinor, apparently recognizing Aurelia's discomfort, suggested that they join Laurie and Cuff, who were upstairs on the mezzanine—relieving Aurelia from having to say anything more about Oliver.

Overall, the night had reset her relationships with the characters. She'd been so focused on Vronsky's story for so many months that it was good to have a night of reconnecting with the rest of her friends. And when they disappeared at dawn, she didn't feel sad. Instead, she felt a deep satisfaction knowing she'd be seeing them all again that night.

44

Although it was a Sunday, Aurelia woke earlier than she'd planned or hoped. As the sun made its way through her blinds, Fezz took this as a sign that it was time to encourage her to get out of bed.

Once she had her cup of tea in hand and an album playing softly on the record player, she settled herself in the armchair overlooking the square. Looking at the clock on the wall, she decided David would certainly be awake by now.

Almost as soon as she'd said hello, he asked, "Are you calling to tell me how swoony Oliver is?"

"David!" she scolded. "No, in fact, that's *not* why I'm calling."

Aurelia had forgotten that David knew she was working with Oliver and would want to discuss him nonstop at the first opportunity.

"Let's pretend it is. How is he? Are the sparks flying this time around?"

"I'll hang up if you keep at it."

"Oh, come on. You ought to know I'm going to tease you mercilessly about this."

"No, David, please. I'm not up for it this morning," Aurelia said in her most petulant voice.

"What's wrong? James said Oliver's in his mad editor mode—is he editing your book into oblivion?"

"He is, a bit. But I can't get a read on him." Aurelia paused, debating how much to share before deciding she needed David's input—even if it would overexcite him. "We had dinner the other night and I think he was hinting he's open to a relationship."

"Well, he is."

"Isn't he trying to get over his ex-girlfriend?"

Aurelia couldn't bring herself to mention the other issue—the fact that he'd once told her in no uncertain terms that he didn't want to date her seemed to contradict his hinting.

"That was months ago. The last time I saw him at one of James's work things, he mentioned something about being ready to move on."

"Hmm," Aurelia intoned noncommittally. She wasn't sure what to do with that new information, so she tried for a change of topic. "What are you and James up to today?"

"We're heading out to see his parents, but we'll be home for dinner. Do you want to come round?"

"Will you be in the kitchen again?"

"No, we're doing takeaway. James begged for a break from my 'historically weird culinary arts,' as he's now calling it."

"Actually, I was going to stay in tonight. But maybe we can meet for a coffee?"

"You do realize I never see you outside of daylight hours anymore? Every time I suggest dinner, you'd rather do lunch or coffee. Don't think I didn't notice you saying you had *dinner* with Oliver."

"I did meet him for dinner—one time," Aurelia admitted. "But I'm trying to keep up progress on the book, and it's easier to write at night. There's a lot to do if I want to get it published this year."

"This year? Is that even possible?"

"I don't know... I hope so?"

"What did Oliver say?"

"He said we could try."

"I'm proud of you, you know that, but why the rush? You're like a thing possessed."

"I'm not possessed. It's just something I've set my heart on, that's all."

Aurelia hoped he'd leave it at that, as they were veering dangerously close to all the reasons she couldn't explain for wanting to get Vronsky's story ready to test out as soon as possible.

David sighed. "Not possessed, then. Obsessed, maybe."

"Yeah, I'll give you that. Can we meet for coffee or lunch this week? I want to see you—I do."

"Alright, I'll call you for lunch later this week," David said, sounding temporarily placated.

After ringing off, Aurelia sat for a moment, feeling as though she'd dodged a more serious telling-off that she probably deserved. She stood up and was about to head into the bathroom to shower when her phone rang.

"How could you tell I needed you?" she asked, knowing it would be Antonia. Moving back to the armchair, Aurelia sat and nestled in again. Fezz strolled over, jumped up on the chair, and settled in next to her.

"If you need me so badly, why haven't I heard from you in days? I tried calling last night, and when you didn't answer I started to worry."

"I'm sorry, I've just been busy with the book."

Aurelia hesitated. She didn't want to tell Antonia that David had just scolded her for not wanting to go out at night. And her recent argument with Vronsky wasn't something she could mention either. It seemed she was walking a very thin line with everyone these days—precariously balancing between what she could share on one side and what she needed to hide on the other. She decided the safest bet was to focus on her dinner with Oliver, which she was sure Antonia would find just as tantalizing.

"You remember I told you about my editor?"

"Yes—Oliver."

"Right. Well, we had dinner on Friday."

"Dinner? *Indeed*," Antonia said roguishly.

"Yes, his aloofness is dropping," Aurelia acknowledged. "He hinted that he's open to a relationship."

"Good—so are you."

"I am not."

"Yes, you are, Aurelia! You're single, and you've said he's cute."

"He is."

"Alright, then." Antonia's tone suggested the matter was settled.

"I'm not going to call him up and ask him on a date right now!" Aurelia said, exasperated.

"Why not?"

"Because he's not interested in me," Aurelia said lightly, though she was sure Antonia could hear the sting of it in her voice.

"I doubt that. But if he wasn't before, maybe he's changed his mind."

"I don't know," Aurelia said quietly, not wanting to read too much into their recent conversations at the risk of getting it all wrong.

"So what's the problem? You've said he's smart and cute—forget whether *he* likes you. Is it conceivable that *you* might like him?"

Aurelia rolled her eyes to the ceiling, not needing much time to think the question over.

"It's conceivable."

"Can you imagine kissing him again? Holding his hand while walking down the street? Having him round for the night?"

Aurelia drew in a deep breath. She thought about the moments his guard dropped and he gave her a smile that reached his eyes, or he got excited about an idea for her book. She thought about sitting across from him at the restaurant and what it might be like to have him walk her home, kiss her goodnight, or come up to her flat. She couldn't deny that the tugging sensation in her belly stretched all the way to her chest as she let each thought pass through her mind.

"Confirmed—I can definitely imagine all that."

"Alright, that's something, then. This isn't a marriage contract—just ask him out on a date."

"Antonia!"

"If he says no, or if he says yes and then you decide you don't feel those special magical sparks, then just tell him. No harm done."

"That would be *so* awkward. We'd still be stuck working together."

"Maybe, but you'd get over it. And the alternative is never trying and maybe missing out on something great just because things *might* get awkward." Antonia paused. "I don't want you missing out on things."

"It's not just that..." Aurelia took a deep breath. "I'm still not ready."

"It's been over a year, Relia," Antonia said gently, intuiting exactly what her sister meant. "You're allowed to fall in love and be happy."

Aurelia knew she was right but still felt guilty at the idea, as if it meant forgetting too.

"Whether it's Oliver or someone else, just don't shut out the possibility," Antonia continued. "Leave that door open, okay?"

"Okay," Aurelia promised.

They talked until Aurelia's mug of tea was empty and they'd agreed that Antonia might as well make the most of her Sunday and go out for a long lunch with her husband. Aurelia decided to make the most of her day too. The weather had cleared, and the early spring sun was surprisingly strong as it streamed in through the windows of her flat. She showered and changed, then made her way to Richmond Park for a long walk in the sunshine.

45

The weather was not, as it turned out, as warm as it had seemed from inside her cozy flat. There was a brisk wind that sent Aurelia into a café on her way home, just to try and get the feeling back into her fingers while holding a cup of hot coffee in her hands. She was so focused on getting warm again that as she stepped out of the café, she nearly bumped into someone who was trying to get inside. They both began to make their apologies when they recognized each other.

"Oliver!" Aurelia almost felt nervous, as though he might have known she'd spent the morning talking about him.

"Aurelia, hi." His tone was a little cool, bringing back the memory of how she'd rushed out of the restaurant on Friday.

"Actually, do you have a minute?" she asked.

He hesitated. "Sure. Do you want to grab a seat while I get a coffee?"

She found a table and tried not to stare at him as he waited in line to order. He was wearing dark jeans and an old, slightly ragged, woolen jumper that looked like it could become one of her favorites if she ever got the chance to take it from him... or off him.

Aurelia! she scolded herself. Clearly her thoughts from that morning—what it might be like to kiss him or take him home—were hard to swat away. It didn't help seeing him looking more relaxed and less like he'd just stepped out of a board room.

He picked up his coffee and then joined her, and she tried harder with the swatting.

"This is off the beaten path for you, isn't it?" he asked.

"A little. I was just walking around Richmond Park."

"What, the whole thing?"

"Most of it, yeah."

"That's a good long walk," Oliver laughed, impressed.

"It is—it was. I'm sort of a walker. I like going out and hearing bits of conversation, doing some people watching—anything I can use for my writing."

It wasn't a secret that she liked going for walks, but the words had tumbled out of her mouth like a confession, and she looked down at her coffee to recover.

"Lately, I've become a bit of a walker myself. It's a good way to explore the city. Somehow there are still corners I've missed after living here for years."

"Exactly," Aurelia said eagerly, grateful he hadn't made fun of her 'I'm a walker' declaration. "Were you out walking too?"

"No, I live a few streets over," he said, gesturing behind him. "This is my usual coffee spot."

They experienced one of their old, stilted pauses before he asked, "You wanted to chat?"

"Yes, I'm glad I ran into you. Literally, as it happens." She gave a quick laugh, still unsure of herself. "I wanted to say I'm sorry for being... off the other night. I wasn't really feeling like myself."

"That's alright."

His tone was neutral, giving nothing away.

"I didn't write much this weekend, but I'm hoping to dive back in tonight. I should have some new chapters for you by the end of the week."

"Have you thought any more about a love interest?"

Aurelia's eyes widened, misunderstanding for a moment and thinking he was asking about their own nonexistent relationship before she realized he was, of course, talking about her book.

"Oh, no. Well, I have thought about it, quite a lot, but... I can't do it. I actually agree with you—that it might be an interesting story with that added in—but I just don't think that's what he would want."

"Not what *he* would want... Do you mean *Vronsky*?"

"I know, it sounds strange," she said, wrinkling her nose in acknowledgment of her apparent madness. "But I don't know how else to explain it."

"I do think it would be better with a love interest, but I've said that already."

"You have. Is that it, then?" she asked. "Am I out of luck having you publish my book?"

He sat back, considering.

"No, let's keep at it. I'd like to see what happens and how it will hang together without this love interest that Vronsky doesn't want."

His tone was teasing, but not unkind, and Aurelia's face broke into a smile. That smile quickly faded as Oliver stood up from the table. She wasn't ready to end their conversation just yet and she fumbled for something else to say.

"Um... When should I get you the next draft?"

"Whenever it's ready. You can drop it at my office."

She felt dismissed and was annoyed until she remembered that her odd behavior on Friday might still require some smoothing over. Oliver gave a smile and nod as he turned for the door.

"What about lunch?" she blurted. He stopped and turned around slowly, looking puzzled.

"Now? It's nearly four."

"No, sorry, I meant once you've read over the next draft. Should we meet for lunch to go over your edits?"

Aurelia waited, her eyebrows traveling up her forehead the longer he took to respond.

"We don't have to meet if you don't want to," he said at last. "I can just call with my edits."

"Okay," she said slowly. "If you'd rather."

"It's not that I'd rather. I just don't want you to feel like we have to go over edits in person if that's not your thing."

They were both flummoxed now, each trying to give the other an out.

"Look, I'm always going to be tetchy about someone else's edits. Whether we meet in person or talk on the phone, I can't promise I won't be. But I'll try my best either way."

She gave an apologetic smile and he smiled back. It was one of those smiles that reached every one of his features.

"Why don't you get me the next pages when you're ready. Once I've read them, I'll call and you can decide whether to meet or go over them right then on the phone."

"Perfect! I'd best go home and get back to writing, then."

They walked out of the café together and said goodbye, each heading in a different direction. An irrepressible smile spread across Aurelia's face as she walked toward the Tube stop that would take her home, feeling relieved. She might not be ready to set her heart on him yet, but—Antonia would be pleased—she now knew that she wasn't ready to close the door on him either.

46

Over the following week, Aurelia flew through the next few chapters of Vronsky's story. They wrote together at night, but her daily editing sessions began to incorporate more and more additions. Each night Vronsky would review what she'd written on her own, nodding his approval or pointing out something he didn't like. Both of them felt pressure now, wanting to finish his story so they could get it published and try their experiment, relieving him from his monotonous ending.

But something else was driving her, too: she was finally *doing it*, finally writing a novel after years of wanting to without getting very far. She'd written short stories before but had never written more than a few chapters of a novel. Now she had an editor and a publishing contract; she'd proven she could do it. And she'd never felt this confident with every word she wrote, with every paragraph she finished. The positive feedback she'd gotten from the characters—and Oliver, too—was wonderful, but what kept her going wasn't just that she was helping Vronsky; it was also that she was doing the thing she'd always wanted to do, doing it well, and feeling so very good about it.

By Friday afternoon, Aurelia dropped off the next draft with the receptionist at Oliver's office. But later, after so many late nights and long days of writing and editing, she missed her evening alarm and woke up disappointed the next morning—and still tired even though she'd had a few extra hours of sleep.

That night, she stepped forward as soon as the characters appeared, catching Elinor and Marmee first.

"I'm sorry I missed you all last night," she began. "I didn't wake up to my alarm—I was a little overtired, I think."

Marmee's eyebrows drew together as she took in Aurelia's worry.

"We understand there are times when you'll miss a night. You need to live your life and see your friends and family outside the shop."

"Oh, right. Yes." It was Aurelia's turn to knit her brows. "Still, I'm sorry I wasn't here."

"I do not believe we have heard you speak of your friends for quite some time," Elinor said. "I trust they are well?"

"Yes, they're all fine. They're annoyed that I've been so busy with the book, but they understand."

Before Marmee could give her a lecture, Aurelia made her way over to her desk, eager to get back to work on Vronsky's story.

———— ☾ ————

Opening her eyes several hours later, it took Aurelia a moment to process where she was and what had happened. She sat up, rubbing the spot on her cheek that had been resting against the papers on her desk.

"Oh," she said, looking around at the characters who were quietly observing her. "I fell asleep? I'm so sorry."

She stood, stretching her strained muscles.

"Have I wasted the entire night?"

She looked to the clock and saw that there was only an hour or so left until dawn.

"I'm sorry," she said again, finding Vronsky's face in the crowd.

"Please, do not apologize," he insisted. "Most people do sleep at night, Aurelia."

"Yes, we worry you're not taking care of yourself as you ought. Perhaps you should go upstairs now and rest a bit more?" Elinor suggested as she walked over to her.

"No, I don't want to lose any more time," Aurelia insisted, running her hands over her eyes and holding back a yawn. "Let's keep working."

Marmee joined Elinor and Aurelia, reaching out a hand as if to rest it on Aurelia's arm as she said, "There is a particular story about your Aunt Marigold that I have yet to share with you. I think it might be time for you to hear it."

"I thought I'd heard all of Marigold's stories by now?"

"I was not inclined, at first, to share this particular story. I thought if Marigold hadn't told it to you, perhaps she had her reasons. But I see now that it may benefit you to learn about this chapter in her life. Shall we make ourselves comfortable?"

Marmee gestured to the mezzanine. Aurelia looked to Vronsky, who nodded, refusing to rescue her from what Aurelia suspected was the lecture she'd avoided earlier. She reluctantly followed Marmee and Elinor up the spiral staircase and by the time they sat down on the window seat, Rachel and Marianne were right behind them.

"May we join?" Rachel asked. "We sensed some intrigue on offer."

They arranged themselves across the window seat, with Marmee and Aurelia in the middle.

"As I've told you, I knew your Aunt Marigold," Marmee began. "I met her during the first year that she owned the shop, and I visited her many times throughout her lifetime. I considered her a dear friend," Marmee added warmly, leaning toward Aurelia.

"Not long after she had been running the shop, I appeared one night and met a dashing young man named D'Artagnan."

Aurelia's breath hitched at the name. It had been weeks since Mark had mentioned *The Three Musketeers*, and she'd completely forgotten to ask Marmee about it.

"D'Artagnan was from a French novel called *The Three Musketeers*," Marmee explained to Elinor and Marianne, whose own book was published before Dumas' novel.

"Like Count Vronsky, D'Artagnan was the only character to appear from his novel. Also like Count Vronsky, D'Artagnan first came to the shop feeling the pain of knowing that a woman whom he loved had lost her life."

Aurelia only vaguely remembered the novel, but she tried to conjure up the storyline as she listened.

"It wasn't long before all in the shop understood the deep feelings that were developing between D'Artagnan and Marigold," Marmee continued. "They made each other very happy and spent many hours talking and laughing together."

"They were in *love?*" Aurelia asked incredulously.

"They were indeed," Marmee said with a smile.

Aurelia found herself smiling, too, at the thought of her aunt's secret romance.

"I visited the shop many times over several years, and each time I could see that Marigold and D'Artagnan's love was just as strong." Marmee paused. "And yet, there came a time when they began to argue, and it was difficult not to hear the nature of their arguments."

Hypnotized by the story, Aurelia gave a nod, encouraging Marmee to continue.

"Time does not pass for us since we remain just as we were at the end of our story. D'Artagnan was a noble man, something like a knight, and he began to feel that his love for Marigold was keeping the rest of her life in abatement. She had to sleep at odd hours in order to stay awake every night, and she spoke less and less of her friends and family. Marigold insisted she would not trade her love for D'Artagnan for a normal life, but he would not relent. He asked her again and again to take his book off the table and allow herself to maintain a life outside of this shop."

The small audience gathered around Marmee had hardly taken a breath. Marianne wiped a tear from her eye and Rachel clasped her hand consolingly.

"Marigold was heartbroken, truly. But I think a part of her knew that he was right. What kind of life could they share with Marigold shut up in the shop and D'Artagnan living his novel during the day, their only contact happening during the few hours between midnight and dawn?"

"And did she accede to his request? Did she cease to place his book upon the table?" Rachel asked.

"She did. For a time, he refused to speak with her until she agreed. Their last week together was very difficult, but they made their peace with one another before parting."

"That is the most tragic tale I believe I have ever heard," Marianne said, sniffling.

Rachel placed an arm around her and they rested their heads together.

"It truly is a sad story," Elinor agreed.

"I think Marigold mourned D'Artagnan for a long time," Marmee continued. "But I also think they were right to let each other go. Marigold later admitted that she had indeed spent so much time with him and the rest of the people who gathered in her shop each night that she had let her friendships and family fall to the wayside. Do you not see a parallel in your own experience?" Marmee asked cautiously.

"You're not suggesting...? Count Vronsky and I are just friends—"

Aurelia could hardly get the words out in her shock at thinking anyone would interpret their friendship as something romantic.

"Oh no, dear! I only meant that you seem to have become just as absorbed in the shop's evening activities as Marigold did, even if your interests are distinct."

"Well, I'm busy with the book, of course, and I like spending time with all of you. But I'm making it work."

"You may not think it now, but I fear the time we've spent together has kept you from a life outside these walls. A life with friends who exist beyond the page," Marmee said.

"No, everything's fine! Things will get easier once I'm done with the book," Aurelia insisted. "Until then, my friends just have to understand that I need to spend my time writing."

"And what of Oliver," Marianne whispered, suddenly mischievous after her tears. "Are you finding time to become better acquainted with him?"

"Marianne!" Aurelia groaned. "He's just my editor—and friend, I suppose."

"If you insist," said Marianne with a smile. "But perhaps he could be *your* D'Artagnan, Aurelia? If you gave him more of your time?"

Aurelia rolled her eyes and shook her head, laughing to see everyone looking at her hopefully. Then she spotted Vronsky sitting at her desk, waiting for her.

"Thank you for sharing, Marmee. I should get back to writing, though."

She headed for the spiral staircase, hearing whispers and laughter behind her, and shook her head again. Marmee's warning had a ring of truth to it. There was a certain kind of comfort and safety in spending time with characters who would never change, never grow old, and never get ill, but she was hardly a shut-in. She still went out for her walks, and she talked to Antonia, David, Kali, and her dad every week, even if she didn't see them every day. She told herself once again that her life would get back to normal after the book was finished—giving her all the more reason to keep working on it.

47

I t had only been a few days since she'd given Oliver her latest draft, but time seemed to drag on until he finally called to let her know he was ready with his next round of edits. They made a plan to have lunch the next day at a spot around the corner from her shop, and she suspected he was testing the waters to see if she could handle hearing his critiques in person again. It reminded her to try and take his edits with a little more grace this time around.

Oliver stopped by the shop to pick her up for lunch, instead of meeting her at the restaurant as they'd planned. She liked seeing him there amongst the books as it seemed to soften his edges and also put her at ease.

"It looks like you've got every Dickens title here," he observed as he scanned the bookshelves.

"I have."

"I never got the appeal. *Tale of Two Cities*, *Great Expectations*, *Oliver Twist*—they're alright, but I was never blown away by his writing."

"But what about *Bleak House*? That's an amazing book. And so is *Little Dorrit*. You have to admit those are good."

"I haven't read them. Once I read the shorter ones, I just didn't see the point in diving into his thousand-page doorstops."

Aurelia's mouth fell open.

"You work with books, and you gave up on Dickens because his are too long?"

"That's not what I said," he told her reprovingly. "I gave up because his books were nothing special."

"No, unacceptable," Aurelia said, shaking her head and walking over to join him. "I can't let you leave here thinking that. Alright, I agree—*Tale of Two Cities* and *Oliver Twist* aren't my favorites either, but you're absolutely missing out if you stop there."

She looked at the shelves, assessing the options.

"Doesn't think he likes classic literature, but he's never read *David Copperfield*," she added in an undertone—knowing full well he could hear her—before saying, louder now, "How am I supposed to choose? *Our Mutual Friend* is my favorite, but I think you really should start with *David Copperfield*. But then there's *Nicholas Nickleby*... and *Bleak House*..."

She finally pulled copies of *David Copperfield* and *Little Dorrit* from the shelves and walked over to her desk, placing them in a canvas shopping bag. Oliver sighed and walked over to join her, pulling out his wallet.

"Oh, no," she said, shaking her finger at him. "This is a literary intervention. These are on the house."

"You can't give your books away! You'll go out of business," he laughed.

"It'll be worth it if I can convert you to Dickens."

"Tell you what, I'll buy one and you can give me one."

Aurelia narrowed her eyes at him in a challenge.

"Final offer," he added.

"Alright, then," she said, reluctantly giving in.

Once he'd paid for his copy, they walked toward the door.

"Start with *David Copperfield*, then read *Little Dorrit*. And I want a full report on each, so don't try skimming them."

"Yes, Miss Lyndham," he teased.

Aurelia laughed but then caught her breath, tears filling her eyes as she realized their exchange was exactly like one of many she'd seen between Aunt Marigold and her customers. The memory came on so quickly that she hadn't had time to prepare herself. She'd thought she was over these unexpected bouts of sadness, but obviously she'd been wrong.

Oliver's amused expression turned to concern and she was immediately embarrassed.

"Sorry, I just... Sorry."

"Is everything okay?"

"Yes—yeah, I'm fine," she said lightly, though her voice was breaking. "Let me just run and get my coat."

She hurried upstairs and closed the door to the flat behind her, leaning against it. *Damnit*, she said to herself, *can't you keep it together for once?* She took a few deep breaths, then wiped at her eyes. Shaking her head in frustration, she got ready to face him again. It was a warm day, but—remembering her excuse—she pulled a coat from its hook and went back down to the shop, making sure to smile reassuringly as she led him out the door.

They walked to lunch discussing Dickens, giving her a chance to shift gears and try to let go of her shame over nearly breaking down in front of him. She became animated by their talk of books, forgetting that they were about to sit down to discuss what he didn't like about the latest draft of hers.

As it turned out, he had plenty of edits, but he'd softened his delivery, making her wonder if James had told him to be a bit gentler with his critiques. There were no major suggestions—nothing that would set Vronsky off—and she was breathing easier once they'd finished lunch and were walking back to the shop again.

Her relief was short-lived, however.

"Earlier, in the shop, you seemed... upset. Did something happen?"

"Oh, nothing happened. I just, um... I was thinking about my aunt and it sort of caught me off guard. She was always pushing books on people, insisting they *had* to read something or other," she said, trying out a laugh. "Pushing Dickens on you made me think of her."

"You must miss her. It sounds like you had a lot in common."

His tone was kind, but Aurelia was convinced she'd shared too much, asked too much of him. She'd nearly cried in front of him, the poor man.

"I'll work on those edits and get another draft to you soon," she said, back to business as they neared the shop. "I can probably get them to you by the end of next week."

"Sure, drop them off when you're ready and I'll give you a call when I have some notes."

"Which will also be the perfect opportunity to tell me what you think of *David Copperfield*," she reminded him, pointing to his bag of books.

He smiled. "You're determined to keep me reading."

"It's sort of my job," she laughed.

Once again, Aurelia watched as he walked away from the shop. Once again, he turned and waved, and they exchanged smiles.

Back inside, though, a frown began to crease her forehead as she remembered how decent he'd been about her emotional meltdown. *So much for keeping the proverbial door open*, she thought. He'd just had a window into her fragile state, so why would he want to walk through a door? She was doing much better than she'd been back when her ex had broken up with her over her tears and her grief. But obviously she still wasn't ready to date anyone; this was just further confirmation of what she'd been telling David and Antonia.

She shook her head. *Friendship it is, then*. She'd just started to allow herself to get used to the idea of him too. It was hard to ignore the tightening in her throat that threatened more tears, and she was angry at herself for being weepy without end.

Catching sight of her laptop, Aurelia made herself think instead about what would happen to Vronsky next. Last night the characters had been begging for an update on his story, and she didn't want to disappoint them.

48

Aurelia's drive to keep writing was coming at a cost. More and more she missed a deadline to pay an invoice or bill for the shop, or forgot to place a special order for a customer only to have them show up wanting to collect it. Days started running into one another, so that she'd open the shop on a Sunday for a few hours before realizing her mistake or forget to open it on a weekday.

One morning found Aurelia sitting in her flat revising a chapter of Vronsky's story when she heard faint knocking coming from the street below. She thought it might be a mistimed delivery for the shop and made her way downstairs, pages and pen in hand. When she spotted Mark through the blinds, she quirked her head in surprise before letting him inside.

"I wasn't sure whether you were on holiday, only you didn't mention anything last week," he said by way of a greeting.

"No, I'm not on holiday—I was just upstairs editing," Aurelia said, waving her pages. Her face fell in shock. "It's not Monday, is it?"

Mark nodded with a laugh.

"What time is it?"

She looked behind her at the mantel clock and couldn't believe it was nearly half past ten.

"Oh, honestly," Aurelia said, shaking her head at herself. "Come in, come in! I was lost in revisions. I can't believe I almost missed you!"

A few minutes later, after Aurelia had raised the blinds and made them both tea, Oliver appeared.

"I'm just on my way to meet one of my authors, but I thought I'd stop by for a quick hello," he announced. Seeing Mark with his mug of tea, he added, "Good morning."

Aurelia introduced them. She'd told Oliver about some of her regulars but hadn't told him Mark's story, worrying that Oliver might take it lightly or make fun of him. As it turned out, Mark wasted no time in telling Oliver himself, and Aurelia was pleased to see that Oliver seemed touched by Mark's love of the shop and Marigold. They chatted quietly outside of Aurelia's hearing for a few minutes, making her slightly nervous that they might be discussing her tendency for tears. But when Oliver turned back to join her at the desk as Mark continued wandering the shop, he seemed normal—no looks of sympathy or concern.

"I wanted to ask—since we both like walking around the city—would you want to walk together? Maybe tomorrow?" he asked.

"Walk... together?"

Somehow, those two words weren't making sense. He wanted to go for a walk. *And* he wanted to go for that walk with her?

"We could talk about the book," he added quickly. "I usually take a break to walk in the early afternoon, so maybe you could pick a spot for us to meet and we can go from there?"

Aurelia's mind was still trying to process this: a walk, with Oliver. Something about it felt like a date, but no, he'd said it was to discuss her book. She looked over at Mark, who was nodding encouragingly, and she started nodding too as she turned back to Oliver.

"Sure, that sounds great."

They made a plan to meet at two o'clock the next day at Russell Square.

"What do you think?" Aurelia asked Mark as soon as Oliver was out the door.

"He's a lovely fellow," Mark said, sounding confused. "When you first mentioned him, he sounded a bit..." He trailed off and Aurelia could just imagine the colorful words she'd used to describe him.

"I might have been a little quick to judge," she admitted with a wince. "But I think we're friends now."

"Well, you let me know when that book of yours is finished. I'd like to see the result of all this hard work. Will you be selling it here?"

"Here?"

Aurelia hadn't thought about selling her book in the shop. She hadn't thought about selling it anywhere, come to that. She was just working toward having one published copy to put on the table for Vronsky.

"I know it might seem out of place with all the old books, but I think customers would like buying a book from the author herself."

"Maybe," Aurelia mused. "I'll have to think about it."

After Mark left, her mind continued working over their conversation. Time was racing forward and her time with Vronsky was growing shorter as they got closer to having a published book for their big experiment. She hadn't taken much time to think about the mechanics of what would happen once they put his new book on the table. Would Vronsky and another character come out of the new book? What would this 'new' Vronsky be like? Would he remember her? What if Vronsky didn't come out at all?

As questions ran through her mind, she decided to see if Sergeant Cuff had any answers, as he so often did.

Aurelia had wanted to catch Cuff on his own that night, but Vronsky was at her side before she could slip away.

"I'm just going to speak with Sergeant Cuff for a moment," she said, hoping Vronsky would wait for her by her desk. Instead, he stepped in alongside her.

"Does this concern our experiment?" he asked.

"Well, yes. How did you know?"

She'd stopped walking and Vronsky had to turn back a few paces to stand beside her again.

"We are nearing the date when you will have a book to place on the table," he said softly. "I myself have questions about how to proceed."

Aurelia nodded, saying, "We've been so focused on writing the book that I haven't had time to think about what's actually going to happen."

She stopped short of listing all the questions that had been spinning through her mind that day, but she was sure Vronsky had thought of them too.

"Let us ask Sergeant Cuff if he can enlighten us further now that we are so near the end," he suggested.

They found Cuff sitting in the armchair, with Marmee and Laurie standing beside him as they discussed Laurie's hothouse and its various roses.

"I would only need one guess as to why you are here, and I assure you that would be sufficient to get at your reason," Cuff declared as he spotted them.

"I see you anticipate our every maneuver, Sergeant Cuff," Vronsky replied with a charming smile. "You would make a formidable chess opponent."

"I am satisfied with having been a formidable opponent of lawlessness prior to my retirement," Cuff said, puffing up at his own compliment.

"Sorry to interrupt," Aurelia said. "We were just hoping to ask you a few questions about the experiment."

"Yes, time is drawing near, is it not?" Cuff asked. "When will you have a book ready to set out on the table?"

"It'll be a few months still."

"Time is indeed drawing near," Cuff said again, now with a dramatic flick of his eyebrows.

Although Aurelia had hoped to speak with Cuff confidentially, a crowd was gathering around them. Everyone else seemed curious to know what would happen next, and Aurelia couldn't blame them. They were all invested in Vronsky's new story since they'd been witnesses to the making of it.

"If we put the new book on the table, you think Alexei might appear from it, right?" she asked.

"Ah, that I cannot say for certain," Cuff said as he shook his head. "The characters who appear vary each time their book is set out."

"But perhaps two other characters would appear that could give a good report of Count Vronsky?" Marmee asked.

"I should think so."

Aurelia knew that was the goal—to be assured of Vronsky's happiness—but still her heart sank to think she might not get to hear about his new life directly from him.

"And if he doesn't appear from the new book, and we put his original book back on the table, will he come back to the shop again?"

"That I also cannot say," Cuff said sadly. "It may be considered a new selection, in which case different characters may be due to appear. If the experiment has worked, two new characters might appear, rather than Count Vronsky alone. He may be one of the two, or they may be two different characters entirely."

Aurelia's and Vronsky's eyes met, both looking uncertain over how they felt about Cuff's theories. She realized she would have to speak next, to give permission for him to leave despite the fact that it might mean losing one of her closest friends. She took a deep breath, looking around at the faces of the characters she'd grown to love as they waited for her to speak.

"We've come this far—we can't let fear stop us now. Once your new book is published, we'll pick a date for me to take your old book off the table and put the new one in its place."

She tried to sound decisive but wasn't sure she'd convinced anyone that she was confident about that plan.

"But you mustn't put our books away," Rachel said suddenly. "We should like to see if the experiment works, and to ask Count Vronsky how he likes his new life."

"You would never put us away before then, would you?" Marianne joined in.

"No, of course not. We should all get to hear how he's doing in his new book." Aurelia smiled, trying to feel the encouragement she was giving everyone else.

"I should like that very much," Vronsky said, looking around and nodding at each character in turn.

The others seemed satisfied and began to wander back into small groups. Aurelia and Vronsky thanked Cuff and walked to her desk, where they took their seats and sat silently for a moment.

"I would like you to promise me something," Vronsky said in an undertone, looking around to make sure the others weren't listening.

Aurelia caught his eye and saw that his expression was heavy.

"Once you have removed my old book from your table, promise me you will not put it back again."

"I'm not sure I can make that promise," she said, stunned by his request. "What if you don't come out of your new book? What if I never see you again?"

"As Marmee said, you will know from the other characters in my new book that I am well and that we have succeeded in changing the course of my life for the better." He paused, waiting for her to meet his eyes before continuing. "I look forward to living the new life you have created for me, and to letting go of the past."

She knew he was right, but it was hard to accept the possibility of losing someone who'd come to feel like family.

"If I do not return to the shop, you must not think of my loss as something to grieve over, Aurelia. You have truly given me a gift, and we must both ensure that I make good use of it."

Words failing her, she nodded her understanding. They looked at each other for a long moment, then she attempted a smile. Turning back to her desk, they kept working on his new story, sobered by the knowledge that their progress was also bringing them closer to what might be his last night in the shop.

49

Vronsky's potentially imminent departure overshadowed Aurelia's thoughts until lunchtime the following day, when she had the idea to take a break and head out for a walk. That's when she remembered: she'd promised to walk with Oliver in just over an hour. She felt nervous but told herself that they were only going to talk about her book. They'd done that plenty of times before—over lunch, over coffee, while sitting in her shop—so throwing in some exercise wasn't a big deal. It didn't make it a date, she reminded herself.

She was a few minutes early when she arrived at Russell Square, so she took a seat on a bench and watched people passing by. Some looked like they were cutting through the square on their way to or from work, others were sitting on benches chatting on the phone or reading a book, and some were walking dogs. One little dog caught her eye, and she couldn't help but laugh as he bounced around the grass, chasing pigeons and dragging along whoever was at the other end of the lead. The dog was an absolute mutt—it was short as a corgi, had blond fur that was wiry like a Jack Russell terrier, and was as goofy as a labrador. Completing the picture were floppy ears and a tail that was almost as long as its body.

As the dog came nearer, Aurelia looked up to match the dog with its owner in case she might want to use them in a story.

"*Oliver?*"

"Yes, hi. I'm sorry."

He didn't say for what, but then the dog began jumping at Aurelia, pawing at her legs as it tried and failed to jump up on the bench next to her. Aurelia bent down to pet it, laughing as it tried to lick her hands and face before turning to Oliver, circling around his legs and nearly tripping him with the lead, then doubling back to Aurelia to say hello again.

"This... This is not your dog."

It couldn't be. Oliver was reserved, always careful with his appearance, and this dog was... chaos and joy and likely to cause a mess.

"It is," he sighed. "I was going to leave him at the office, but someone asked if I was going for a walk and he got too excited for me to leave him."

"Did you? You got too excited? You wanted to come and join us?" Aurelia's voice automatically took on a higher pitch, the same way it did when she talked to her father's dogs (but never Fezz, who demanded a much more sedate tone).

"You have a dog," Aurelia declared as she looked back at Oliver.

The fact of it was startling, like learning that Oliver wasn't an editor at all but a race car driver. It didn't compute, not least because the dog was all jumps, licks, and tail wags.

"What's your name?" she asked the dog as she squatted down to try and pet him as he hopped all around her.

"It's, um, Biscuit," Oliver answered for him.

"Biscuit? What a very silly name for a very silly dog!" Aurelia gave the dog a few more rubs on his sweet little head before the dog's name finally sank in. "*Biscuit?* Really?" she asked Oliver.

"It wasn't my idea," he said morosely.

Aurelia's laughter began as an uncontrollable giggle before exploding into a burst of noise.

"No, I imagine it wasn't," she managed to get out.

"I've tried everything else starting with a B—Billy, Beau, Buster, Buddy—but he won't answer to any of them."

"Only Biscuit will do, eh?" Aurelia asked the dog before standing up.

From his name to his blond fur, Biscuit couldn't be further from the dog Aurelia would have imagined for Oliver.

"You have a dog," she said again.

"This is him, yes."

Biscuit started pulling Oliver toward one of the gates that led out of the square and into the city beyond.

"I hope you're ready for that walk?" he asked, trying to hold steady as Biscuit tugged him ahead.

Aurelia laughed, then said, "I don't think we have a choice."

Once they were a few streets past the square, Biscuit began to settle down and they were able to go at a steadier pace.

"So: Biscuit. Name origin story, please," Aurelia demanded.

"Ah... My ex-girlfriend surprised me with him a few months before we broke up."

"Did she even know you?" Aurelia burst out with a laugh before remembering herself. "I'm so sorry, it's just... No, I'm sorry."

"No, it's alright. The answer is apparently not. I never said I wanted a dog—I never did. I think it was a 'let's have a baby and see if that fixes our broken relationship' type of decision."

"Oh, those are terrible decisions."

"Very. She brought him home, named him like he was a tiny show dog, and then insisted on keeping him after we broke up. But Biscuit was always sort of *my* dog. I didn't try to make him mine. He just... was. Is. Then last month she brought him over to my flat and said she was giving me 'full custody' because he was too depressed without me."

"Poor Biscuit."

Aurelia was trying not to laugh at the whole situation, but she saw Oliver was smiling. At least he was at a point where he could see the humor too.

"Hang on," Oliver said.

He stopped to pick up the dog as they passed a woman dragging a wheeled suitcase. Biscuit whined and turned his head away from the woman until the sound of the wheels bumping over every crevice in the pavement had passed. Oliver put him down carefully—so carefully—and ruffled the fur behind his ears before continuing to walk. He looked over and caught Aurelia staring at him, waiting for an explanation.

"He doesn't like rolling bags," Oliver said sheepishly, as though she might laugh at him or Biscuit.

She didn't want to laugh at all, though. Instead, she was working very hard to keep her face from melting into the soppiest of smiles. He hadn't wanted a dog, didn't get to pick the dog's name, and now was stuck with the dog—but he clearly had a soft spot for him just the same. Aurelia had seen quite a few sides to Oliver by now, but this sweet side turned that all-too-familiar tugging sensation in her belly into a brand-new feeling. Like she was on one end of a line that was pulling her entire being toward him. As they walked, she wanted to lean into him, to be nearer to him, but she held herself back. They were colleagues now, and friends. She didn't want to cross a line he'd already drawn, even if she was starting to wish he would erase it.

They walked for nearly an hour, until Oliver had to get back to work and Aurelia had to open the shop again. Biscuit flopped at their feet as they said goodbye, his little legs clearly tired from the dozen or so steps he'd taken for every one of theirs.

"We didn't get to talk much about your book," Oliver said.

"No, that's right." She tried to keep her tone light even though she felt disappointed at the reminder that this had been a work date, not a real one.

"Maybe we could walk again this weekend," he suggested. "Have you been to Highgate? Dogs aren't allowed, but I think it'd be too long of a walk for him anyway."

Aurelia's face fell at the name. Highgate was a beautiful nineteenth-century cemetery in the city, full of crumbling old tombs and giant trees. She used to love walking through it, writing down names from tombstones that she might use for characters, and basking in the quiet escape it offered from the hustle of city life. Her aunt and mother weren't buried there, but the idea of going to a cemetery again felt too painful.

"Oh, Aurelia, I'm so sorry," Oliver said, stepping closer before nearly tripping over Biscuit. He took a second to get his footing again before adding, "That was thoughtless of me—I'm sorry."

"It's fine! No need to apologize. Um, I don't think I can go this weekend, but maybe another time, okay?"

"Sure. Or we could try the Embankment? Biscuit likes it there, and it's not too far for either of us to get away during the week."

She appreciated his quick thinking, but it just reminded her that he was all too aware of her constant grieving.

"The Embankment... That sounds good. We could go later this week, once you've had a chance to read my latest chapters? Then you can tell me what you think while we walk."

"Right. Yes. We can work on your book."

They waved goodbye and Aurelia watched as Oliver gently prodded Biscuit back to his feet for the short walk to his office. *Work colleagues*, she reminded herself. *And friends. That's it and that's good enough.*

50

The pattern of Aurelia's life shifted yet again. She and Vronsky came closer and closer to finishing the book, and seeing Oliver a few times a week became a regular thing. Sometimes he would pop in to say hello on his way to a meeting, other times they would go out for coffee, lunch, or a walk with Biscuit.

Aurelia was convinced that he'd filed her away as a friend and colleague, just as she'd done with him, and she understood why. Still, there was something about the *presence* of Oliver after so many nights spent in the shop with characters she couldn't touch. At random moments, she found herself thinking back to the nearness of his body as they'd walked next to each other through a park, or as he'd sat across from her at lunch or next to her in the shop. But Oliver was more than just a solid body; he was also a puzzle that she found herself wanting to work out.

It didn't matter, though, as she knew she'd ruined any chance of being more than friends with him, even if she had been ready to start dating again. Anyway, as she frequently reminded herself, she shouldn't let herself get distracted so close to the end of her writing project. Then, of course, there was also the matter of timing—between running the shop during the day, spending time with the characters at night, and working on her book in between, she felt certain that adding one more element to the mix might overbalance her life and send everything toppling over.

Oliver wasn't the only one Aurelia had pushed to the sidelines of her life; other friends, too, had been patiently waiting for her to return to a normal routine outside of her shop, her flat, and her book. David, for instance, had announced that he wanted a blow-out night for his birthday that year, which he'd translated for Aurelia as a big dinner out with friends followed by dancing and many, many drinks.

"That's *dinner*, Aurelia," he'd informed her. "After dark, you understand? You'll have to leave the shop and join me and other people *after* the sun has set."

On the night of the party, David's crowd of friends helped him to celebrate his birthday so thoroughly that by eleven o'clock, he was too busy drunkenly singing along to the music blaring in the bar to notice Aurelia checking her watch every few minutes. Once she saw that it was nearly midnight, though, she knew she'd never make it home in time. The realization allowed her to relax and enjoy herself, and she threw herself into the festive spirit with the rest of them. She couldn't think of the last time she'd danced so much or laughed so hard. It was a perfect party other than the one moment when she found herself wishing that Oliver had been able to join them instead of having to attend a launch party for one of his authors.

When the party finally started to break up, David cornered her, a look of drunken determination on his face.

"Aurelia," he slurred. "You're overdue for a telling-off."

She raised her eyebrows as if to challenge him, but she was just as wobbly as he was.

"So busy, no time for anything but your book," he continued, pointing a finger at her that slowly started dipping to the floor as he tried to keep steady.

"I know," she said, putting on her best apologetic face. "But it's almost finished, I promise."

She reached out to hug him, but he stepped away, nearly falling over before recovering his balance.

"You're blind to everything but that book. Including the fact that Oliver likes you."

"David," she began, swatting at him ineffectively in her inebriated state.

"No, Aurelia," he said, pulling himself up. "Don't 'David' me. He *likes* you."

"He doesn't," she said, suddenly sobering up. "He told me—made it quite clear that he doesn't like me at all."

A sudden slideshow played in her mind of all the times she'd seen him lately—how she sometimes felt there might be something else there—but she shut it down, sending her mind back to his first visit to the shop to cure herself of those more recent memories.

David frowned, thrown from his conviction that she and Oliver were a project he could make happen.

"It's alright," she said, throwing her hands up as though she couldn't have cared less. "I have you, don't I?"

She felt her forehead pucker in disappointment, completely undermining her declaration. She cursed her drunken state, blaming that instead of the hurt she felt thinking that Oliver wasn't—would never be—an option. David's face crumpled in sympathy and he pulled her into a hug. But what started as a genuine hug of consolation led to each of them trying to keep the other upright, which set them laughing again. They stumbled out of the bar and into the cabs James had found for them, waving goodbye as each left in opposite directions.

She'd been laughing as her cab pulled away, yet somehow, on the ride home it was hard to tamp down her disappointment that David had finally seemed to accept that Oliver didn't like her, which meant there was no one left to push them together.

That disappointment doubled when she remembered she'd be returning home to an empty shop.

51

It pained Aurelia to get out of bed to open the shop the next morning, and she doubled-up on coffee in an effort to both wake up and defeat her headache. She waited until noon to call David to check in on his hangover, but James answered David's phone to report that David was incapable of speech or movement until further notice.

Oliver was due at the shop that evening to walk through his latest edits, giving Aurelia a few more hours to recover before she'd need to get her brain fully functioning. She'd gotten marginally better at taking his feedback. They sometimes argued, and other times nodded together in agreement over a scene that needed to be moved, or a theme that had developed late in the novel and needed to be worked into earlier scenes. With each passing day, Aurelia saw the novel coming together, getting better and stronger, and she thrilled at the feeling of pride. They were closing in on the end now—early chapters polished and ready to go, and later chapters nearly finished but not yet finalized.

When Aurelia met Oliver at the door to let him in after closing, he was holding a takeaway bag filled with food while carrying Biscuit.

"Rolling bag," he explained, nodding toward the street.

Aurelia still laughed every time she saw the dog—especially now, as Oliver put him down and he nearly tripped Oliver in his eagerness to be as close as possible to his favorite human. Fezz was up on the window seat, pretending to be asleep and unbothered by the new arrivals. He'd seen Biscuit a few times now, and he treated him just like Mrs. Smith's dog—with cautious indifference.

An hour after Oliver had arrived, they were sitting at her desk with takeaway boxes strewn over her notes and his edits, and Biscuit asleep at their feet. Oliver was pointing to the pages of a scene he claimed wasn't working.

"He'd never say that," Oliver insisted.

"He would and look—there he is," she said smugly, pointing to the page in front of them, "saying just that."

"That's not Tolstoy's Vronsky."

"No, you're right. He's changed a lot since Anna died."

Oliver shook his head and opened his mouth to argue.

"You can disagree with me," she continued, "but it's staying put because I know I'm right."

"How? How do you *know*?" he challenged her with a grin.

She answered with one of her own as she said, "Because he told me so himself."

Oliver rolled his eyes, all too familiar now with her insistence that her characters spoke to her, never guessing that her fib about her 'process' was closer to the truth than she'd let anyone else get. Aurelia enjoyed those moments of being honest with him, even enjoyed how much it annoyed him. It was their own private 'joke.'

"Right," he sighed, a hint of surrender in his voice.

"Exactly. In it stays."

She turned the page before he could press the point. He slid the manuscript away from her and began flipping through to his next edit. As she watched his fingers moving over her words, searching out his next attack, the mantel clock behind them began striking the hour. Aurelia turned idly to the clock, saw the time, then turned back to Oliver as he set the pages down. She was about to argue on principle before even hearing what he was going to suggest, when she jerked her head back to the clock again. Could it really be ten o'clock? They might have another hour of work ahead of them, and she'd missed her chance for a nap.

"You okay?" Oliver asked.

"Yes—yeah."

"Do you want a break? We could walk around the square, stretch our legs," he suggested, nodding to the door.

"No, I'm alright. Unless you need a break?"

"I'm fine. Here—this line here," he said, diving right back into his notes.

She tried to focus on his words, but her brain kept dragging her back to thoughts of the characters, of wanting to show Vronsky what they'd been working on. Though, at the same time, she was enjoying her time with Oliver and had to admit she didn't mind being secreted away with him in the shop. Just the two of them... Side by side... Talking so passionately about the words she'd written...

"What do you think?" he asked.

"Um, I think that's probably fine," she answered dreamily, her voice far away.

"Seriously? I thought you were going to fight me tooth and nail on that."

She stared down at the paper, willing herself to focus.

"Wait, no... No! That doesn't work at all," she said shaking her head emphatically.

"That's what I thought you'd say. You know, this would be much easier if you'd just zone out and let me have at the book on my own."

She shot him a death glare and he laughed before starting to talk through his next edit.

Again, she lost the thread of it as she wondered how he could stay out so late. Surely he wasn't dating anyone new? Wouldn't a girlfriend mind him being away for so many hours a day? Of course, he was only here working—they were just editing her book together. That was his job, after all. They'd become friends too, after all these months, but that was it. Thanks to her tears—maybe even thanks to her stubbornness with his edits. Then there were her midnight visits with fictional characters that, if he ever guessed they were more than a shared joke, would surely send him running.

"I'm losing you. Let's call it a night," Oliver said, patting her on the shoulder as he stood and gathered his things.

"What? Why?"

She'd been caught up in her thoughts again and had no idea what had happened.

"You're drifting off. I know it's late."

"No, it's fine! I'm used to late nights. Really," she said as she got to her feet.

"We can pick it up again another time."

He started walking to the door, Biscuit at his heels, and Aurelia turned to check the clock again. If they kept working, she might not get to see the characters, but, for once, spending a few more minutes editing with him seemed worth the risk of missing them.

"I'm sorry, let's keep at it," she said, following him to the door. "I know it's late, but I appreciate you coming over, staying to help me tie things up. We've made such good headway tonight. You're very dedicated."

He turned to her as he pulled open the door and suddenly they were standing extremely close to one another.

"I am," he agreed softly. "Very dedicated."

Aurelia's eyes widened. Was that... Was he...? Her mind flashed to a memory of them standing in that same spot just months ago, when he'd told her they could be friends—just friends.

"Well, thank you," she said quickly, annoyed at herself for having misread the moment. "See you later, then?"

"Right. Goodnight."

Leaving Aurelia behind at the shop door, Oliver stepped out into the night and turned to wave as he and Biscuit crossed the square.

52

The next morning, sitting at her desk with a mug of tea, Aurelia stared at the pages in front of her, which were crisscrossed with Oliver's notes. Her face crumpled into a scowl at the thought of what Marmee and Marianne would have said last night if she'd told them about his visit—how she'd worried over whether to meet with all of them or spend time with him.

That thought reminded Aurelia of the story Marmee had told her—how Marigold had spent too much time with the characters and lost touch with the real world. Though Aurelia hated to call her life during daylight hours the 'real world,' as if the characters mattered less because they came from books and couldn't leave the shop. They'd become real to her, but still, she understood the point of Marmee's story. And Marigold had said the same to Mark all those years ago—*it doesn't do to live in fiction*. These past months, spending time with the characters was like waking up to a world in color after living in black and white for far too long. At first, the color had only bled through inside the shop, but now... Now that she was writing again, now that she'd made a friend out of Oliver, now that Vronsky's story was almost done, the color had flowed out the shop door and into the wider world, making her want to experience it again instead of keeping herself locked away.

Aurelia stood, carrying her mug to the front of the shop and opening the door to take in the warm spring morning as she watched people enjoying the square beyond.

Visiting with the characters didn't have to be an all-or-nothing thing anymore. Maybe it never had; she'd just done it without really stopping to consider why. True, sticking close to the shop had helped her get through Vronsky's book faster than she might have if she'd had a few extra lunches with Kali, or a few extra dinners (preferably non-historical ones) with David. But now it was nearly done, it was time to find a new 'normal' that involved going out and being in the world. She had the thought that getting out naturally included Oliver since he was a friend now too. They'd gone out for coffee and walks to work on her book, but maybe now they could get together just because—no talking about her book required. And treating him like a friend might help her put to bed certain feelings that were decidedly more than friendly.

"*Put to bed*," she mumbled to herself, rolling her eyes as she closed the door and went back to her desk. If they were really going to be friends, she'd need to think of metaphors that wouldn't make her blush or give him the wrong impression. She'd also need to think of some way to show him that she saw him as more than just her editor. What would be a nice, friendly gesture? she wondered. A walk at Highgate might be good—though she snorted a laugh at the fact that her first idea for a friendly gesture was to invite him to a cemetery. But he'd suggested it before and she felt bad for how she'd refused. She might very well cry—going there could easily bring up feelings of sadness and grief—but he was a friend now. If she needed to cry, then she would cry, and they'd move on.

Aurelia nodded decisively, then called Oliver to set a date—no, *to schedule* their walk, she corrected herself.

53

A urelia arrived a few minutes late to meet Oliver at Highgate, and when she saw him standing alone—no Biscuit on a lead at his side—her steps faltered. She'd forgotten that dogs weren't allowed inside, and somehow the absence of Biscuit as a buffer, with his energy and joy, made her a little nervous. As she got closer, though, she saw that Oliver looked a little nervous too. Maybe he'd also realized they wouldn't have any buffers—no dog and no edits to discuss since she hadn't given him a new draft yet. But then Oliver waved and started walking over to her, a smile on his face, and she decided maybe they didn't need any buffers after all.

"What d'you reckon?" he asked once they'd said hello and made the requisite comments about the weather. "Should we start with the East Side or the West Side?"

"The West Side was always my favorite—all those giant gothic flourishes. Start there?"

Once they were through the gates, it only took them a few minutes of slightly awkward fits and starts of conversation before they were comfortable again, just like they'd been the other night in the shop.

"I've always loved it here," Oliver said as they moved deeper inside, where the trees were ancient and looming, and the mausoleums leaned precariously but charmingly against each other.

"I thought you didn't like old things?" Aurelia teased.

"I like newer books, but I love everything old about London," he said, looking wistfully at an old headstone as they passed it.

She was surprised by the note of nostalgia coming from Mr. Ebooks Are the Future, but she liked it. Without realizing, she was watching him, factoring this new aspect into her ever-evolving understanding of who he was. He looked over and caught her looking at him—gazing at him, really. She was sure he could see her feelings for him written all over her face.

"You like everything old—is that why you like it here?" he asked.

Aurelia was glad for the question and the distraction from the track her thoughts had been running on.

"It's one reason. I like the idea that generations of people have walked through here, maybe even reading the same books I've brought in to read on one of the same benches, under one of the same trees. And... This is kind of embarrassing, but... I like looking at the tombstones and mausoleums and writing down names that might work in whatever I'm writing."

"I don't think that's embarrassing—it's a nice way to honor someone. Even if you didn't know them, using their name is a way of keeping their memory in the world, isn't it?"

Aurelia was at risk of gazing at him again.

"That's exactly why I like doing it. A little memorial that's just between me and them, whoever they were."

Oliver was smiling as he listened when his eyebrows drew together in a frown.

"Are you alright, being here? You'll have to tell me if you want to leave—it's no problem if you do. We could go and get a coffee instead."

"I'm okay, actually," Aurelia said, realizing in that moment that she was, in fact, very okay. Being surrounded by memorials to lost loved ones wasn't exactly a cheerful activity, but the good company helped. "It's nice being back here."

Oliver smiled again and Aurelia smiled back, the moment stretching as their steps slowed. She'd been looking at him for too long, though, because she tripped over a tree root and had to grab him to right herself.

"Sorry!"

"It's fine. Are you alright?"

"I'm fine!"

She realized she was still holding onto him and let go, stepping back to reinstate a friend-like distance between them.

"Should we cross back over to the East Side?" she asked quickly, nodding in that direction as she led the way.

Later, as they were heading for the gate to leave, Oliver stopped in front of a small, worn headstone. It was tipping forward with age and he squatted down to gently brush away the dirt and weeds around it.

"'Vivienne Paumier, 1850 to 1885,'" Oliver read aloud from the stone.

"Oh, she was our age, wasn't she? How sad."

"There's a saying here—a quotation, I think, but it's too hard to read."

Aurelia squatted next to him and moved her hand over the carvings in the stone as she tried to read it too, but time and weather had worn the words away. They kept a moment of respectful silence before standing and looking down at the headstone again.

"Her name sounds French," Oliver observed. "Like someone Vronsky might have met if he'd lived your sequel."

"It does," Aurelia agreed, smiling as they continued walking back out into the London bustle.

Even after they'd said goodbye and made plans to meet soon to go over the next round of revisions to Vronsky's story, the name Vivienne—her short life and lost future—stuck in Aurelia's head, like a burr that wouldn't shake loose.

54

Two weeks passed and it was June, full of fine weather and longer days, but shorter nights to spend with the characters. She and Vronsky had worked hard in the time they'd had to add to his story and build in each new round of edits from Oliver. All of a sudden, on a Friday late in the month, they were finished.

"That's it," Aurelia said as she made a final note on the page they'd been editing.

"It? What is 'it'?" Vronsky asked.

"It's the end. We've finished the book."

She'd known it was coming and thought it might happen that evening, but she was still awestruck to be drawing her hands away from pen and paper in an act of finality. She turned to look at him, smiles breaking out on both their faces.

"My story is complete," he said, as if trying to believe it.

"It is—we've done it!"

Others came over to join them, asking if it were true and congratulating them. She and Vronsky were swept up in the excitement, joining in their cheers. Aurelia watched as everyone shook Vronsky's hand or clapped him on the back and she wished she, too, could hug Marmee or shake Cuff's hand. They all agreed that the following evening, she would read them the final chapter of his story and they would celebrate as they had after hearing the first few chapters all those months ago.

"And now, Aurelia? When will you have a copy of the book?" Marianne asked.

"We've been aiming for an autumn publication date, so it should be just a matter of months. I'll type up these changes tomorrow, then call Oliver and let him know we're done."

Aurelia wasted no time in calling Oliver the next morning to give him the news. In honor of the occasion, he wanted to take her to dinner that night to celebrate. She tried to argue for a celebratory lunch instead, but he was resolute. Aurelia looked around the shop, worried at the possibility that she might get home late and miss the characters and their party. But she reminded herself of her new resolution to get out more, and knew this was the perfect opportunity to do just that.

Aurelia sifted through the options in her closet that evening and began to realize that dinner with Oliver seemed like a date. She saw him in the shop or out for coffee or lunch almost every week, but a nice dinner and dressing up felt a bit more serious. Her thoughts were a muddle of excitement and worry and she shook her head in exasperation, determined to find something to wear that wouldn't scream 'date.'

Stepping out of a cab in front of the restaurant, Aurelia thought she might have overshot her outfit. She was wearing a deep green dress with short sleeves, a high collar and an open back, along with her mother's pearl drop earrings and a pair of wedge heels that wouldn't risk life and limb on the uneven streets of Soho. She walked to the door of the restaurant and was about to pull it open when she heard Oliver's voice behind her, calling her name. She turned and caught sight of him as he walked to join her.

He was in a navy suit and a white oxford shirt with two buttons undone instead of his usual one, and the grin on his face was contagious. Aurelia let go of her worry about whether their dinner was a romantic overture and gave in—just for a moment—to the full-on tingles running over her skin at the sight of him.

"Look at you," she said approvingly, trying to keep her tone light.

"You look... *amazing*," he replied, shaking his head as he took her in.

He held the restaurant door open for her, giving her a chance to enjoy his compliment unobserved as she walked ahead of him.

Later, as they sat waiting for dessert to arrive, Oliver quirked his eyebrow at her.

"You remember our first date?"

After all these months, she was surprised to hear him mention that night since it had seemed like a forbidden topic.

"I do, in fact."

"You were so incredibly rude—yawning, drifting off every time I started talking."

His smile told her he was teasing her, wanting to get a rise out of her—and it worked.

"Me? What about you? Droning on and on, barely a smile, looking like it was torture to be in the same room with me!"

"*Me?*" he mimicked. "I recall you making all sorts of faces at that dinner with David and James, like *you* were in agony being in the same room with me."

Aurelia covered her mouth, mortified at having been caught all those months ago. Oliver laughed and she joined in, glad they were both finally acknowledging the rough start to their friendship.

"Well, you still yawn on occasion, but I've mostly been able to keep your attention since then."

"And you've thawed out quite nicely."

Aurelia's tone was more flirtatious than she'd intended, and her smile faltered.

Oliver clearly noticed, because his eyes were steady on hers as he said, "I know I've said it before... I'm sorry if I confused you, at the end of the date. But... I haven't regretted that kiss."

Aurelia tried to hold his gaze but had to look away. It seemed impossible that he could really mean that after she'd spent ages reminding herself that he didn't think of her that way—as someone he wanted to kiss. Their dessert arrived and she pretended to be distracted by the business of refilling their glasses with more champagne and commenting on what each of them had ordered and whether they'd be willing to share.

By the time they left the restaurant they were both silly from the bubbly and the excitement of the evening. Oliver offered to walk her home, but Aurelia solemnly pointed to her heeled shoes and shook her head, so they compromised by taking the Tube. Once they were out of the station and walking toward the shop, though, their celebratory mood began to dissipate. Aurelia struggled to find things to say, and Oliver grew serious. She felt as though each step they took was bringing them closer to a decisive moment.

As they arrived at the shop door, Aurelia understood—the decisive moment was their goodbye, which would determine once and for all whether this had been a date. She grew restless, fiddling with her bag, her coat, her keys. She didn't want to make eye contact with Oliver. She was worried she might reach for him and put him in the terrible position of having to correct her mistake—*Oh, I'm sorry. You didn't think I liked you—not like that?*

"Aurelia?" He was trying to catch her eye, and she finally had to relent. She looked into his eyes and felt her heart leap. She was unaccountably scared, as though she were being backed toward the edge of a cliff.

Oliver stepped forward, reaching a hand to her arm and drawing nearer to her. She braced herself, knowing that if he got any closer she wouldn't be able to stop herself from leaning in to brush his lips with hers.

"It's almost midnight!" she burst out.

He drew back for a moment, looking appropriately confused by her sudden declaration.

"Are you afraid you'll turn into a pumpkin?"

"No," she laughed. "And anyway, Cinderella doesn't turn into a pumpkin—her coach does. You need to brush up on your fairy tales."

Aurelia pushed at him playfully and he took the opportunity to pull her toward him and kiss her. Despite her earlier resistance, she felt her body relax into his as she kissed him back. It was just as good as it had been on their horrible first date. No, she realized quickly, it was *better*.

She lost all sense of where she was until she heard the faint sounds of the mantel clock inside the shop as it began to toll the hour. She was very aware of the fact that they were standing in front of the shop and that she was usually inside, waiting to meet a collection of fictional characters. The thought of them—and what Oliver would think if he even suspected her nighttime routine—jolted her back to reality and she drew away from him.

"I'm sorry, Oliver. I... I don't—" Aurelia shook her head and closed her eyes, wishing for the words to express what she was feeling—wishing she could put her finger on what, exactly, she was feeling for that matter.

He stepped back, a crease between his eyebrows as his eyes traveled her face, trying to figure out what had happened.

"You said you weren't interested in me," she mumbled.

"I never said that," he said decisively.

"You did—when you came by the shop after our date."

"No, I said I was sorry for surprising you. And then you said you weren't ready to date just then."

"But I thought..." she began before trailing off. She'd been reminding herself of that conversation for months—did she really have it wrong all this time?

"Anyway, that was ages ago, Aurelia," he reminded her, smiling. "We'd only just met. I've seen you almost every day these past few months." He paused. "You remember telling me that I was dedicated?" He took a step nearer, tentatively reaching out to run his thumb over her cheek as he added, "Did you really think I only cared about your book?"

Aurelia frowned as she tried and failed to reconcile this new information with what she'd been telling herself over and over for so long. And he *had* just kissed her—you don't kiss someone you don't like. But then again, hadn't he done just that on their first date?

"I did—no, I... I don't know. I've been so focused on getting through the book," she tried to explain. "I haven't really thought about... us."

She knew the lie was obvious as soon as it escaped her mouth and was about to continue trying to cover up the fib, but he held up a hand to stop her from explaining. She reached for his arm, momentarily dazed by her ability to grasp it in her hand after so much time spent with characters she couldn't touch.

"It's alright," he said. "I'm sorry for thinking—"

"No, don't say that," she said quickly as he backed away from her again, her arm dropping as he stepped out of her reach.

"It's fine," he said. "You've got your book and your shop. That doesn't leave much time for anything else."

It was Aurelia's turn to feel hurt. The echoes of conversations with David and Marmee made her feel all the more bruised.

"It's not just that. It's a lot of things. I guess I'm just... too much of everything right now."

"You seem just right to me," he said quietly.

"No, it might seem like that, but I'm not." *Why was he trying to confuse her?* "I'm sorry," she added miserably, shaking her head as if that could order her thoughts.

Oliver nodded slowly and she felt like something had shifted between them.

"I'll bring the final chapter by on Monday, okay? I've made all your edits this time, so you'll be very pleased."

Her forced, cheery tone was grating even to her own ears, but he made an effort to smile and she was grateful for it.

"Thank you for a fantastic celebration," she added. "My feet are killing me, and I'm stuffed, but it was perfect."

Oliver looked desperate to leave. She took out her keys, wanting to hurry inside to give him an opportunity to escape.

"I'll be expecting a Michelin-star meal when the book is published—you've spoiled me completely," she added as she opened the door.

"Well, it's quite an accomplishment. You should be very proud, Aurelia. Goodnight."

She watched him walk away as she stood in the doorway, and of all their goodbyes, it was the first time he didn't turn around.

"He didn't wave," she said under her breath, feeling all too keenly that she might have just made a very big mistake.

As his outline faded into the distance, she remembered that it was now past midnight and the shop behind her was empty.

55

I t was Sunday, leaving Aurelia with an entire day to play over her bungled night out with Oliver. She was more convinced than ever that she'd done the wrong thing but wasn't sure how to fix it now that they were so very far off course. Did he really like her now? And, if he did, was she ready for all that would mean?

She and Kali met for brunch, but Aurelia wasn't very good company. Kali asked her a few times if she was alright and Aurelia finally came clean about her night out with Oliver. Once again, Aurelia found herself answering the question *Do you like him?* in the affirmative, but how could she explain why liking him didn't feel like enough to get over the hurdle of diving into a relationship when she couldn't tell Kali about the shop and its characters? But, if she were honest with herself, it wasn't just about her secret life in the shop, so Aurelia finally came clean about her ex's parting words.

"'Too much'?" Kali asked, frowning. "What was that supposed to mean?"

"I was really down about my mum dying, and then with Marigold getting sick, I think he just realized he was in for an indefinite period of me crying all the time."

"Yes, that's what happens when someone's grieving," Kali said, angry on Aurelia's behalf.

"But it was a lot to ask of him, to stay by me through that. And I'm still in it. I'm better now, but I think it's still too much for someone to take me on."

"I don't like this," Kali insisted. "That stupid Brendan made you feel ashamed of being sad when there's no shame in it at all. What about Oliver—has he ever seen you get upset over your mum and Marigold?"

"Yep, a few times," Aurelia admitted with a grimace.

"Well, after everything he told you last night, it doesn't seem like he has a problem with that, does it?" Kali asked kindly.

Nodding slowly, Aurelia thought back over their Highgate walk, how Oliver had checked in to make sure she was alright, how it seemed like he wouldn't have minded if she'd taken him up on his offer to leave and go for coffee instead. If Brendan had made her feel ashamed about feeling sad, Oliver made her feel like it was no trouble at all if she needed time to process those feelings before she could move past them.

After brunch, Aurelia was still thinking about Oliver, only this time she felt like she was seeing everything that had happened between them a little more clearly. She thought about how kind he'd been each time he'd seen tears brimming in her eyes. How sweet he'd been last night in wanting to celebrate her book with her. He'd shown her—not just last night, but for weeks—that he liked her. And maybe now, after what he'd said last night—that she was *just right*—it was time to believe there could be something more than friendship between them.

But there was still the small problem, the very minor one, of how she spent most of her nights.

That night, Aurelia was prepared to apologize to the characters for missing the party the night before, but then she remembered that they wouldn't have noticed since she hadn't been in the shop at midnight and so neither had they. She debated telling them but decided not to bring down the party mood with apologies and explanations—especially when Marmee might take it as a sign, one Aurelia would have to acknowledge this time, that she wasn't prioritizing her 'real' life as she should.

After a few hours of celebrating the end of Vronsky's new book, the characters had split into smaller clusters around the shop. Aurelia was standing alone with Elinor, whose perceptive nature meant she had no trouble sensing Aurelia was out of sorts.

"Has something happened, Aurelia? Your thoughts seem to be carrying you somewhere else this evening."

"Do they? I'm sorry, I've been very distracted today. I'll try to be more in the moment," Aurelia said, making an effort to smile.

"Or you could share what has you looking so concerned?" Elinor suggested.

Aurelia scanned the room, careful to make sure no one else was within listening distance.

"We've talked before about Oliver, my editor," she began.

Elinor smiled knowingly.

"Yes, we have indeed."

"The other night... He let me know he's interested in being together—as something more romantic than friends, or editor and writer."

"As well he should. You are a successful woman of business and now letters. Do you share his interest?"

"I do—part of me does. But the other part is still unsure."

Unconsciously, Aurelia's eyes traveled around the room again, taking in the characters she'd grown to love.

"You have finished the book that will set Count Vronsky free from his past and ensure him a new future, but it seems there must be some way for you to do the same—ensure a new future for yourself, one that will allow you to open your heart to Oliver, or whomever you choose." Elinor paused. "I am reminded of the story Marmee told us some weeks ago about your aunt, Marigold. Are we holding you back from returning Oliver's affections?"

"If anyone is holding me back, it's me," Aurelia said with a grim smile. "I just can't imagine trying to be in a relationship with someone when my nights are spent here, with all of you."

Elinor opened her mouth to protest, but Aurelia quickly continued.

"No, sorry, that's not what I meant. I've been better about getting out, I promise! It's just that, with the shop being so... out of the ordinary, I'm not sure how I would keep a secret like that from someone. I mean, I've been keeping it a secret from my friends and family, but somehow it seems like keeping it from a boyfriend, from Oliver, would be too hard."

"Too hard to even attempt?" Elinor asked.

"I think so. It's easier to just keep things as they are. I'm happy enough for now."

Elinor was thoughtful, looking first at Aurelia, then across the room at Vronsky.

"'Happy enough'? You and Vronsky are cut from the same cloth, it seems."

Elinor, who was usually so even keeled and gentle, surprised Aurelia with her sharp tone.

"What do you mean?"

"Both of you are all too willing to settle for *happy enough* without trusting that a greater happiness is possible."

"*Possible*, sure, but there's no guarantee."

In spite of Aurelia's attempts to keep her voice down, Rachel—who had been standing nearby—seemed to have overheard them.

"I am thoroughly perplexed by you, Aurelia," she said, her tone just as sharp as Elinor's. "You told us that women in your time can do anything they like, be anything they like. There are no barriers, correct?"

"Yes, but—"

"In our time, barriers are put up all around us, by others. And here you sit, manufacturing barriers of your own when you could live as free as you choose."

"It's not that simple, Rachel—"

"Of course it is. You've found a way to spend nights in the shop with us, a way to run this shop on your own, a way to write a book, and help a friend. There can be no possible reason not to follow your heart if you love this man."

"*Love* him? I don't know if I—"

Almost instantly, Aurelia thought about that pulling, all-over tingling feeling she felt every time they'd been together over the past few weeks, and found she did know.

"But... even if we were together," she continued, struggling under the weight of her realization, "we could make each other miserable. Or he might find out about all of you and refuse to see me again."

"Or one of you could become ill. Or worse," Elinor said, catching Aurelia's eye to make sure her point hit home. "Or you could find yourselves happier than you ever imagined, and you could live out a long and happy life together. Good and bad are possible, Aurelia."

"It's true that Alexei's old story had an unhappy ending," Marianne said, pushing into their circle just as Rachel had done minutes earlier. "But what about my happy ending?"

"And mine," Rachel chimed in.

"And mine," Elinor said firmly. "You and Count Vronsky think avoiding love entirely is certain to protect you from experiencing the pain of heartache. But it is also certain to prevent you from experiencing the joy and happiness of finding someone you truly love, and from finding your own happy ending."

"But... I've finished Alexei's book and it's just the way he wanted it—there's no love story."

Aurelia suddenly understood what that meant.

"I've sealed his fate, haven't I? I set out to give him a better ending, but then I let him run from a real chance at happiness."

"You said the book won't be published for several months yet. Is there time to correct his mistake?"

"There might be time, if I work quickly. It's possible I could find a way to work something in on my own." Aurelia's mind rushed forward as she began to think of how she could do it, what she would write, when, and how she would tell Vronsky what she'd done. "I think I could manage it. I'm not sure how, but I could try."

"I think you must try. His story is not yet complete. And, it seems, neither is yours."

When dawn arrived and everyone departed, Aurelia wasn't tired at all. Instead of going up to her flat to sleep, she strode over to her desk and pulled out a stack of blank paper, ready to begin writing a new ending for Count Vronsky. Again.

56

A few hours later, Aurelia was so deep into her writing that she didn't register the knock at the shop door until it happened a second time. She looked up, confused. Once she saw that it was Mark, peering in the window at her, the pieces fell into place—it was just past ten in the morning and she hadn't opened the shop yet.

Jumping up from her desk, she nearly knocked over her chair. She rushed to the door to let Mark in, apologizing before it was even fully opened.

"Mark! I'm so sorry, I didn't realize how late it was."

He looked concerned as he took in her tired eyes, her rumpled clothes, and her general state of disarray.

"I hope everything's alright?" he asked.

"Yes! Everything's great. I'm just on a writing jag and I lost track of the time. Please, come in."

Mark had been hovering uncertainly in the doorway but took a few hesitant steps inside.

"I'll make us tea," Aurelia said as she disappeared into the back room.

"Is this the same book you've been working on?"

"It is!" she called out. "I'm nearly done now." She emerged again. "Well, I was done, but then I realized it wasn't actually finished, so I'm adding a bit more."

After she brought out their tea, they chatted for a few more minutes before Mark began his wander around the shop. Aurelia looked longingly at her desk but knew that if she sat down to write again there was a good chance she'd be too distracted to remember he was even there.

When Mark eventually left, she stood at the shop door, debating what to do. She wanted to write and she wanted to sleep, and she couldn't do either while running the shop. She walked to her desk and typed out a note on the typewriter that read, 'Very sorry! Temporarily closed to write a happy ending.'

After posting the note on the door, Aurelia turned the lock and went back to her desk to keep writing.

57

The next few days were filled with writing, sleeping, and editing. Aurelia didn't leave the building, moving only between her flat and her desk as she drafted Vronsky's love story. And she avoided the shop between midnight and dawn, since she wanted to focus on the book—and because she was afraid Vronsky would suspect she was up to something.

By Wednesday afternoon, she'd finished revising the existing chapters and had written a few new ones. Using what she'd learned about Vronsky from their many nights discussing what his life had been and what he wanted it to be, Aurelia had written him a love interest. That evening, she waited at her desk with the revised manuscript clasped in her arms. With all her talk about letting Vronsky choose his own future and no longer being powerless to an author's whim, she was nervous about his reaction.

When the characters appeared, Aurelia greeted them all, but soon asked Vronsky to join her at her desk, where she placed the manuscript between them.

"Has Oliver given you more changes?" he asked. "I thought we had completed his revisions."

"We did. But this is a new draft. I've added something—a few things. I'd like you to read it all the way through before I give it to him."

"I have no doubt I will be satisfied with whatever little changes you have made."

"These are... significant, not little. I realized your story wasn't really done and I decided to try to help you—us—to finish it properly."

Vronsky quirked an eyebrow, intrigued.

"I thought the ending was sufficient, but I am willing to consider your additions."

He looked down at the manuscript, then back at Aurelia.

"Right," she said, realizing the problem. "I'll set it here, and you can nod when you want me to turn a page."

"This will take some time," he said, looking hopefully toward the conversations taking place around them.

"It's important."

Seeing her determination, Vronsky nodded, saying, "I understand. Let me begin."

It took him several hours, but eventually he finished reading the new draft. At times he'd frowned, wrinkled his brow, or scoffed; at others, he'd smiled or nodded. But he didn't stomp away or refuse to keep reading, which Aurelia took as a positive—or at least neutral—sign. Once she'd turned the last page, they were quiet, neither looking directly at the other.

"You have written me into a romance with a bluestocking," he said softly.

Their eyes met, and the corner of his mouth twitched into a smile. Aurelia smiled back in relief.

"Well, I thought you'd need a woman who would challenge you."

"Challenge or harangue?"

"Both, I suppose," she said, arching an eyebrow.

They laughed and Aurelia felt the tension she'd been carrying fall away.

"You saw I didn't introduce her right away. I thought you'd want time—after Anna."

"Thank you for that."

"You'll have to work your way toward her. It wouldn't be much of a story if you met right away and lived happily ever after."

"Yes, how very boring that would be," Vronsky said, smiling.

"I may have put some of my own modern thinking into her, and there are sparks of Marianne, Elinor, Rachel, and Marmee in her too—all intelligent, independent women from a time that's closer to your own."

Aurelia tried to read his expression but couldn't tell what he was thinking, so she asked, "I hope you think she's someone you could love?"

"I believe she is. If I could have, I would have written her for myself."

"Really? I can make a change if there's something you don't like—I can take all of it out if you don't like it, or her. I know I promised you—"

"You did promise me, but it was wrong of me to ask. This is right—it is a better story. It is truer to whom I ought to be and whom I wish to be."

The other characters began asking what had kept them quiet for so long, and as Vronsky told them about her changes, Aurelia felt a sense of ease—like she'd set something right that had been slightly askew. She caught Elinor's eye, then Rachel's, pleased to see them both smiling smugly back at her. Meanwhile, Marianne was busy asking Vronsky all sorts of questions about his new love interest, including exactly how and when they were going to fall in love.

Watching Vronsky as he answered Marianne's questions, Aurelia noticed that he seemed to grow more relaxed as he described the character Aurelia had created, as though this new twist in his future had brought him some measure of peace. She hoped she would feel the same, just as soon as she figured out how to make things right with Oliver.

58

The following morning, Aurelia called Oliver and asked him to meet for a coffee. He was his old standoffish self again, but she held firm, determined to get back the Oliver she'd gotten to know over the past few months. Although he tried a few excuses, she didn't give up until he agreed to meet her at a café that was just a few minutes from the shop.

Knowing his preference for hard copies when he was editing, Aurelia carefully wrapped the manuscript in one of the shop's canvas bags and carried it with her to the café, feeling protective of this final draft now that it was truly finished and had Vronsky's blessing.

Just like their first meeting to discuss the book all those months ago, Oliver sat waiting for her when she arrived, wearing his usual buttoned-up shirt and a light linen jacket. He was at a table at the back of the café, looking cool and collected when she felt the exact opposite. Still, Aurelia squared her shoulders and held fast to her resolve to thaw his icy demeanor all over again.

"I know I promised to get you the final chapter on Monday, but I had a bit of a breakthrough," she said as she sat down.

"Oh?"

"When we first started talking about the book, you told me it needed a love interest and I said no. Then I said no again, and maybe I even said it a third time."

"Yes, you made it very clear."

There was a slight edge to his voice that Aurelia understood had more to do with how they'd left things on Saturday than her writing.

"Well, I was wrong. You were right," she added with a deferential nod. "I've been writing nonstop these past few days to add some new sections and chapters. Here," she said, handing over the bag with her manuscript.

He reached out to take it from her. Holding it in his hands, he asked, "Are you sure? You seemed quite determined about that."

"I was. But time and some perspective opened my eyes."

"And what about Vronsky? Did you run it past him?"

There was a hint of their familiar teasing there and Aurelia loved to hear it.

"I did—it's Vronsky approved."

Oliver opened the bag and began flipping through the pages. He stopped, as if something had caught his eye, and read a few lines before looking up at her.

"There's a new character—Vivienne?"

"There is."

"And she's... Is she the love interest?"

"Mm-hmm. It's a lovely name—it seemed a waste not to use it for an important character."

Oliver's face softened and she thought this could work, that she just might be able to convince him to give her another try. But once they finished their coffees and were standing outside the café, they faced another tense moment.

"Usually I walk you back," Oliver began.

Aurelia knew another excuse was coming and cut him off, saying "That would be lovely, thanks."

He closed his mouth, and they started walking. Aurelia was thinking back to the last time they'd walked to the shop, just days ago, and was certain Oliver was thinking about it too.

When they were at her doorstep, he attempted a quick retreat, saying, "Well, best be off."

"Oliver, wait. Please?"

He drew in a breath, blinking slowly to signal his impatience.

"It's alright, Aurelia. We don't have to talk about it. I really am sorry—let's just move on."

But Aurelia wasn't ready to move on.

"Do you know what?" she asked suddenly.

Oliver's eyebrows drew up a fraction as he waited for her to tell him what.

"I didn't like it when you didn't wave goodbye on Saturday."

"Pardon?"

His face was a giant question mark staring back at her.

"You always turn and wave goodbye—just there—when you leave the shop, but not on Saturday."

"Oh. I must have forgotten."

"Well, I didn't like it."

"Okay... I'll try to remember to wave next time."

He spoke slowly, as if he were responding to a question in school and wasn't sure he had the right answer.

Aurelia took a step forward, moving closer to him. She hesitated, then reached out and felt for the lapels on his jacket. Emboldened, she pulled him a step closer and rested her hands against his chest. She felt the quickening rise and fall under her palms, then realized she was breathing just as quickly as they now stood inches apart from one another.

Something in his jacket pocket distracted her as she felt it through the fabric under her fingers—a business card, perhaps, or a credit card? She ran her thumb along the edge of it as she tried to think of what to say next, unable to meet his eyes just yet.

Oliver reached up and gently took her hand in his as his other hand disappeared into his jacket. She watched as he pulled out one of the shop's bookmarks—not just any bookmark, in fact, but the one she'd given him on their date all those months ago. The edges were worn away and the printed words were hardly legible.

She looked up and into his eyes, then, and saw that his reserve was gone. His face was soft and kind, back to the Oliver she'd come to love.

"This is the bookmark I gave you?"

He nodded.

"But... This isn't the jacket you were wearing that night, when we had our date."

"No."

"So you put it in your pocket today—on purpose?"

"Not just today. Not just this jacket."

She looked at the bookmark again. He'd been carrying it with him all this time, from jacket to jacket. He had spent days, weeks, and months keeping her close to him, in spite of her occasional sadness over her aunt and mother, in spite of her preoccupation with the shop and her book.

Taking the bookmark from him, she carefully tucked it back into his pocket and patted the spot where it lay.

"I'm thinking of all sorts of clichés about bookmarks and saving a place for me."

Aurelia smiled and looked to his face again. He held her eyes and, unlike just a few nights ago, she didn't feel the urge to look away.

"I'm glad you did," she added, running her fingers over his pocket again.

"Are you, really?" Oliver asked.

His voice was almost a whisper as his eyes searched her face, like he was looking for a crack in her sudden resolve. She nodded and he leaned in to close the last few inches between them.

The pressure of his lips against hers, his palm brushing her cheek, his arm around the small of her back—for a moment the world around them disappeared and Aurelia's whole being was focused on each part of her that was touching him.

When he pulled away to catch his breath, she held fast to him, not wanting to let him go just yet. Something behind her caught his eye and he gave a soft chuckle. Turning, she spotted the sign she'd hung on the door on Monday, alerting customers to her urgent writing agenda.

"Lucky for you I put that sign up," she teased him. "It would have taken me a few extra days to get here otherwise."

"I don't suppose the sign could stay up for a bit longer?" he asked, leaning in to kiss her again.

Without answering, Aurelia stood back to unlock the door and, holding his hand in hers, led him inside.

59

The next few months passed in an absolute whirlwind. Managing the shop had become a distant third to finalizing the book for publication and spending time with Oliver as her editor *and* boyfriend. Aurelia had also made what she called a 'tour of apology,' which took her to Yorkshire to visit her father, Paris for a bank holiday weekend to see Antonia and her family, and many outings with Kali, David, and James. Now that the book was out of her hands, Aurelia was determined to do a better job of balancing her life outside the shop and her life with the characters within it.

Mark, Sophie, and even Mrs. Smith were excited about the book's upcoming publication and she'd promised to host a party in the shop to celebrate. Her father and Antonia were coming to London for it, and of course her friends would be there too. She'd promised the characters a party to celebrate the book's release, too, though as the date grew closer, they all felt a mingled sense of excitement and sadness to know Vronsky might soon be leaving them. As for Vronsky, Aurelia had made sure to involve him in every aspect of finalizing the book, from viewing final proofs to options for the cover. He was almost euphoric as the publication date neared, thrilled to be the center of attention and anxiously awaiting the dawn when he might disappear into his new future.

Oliver appeared at the shop one afternoon, carrying a box in his arms as he pushed open the door, pausing to let Biscuit tumble in behind him. After the obligatory few minutes of greeting Biscuit and watching the dance between him and Fezz play out (Biscuit wanting to say hello, Fezz feigning disinterest), Aurelia noticed that Oliver was still holding the box.

"What's that?"

"Something very exciting," he said, waggling his eyebrows before setting the box on her desk.

Aurelia reached out to open it, but he took her hand and kissed her palm instead.

"Can't you guess?"

She finally caught on.

"It isn't?"

He opened the box, revealing two rows of books with the same cover, the same title: her novel. Aurelia drew her hand over them, marveling at her name printed across each copy. Oliver, seeming to appreciate the gravity of the moment, stood quietly at her side.

Finally, Aurelia looked up at him.

"My book," she said simply.

"Your book," he agreed.

She put her arm around him as she continued gazing down at the project that meant so much more than she could ever tell him. Leaning into his side, she smiled, knowing that everyone would be thrilled to see the final product that night.

Before going back to his office, Oliver made her promise not to put the copies on display until the official launch the following week, but he let her keep them in the back room so that she could look at them whenever she liked.

That night, Aurelia played out a similar scene with the characters. She left the box on her desk with the top closed and waited for someone to ask what was inside. Marianne was the first to spot it.

"You have a box, Aurelia."

"I do," she said mysteriously.

"Is there something inside?"

"There is."

Aurelia smiled as she realized she was channeling Sergeant Cuff.

"Will you make me guess or shall you tell us?" Marianne asked impatiently.

Aurelia opened the lid of the box, then tipped it forward so that everyone could see what was inside. Cheers and whoops erupted as they realized it was Vronsky's book, and she held a copy up as the characters pushed in to look. Vronsky stood toward the back of the crowd, smiling and accepting their congratulations as he looked on in amusement. A new burst of excitement sprang up when Laurie noticed a photograph of Aurelia on the back cover, and she had to hold up the book again so that everyone could see it.

Chatter broke out as they began to plan their celebration for the official book launch, but Vronsky left the others to join Aurelia at her desk.

"Your book," he said, nodding to the copy in her hand.

"Our book," she said, placing it on the desktop so he could inspect it. "Do you want to take a closer look?"

Aurelia fanned the pages, landing on one that described Vronsky's first days in France. He peered at it, smiling.

"There is no need. I am quite satisfied."

He looked at Aurelia and the weight of his gaze deflated her holiday mood. She opened her mouth to ask what was the matter, but in the same instant she knew.

"Now? Not yet."

"But when?" he asked quietly. "Waiting will not make our goodbyes any easier."

"I thought... after the party—"

"I would rather the party were a celebratory affair. If we wait, it will only dampen the spirit of the occasion."

"You're sure—quite sure? Even if it works, you might not be one of the people who comes into the shop from your new book."

"I understand the risk. We will simply have to hope that I appear from the new book to reassure you of our success."

Aurelia looked around the room.

"Shouldn't we tell them? You might want to say goodbye, just in case you don't see them again."

Vronsky's eyebrows drew together.

"Yes, I agree. I would hate to depart without taking the opportunity to thank everyone for their friendship and kindness."

Astonishment spread throughout the shop as the others learned of Vronsky's plan, but they soon put aside their disappointment to give him their well-wishes for a bright future.

In the hour before dawn, Aurelia and Vronsky retreated to the window seat, where they reminisced about the first time they'd met—when she'd woken up in the shop and learned its secret. It seemed too big a moment, knowing that it might be their last conversation, to try and cover everything they'd like to say to each other. But as the sky lightened, Vronsky turned serious.

"You remember your promise, Aurelia? You will not put my old book out again?"

"I do—I promise."

Aurelia couldn't stop her tears now that their time was running out. She was saying goodbye to a dear friend, possibly forever. Although it brought to mind her last goodbyes with her mother and aunt, her heart felt lighter knowing she might hear from him, or at least hear about him, very soon.

They joined the others downstairs, where there was much smiling, laughing, and brushing away tears as the minutes closed in on their final goodbyes. Vronsky had been looking at Aurelia, one eyebrow up in a teasing gesture as she laughed through her tears, before the dawn swept him gently away, back into *Anna Karenina* for the last time.

60

It wasn't until the shop closed at five o'clock the following day that Aurelia finally put away the copies of *Anna Karenina*. She'd stood at the table several times that day, resolved to pick them up, but each time she found herself unable to reach out her hands to do it. But with the shop closed, she started to worry that she'd miss some unknown window of time before midnight when she'd need to make the switch.

She carried the copies of *Anna Karenina* to the back room, then brought out a single copy of the new book. Aurelia held it—her book, their book—in her arms and closed her eyes, wishing that the experiment would work and Vronsky would find the love and happiness they'd planned for him. Eyes open once again, she placed the book on the table and walked upstairs to try to sleep before midnight.

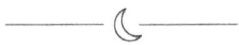

Rest was, in the end, impossible; she couldn't quiet the thoughts and feelings that were keeping her from sleep. Giving in, she finally decided to wait downstairs for the fateful moment. As midnight approached, she hovered near her desk, wondering who, if anyone, would appear from her book.

When the mists finally materialized, she couldn't be sure whether any were from her book and she stepped closer, trying to make out the figures as they came into being.

There were Marmee and Laurie, Elinor and Marianne, Sergeant Cuff and Rachel. And there... There was a man in a uniform that was similar to Vronsky's, but with slightly different epaulettes across the shoulders. He was tall and solidly built, seeming almost too large for the shop, and he had a thick mustache and dark hair that was cropped close to his head. Although he looked imposing, he glanced around uncertainly, like he was shy to meet the small crowd gathered around.

Next to him, a woman had appeared. She had light brown hair and eyes that were somewhere between hazel and green. She was wearing a simple but elegant dress of grey cotton with a white shift underneath. Dashes of paint in various colors appeared on her dress and hands, and there was even a spot of paint on her neck. She looked lovely, her long hair pulled back into a loose chignon and a smile playing across her lips as she took in the shop.

"Vivienne?" Aurelia's voice came out in a whisper.

The woman looked at her.

"Do I know you, mademoiselle?"

Aurelia gasped. It was one thing to see characters she knew from beloved books come to life, but it was something else entirely to see a character she'd created standing in front of her, talking to her. Vivienne's inquisitive look helped to keep Aurelia in the moment.

"No, not yet," she managed to get out. "My name is Aurelia Lyndham, and this is my bookshop. You are very, very welcome here." She turned to the man in uniform. "And you're Prince Yashvin? Count Vronsky's friend?"

"Indeed, Miss Lyndham. It is an honor." He snapped to his full height and gave Aurelia a stiff bow.

"Please, let me introduce you to the others."

Vivienne and Yashvin seemed to have no trouble accepting their unfamiliar surroundings as everyone said hello. Aurelia was afraid to ask about Vronsky, to hear how he was doing and whether it matched up with the plans they'd made. Still, she was grateful when Marianne asked soon after the introductions were over.

"Can you tell us—how is Count Vronsky? He is an acquaintance of ours and we long to know if he is well."

Elinor stepped closer to Aurelia, catching her eye and giving her an encouraging nod.

"Alexei is very well."

Vivienne smiled as she absentmindedly ran a finger over a ring on her hand, reminding Aurelia that Vivienne and Vronsky were recently wed, living in Paris, and sharing a studio where they both painted. Yashvin had just joined them in Paris and planned to settle there to be nearer to his closest friend.

"Last week he was angry when my painting was praised above his at the Salon, but I quickly talked him out of that," Vivienne added with a laugh. "Soon he was bragging that his wife had painted the best piece in the exhibition."

"They have heated discussions, those two, but one cannot deny they are suited to each other. I have not seen my friend as happy in many years," Yashvin joined in.

"He enjoys Paris, then?"

"Oh, yes, truly he does. His French is almost better than mine, but you must never tell him I said this," Vivienne said.

Her ready smile was remarkable—it was just as Aurelia had written it.

"And do you walk along the Seine together?" Aurelia finally spoke up, though she knew the answer.

"We do, almost every night, in fact. Alexei says the lights reflecting on the water inspire him to keep trying to capture them on canvas."

The characters crowded around Vivienne and Yashvin, asking more questions about Vronsky and their life in Paris. Aurelia's heart was full as she watched the characters she knew talking with the two she'd written about in her book. They had done it: Vronsky was happy, in love, and making a life for himself in Paris. She looked around to find Sergeant Cuff standing nearby. He flashed her a very self-satisfied smile, then walked over to speak with Yashvin.

Although she would have liked to see Vronsky, to watch him catch Vivienne's hand or tease her about whose work was best, she was thrilled to know that it had worked—that she'd given him a new chapter in his life to find love.

Aurelia smiled as she thought of Oliver, knowing that, in a way, Vronsky had done just the same for her.

Recommended Reads

Anna Karenina (1878) – Leo Tolstoy

- Count Alexei Vronsky: a confident military man who has everything figured out—until he meets Anna. Their passionate, years-long love affair turns both their worlds upside-down.

The book is long but so good! Hang in there and be rewarded with some truly brilliant depictions of human relationships. I knew how the book ends years before I read it, so I didn't hesitate to reveal it here because it doesn't ruin a thing. Make sure to skim a few pages before picking which copy to read since a good translation makes a big difference.

Little Women (1868) – Louisa May Alcott

- Mrs. March (Marmee): mother to four independent daughters; instiller of wisdom; patient but firm.

- Theodore Laurence (Laurie): neighbor and best friend to Marmee's girls; he longs to be part of the family and eventually gets his wish.

Growing up in New England, it felt like the March sisters were in my DNA. I've loved revisiting the strong, unique women with every re-read, and the many fantastic film adaptations show how this story is just as engaging now as when Alcott brought her characters to life.

The Moonstone (1868) – **Wilkie Collins**

- <u>Sergeant Cuff</u>: a retired, wizened old detective, fond of uncovering clues and obsessed with cultivating roses.

- <u>Rachel</u>: a young woman with strong opinions and feelings who is unwittingly placed in the middle of some mysterious happenings.

I spotted this book at a used bookshop and was drawn in by the back cover describing it as one of the first detective novels. The story is by turns silly and serious, told in the form of letters from various characters who are involved in the search for a missing diamond called the Moonstone.

Sense and Sensibility (1811) – **Jane Austen**

- <u>Elinor Dashwood</u>: the responsible older sister who takes charge of her family's welfare and looks after her mother and two younger sisters.

- <u>Marianne Dashwood</u>: the romantic middle sister who loves poetry and long walks in the countryside.

You get a two-fer with this book: two sisters = two love stories. The pining! The hope! This is a classic romance with a traditional happy ending, but the surprise—and fun—is in how the characters get there.

Each of these books has elements that are timeless—a love story, characters with relatable flaws and vulnerabilities, and beautiful writing. But they also reflect the perspectives and prejudices of specific moments in time. That makes them ripe for critical analysis—did Tolstoy really think his depiction of contented laborers was realistic? Was the curse of the Moonstone Collins' subtle, or too subtle, attempt at criticizing colonialism? Books like these are so important because—even though they're fiction—they give readers a great opportunity to consider what's changed, what hasn't, and what we want to change about our own moment in time.

Acknowledgements

I should start by thanking everyone who has read drafts—often multiple versions—and put up with my Aurelia-ness over their critiques: Alla, Ally, Braden, Caroline, Danielle, Deb, Jaime, Kristen, Liz, Lizzie, and Tara. And if I'm forgetting someone then thank you, too! I so appreciate your time, candor, and thoughtfulness.

Lots of family thank yous: Thank you to Deb for reading very rough drafts, and for patiently listening to the ups and downs of my writing journey during many walks and phone calls. Thank you to Caroline for reading *so* many drafts, for talking through ideas (again and again...and again), and for sharing your creative insight and guidance. Thanks Kai, for your encouragement and for checking in to ask how the writing/editing/publishing was going. And thank you to Mom and Dad, for always asking "Did you try your best?" You taught me to give every project my all.

Many thanks to Jen Prokop for your editorial savvy. Something was missing and you helped me find it! Thanks to Louise Walters and Megan Carroll for your helpful early edits and suggestions.

Thank you so very much to my friends for your support and cheerleading as I wrote, edited, and put this book out into the world. And Braden gets a second thanks, this time with Carlos, for deciding to get married in Porto, Portugal and for insisting that I visit Livraria Lello, the beautiful old bookshop that inspired this story.

Thank you to the many people who helped me get this book into print in various ways: Cassidy at Grump & Sunshine Bookshop (self-pub guidance); Jamie P. Bradley (self-pub guidance); Kristen O'Connell (marketing guru); and Eleanor Smith (proofreading/copyediting). Everyone who has built the resources and infrastructure for indie authors to thrive—from blog posts to websites and services—thank you.

For the beautiful cover that surpassed my limited artistic vision—thank you, Lena Yang.

Readers: thank you for being taken in by the cover, the description, or someone's recommendation and deciding to read this book. I appreciate you spending your time with Aurelia! And last but never least, thank you to the staff of every bookshop and library for working so hard to keep your doors open to book lovers.

About the Author

Emily lives in Maine, her recently adopted homeland, with her three cats. She owns too many books, likes tea and coffee (don't ask her to choose), and is currently knitting more projects than she can count. When she isn't writing, reading, or knitting, she's talking to the wildlife in her backyard. They haven't answered back—yet.

You can learn more about Emily by visiting her website or scanning the QR code below. And if you want to read more about Aurelia, Oliver, Biscuit, and Fezz, her website is also where you'll find a sneak peek at Book Two in the Midnights On the Square series.

www.ewandersen.com

If you have time and are so inclined, writing a review or rating this book on Goodreads, StoryGraph, Amazon, or your local indie bookshop's website would be so very helpful.

Thank you for reading!